P9-CIW-043

HUNT FOR THE PYXIS

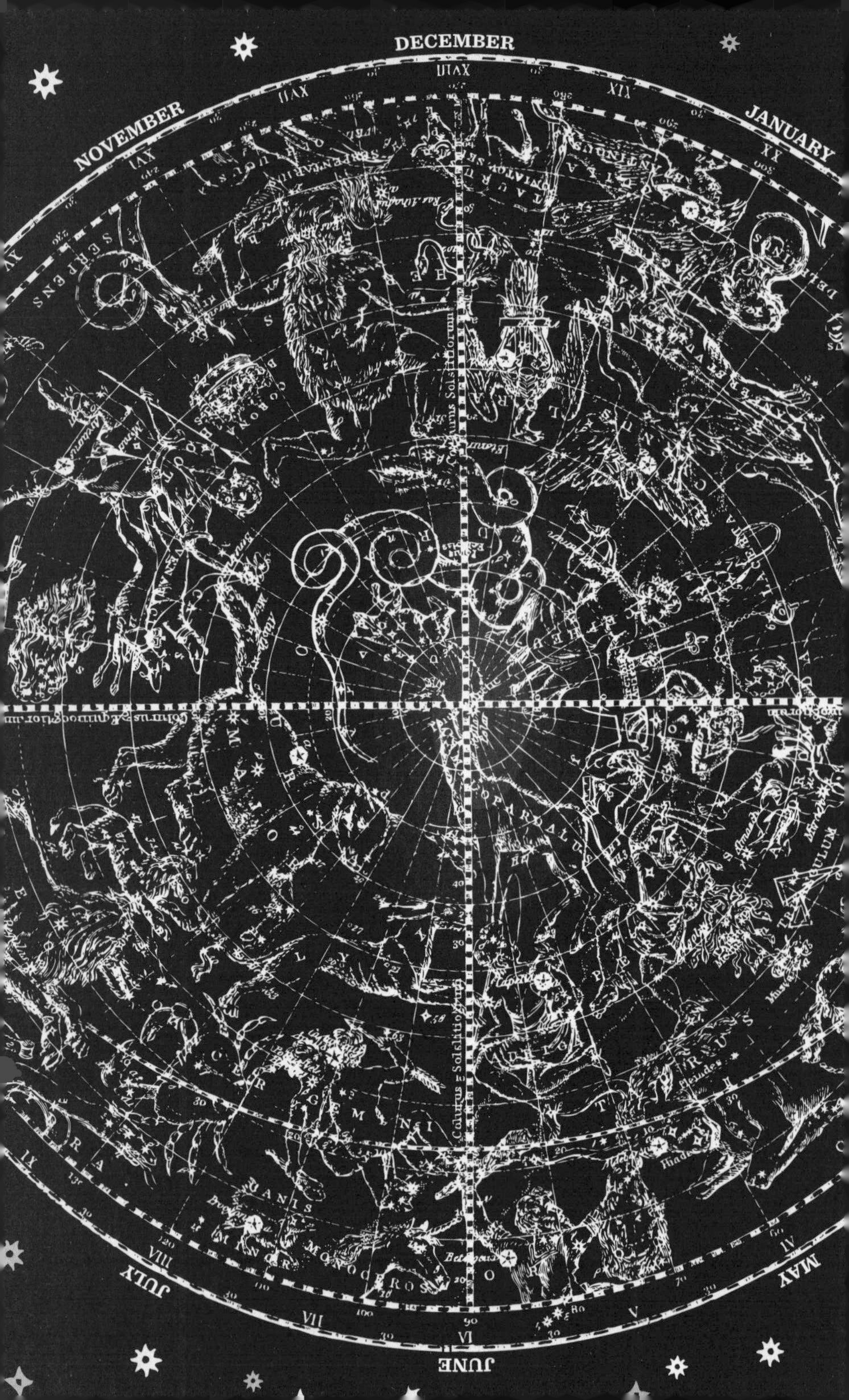
DECEMBER
NOVEMBER
JANUARY
JULY
JUNE
MAY

HUNT FOR THE PYXIS

ZOË FERRARIS

CROWN BOOKS
FOR YOUNG READERS
NEW YORK

This is a work of fiction. Names, characters, places, and incidents either are the product of the author's imagination or are used fictitiously. Any resemblance to actual persons, living or dead, events, or locales is entirely coincidental.

 Published in the United States by Crown Books for Young Readers, an imprint of Random House Children's Books, a division of Penguin Random House LLC, New York.

Crown and the colophon are registered trademarks of Penguin Random House LLC.

Visit us on the Web! randomhousekids.com

Educators and librarians, for a variety of teaching tools, visit us at RHTeachersLibrarians.com

Library of Congress Cataloging-in-Publication Data
Ferraris, Zoë.
The galaxy pirates : hunt for the Pyxis / Zoe Ferraris. — First edition.
pages cm. — (The galaxy pirates)
Summary: After her parents are kidnapped, Emma and her best friend Herbie set out on an adventure that takes them through a galaxy populated by pirates, monkeys, the tyrant Queen of Virgo, and other creatures, human and otherwise, as they try to rescue her parents and protect the mysterious Pyxis.
ISBN 978-0-385-39216-7 (trade) — ISBN 978-0-385-39217-4 (lib. bdg.) —
ISBN 978-0-385-39218-1 (ebook) [1. Adventure and adventurers—Fiction. 2. Space and time—Fiction. 3. Pirates—Fiction. 4. Kidnapping—Fiction. 5. Identity—Fiction. 6. Science fiction.] I. Title.
PZ7.1.F467Gal 2015 [Fic]—dc23 2014042924

Printed in the United States of America
10 9 8 7 6 5 4 3 2 1
First Edition

Contents

HUNT FOR THE PYXIS

CHAPTER 1

That Fish

Captain Tema Gent stood on the top deck of the HMS *Trunchien,* surrounded by a group of her strongest men. They formed a half circle, battered by the wind, their red uniforms made dark and shapeless by the rain. Looking past the starboard rail, Gent noted with disgust that it was beginning to hail.

Standing in the center of the deck, the prisoner made a pathetic figure. She was shivering violently and clutching her waist. Her hair—cut jagged by the surgeon's knife—was flattened to her skull, and her robe was heavy with the icy rain.

"Miss Brightstoke," Gent began, "I will give you one more chance to tell me where it is before I throw you overboard."

Brightstoke looked nervously to port.

"It's not particularly wise to continue this silence," Gent

said, waving her hand at the sky. "With this weather . . . it's a drowning night."

Brightstoke didn't look at her. She had withdrawn into a deep, silent part of herself.

Gent glanced down at her wrist, where her tarantula, Besnett, was beginning the long, tortuous climb up her arm. She was a black creature with fine silvery edges. The white epaulet on Gent's shoulder was her favorite perch.

Gent turned back to her prisoner. "I would have thought," she said, "that after the events of the past few days, you might have come to some conclusions about your captain. Are you willing to die for him now?"

Brightstoke stared relentlessly at the deck. The rain was coming down harder, and the waters of the Strand were churning beneath them, rocking the ship.

"He's no good," Gent went on. "I would have thought you were smart enough to see that. Especially after his betrayal of you."

Brightstoke clenched her jaw.

"Fine," Gent said. Besnett had made her way onto Gent's shoulder, and now she stood clinging to the epaulet despite the buffeting winds and the fierce lashing of Gent's bright-red hair. "You leave me no choice. Under the Articles of Maritime War, piracy and treason are to be punished by execution. Should I fail to carry out your sentence, I would be subject to the same punishment myself. So you can see how my hands are tied." Gent showed her hands and added slyly, "However, I do want to be merciful with you. I would expect the same for myself."

Brightstoke met her gaze. The women exchanged a tentative look.

"Under certain circumstances, piracy is forgiven," Gent reminded her. "I realize that the Pyxis is an important object for the rebellion, but perhaps we could come to an agreement. You give the Pyxis to us, and we guarantee that the Queen will no longer use her power against your systems. This would be enough, in my opinion, to win you a pardon."

Brightstoke blinked against a slash of rain. "How do I know you won't kill me anyway?"

"You have my word," Gent replied.

Brightstoke's eyes narrowed. She had been betrayed by her pirate companions, and Gent could see that it had wounded her.

In Gent's mind, this was all an elaborate ruse to get the prisoner to speak. Of course she would speak. Only a fool would remain silent in the face of a death like this one—being thrown into the memory seas. They'd had her for three days; they'd kept her in the fo'c'sle without food or water. Usually that was enough, because even the stupidest prisoners knew that pirates could only be held for three days before execution was required.

"So what is it, Miss Brightstoke? What will you tell us?"

"Nothing," the prisoner said. "We cannot trust the Queen. The Pyxis has to remain hidden. Forever."

Gent drew closer, eyeing her carefully. "Noble, Miss Brightstoke, but can you guarantee that it will remain hidden? That no one will find it accidentally? Or on purpose?" Brightstoke blinked. Gent was making headway. "Have you secured it properly? Do you have enough men and ships to protect the Pyxis from all the greedy, desperate renegades out there who will spend their *lives* trying to find it?"

Brightstoke looked hesitant, but she steeled herself and said, "I have secrecy on my side. That is enough."

Gent let her breath out slowly and turned to her men. "Crounse, fetch the judgment! Grimble and Bocock, tuskets ready! Let's make this quick."

"You won't kill me!" Brightstoke cried out. "I'm the only one who knows where it is!"

Gent eyed her sharply. "Comfort yourself with this: if you die, then your secret will be safe."

Moments later, Crounse reappeared on deck with the scroll. Gent said through clenched teeth, "Read the judgment."

"'Halifax Brightstoke of Spica,'" Crounse called. "'After judicious decision by the maritime configuration of a war seas council, you are hereby charged with treason and piracy. . . .'"

Gent stared fiercely at the starboard rail. Brightstoke was really going to give up her life? For the *Pyxis*? It was infuriating. They had spent months at sea and lost dozens of lives trying to catch Brightstoke. Her capture had been their only success. Gent felt certain that they would get the Pyxis too. Now everything was falling apart because this little princess was still pretending to be a pirate.

So be it, Gent decided. She didn't need Brightstoke anyway. She would find the Pyxis herself.

"'. . . by law,'" Crounse continued, "'your punishment is immediate execution in a manner to be determined by Captain Artemisia Gent of the sloop *Trunchien* in Her Majesty's service. Graces to the Queen.'"

"Wait!" Fuming, Gent turned to her men. "Go down and fetch the lynx. Yes, you heard me. Bring it out of its cage. And bring me some ballast. Bricks should do it. And I'll need a sheet of canvas, big as the topsail. Hurry! We're going to put her in a Party Bag."

The rain lashed Brightstoke's cheeks, and she squinted

against it, looking defiant. Two men tightened the rope that bound her hands. They raised a sack to her head. Gent told herself that she was ridding the seas of a thief—in this case, a particularly dangerous thief—and a murderer.

"Let this be a warning to others like you," Gent called out. "Piracy is forbidden on the galactic seas."

The lynx's cage was carried onto the deck. The great cat was curled up against the rain. Two midshipmen stunned the animal with a club. The lynx gave a loud, wailing cry and fell on its side with a thump. The men opened the cage and dragged it out, wrapping it quickly inside the canvas. Then they grabbed a struggling Brightstoke and shoved her inside, right next to the lynx, followed by half a dozen bricks for ballast. They began stitching the edges of the canvas together, their fingers working quickly. At any moment the creature might wake and spring at them. It took three men to sew the final seams, but when they were done, the bag formed a nice, tight pouch around its occupants.

No sooner had they finished than the bag began to jump and jolt. They heard Brightstoke's muffled screams, but with perfect naval composure, the men waited for Gent's command. "Go on," she said. They grabbed the bag's edge and dragged it toward the gap in the starboard rail. The bricks thumped angrily against the deck. The occupants thrashed. Everyone stared at the canvas cover. Suddenly, the lynx roared, and Brightstoke gave a heart-rending cry.

Gent motioned to her men. "Tuskets ready," she said. "On my count." The men pointed their weapons at the sky. The long ivory daggers at each tusket's tip glistened in the rain. When Gent gave the order, they fired into the sky, a deafening boom to commemorate an execution on the Strands.

Brightstoke and the lynx seemed to have fallen quiet. Everyone stared at the bag, but nothing moved. Slowly, a dark bloodstain seeped through the fabric.

"Throw it over," she said.

The men gave it a heave, and with one quick swish, the bag flipped over the side and into the dark sea. Everyone ran to the rail. Gent heard the splash and felt Besnett crawl into her collar so that only her forelegs were sticking out. When the men turned around, she saw from their faces that the deed was done.

"Captain?"

She turned to see Dr. Vermek, his scrawny form coming up from the depths of the ship. Clutching whatever he could grab against the lashing rain, he shouted, "Where is the prisoner?"

"What is your interest in the prisoner?" Gent asked.

"She was pregnant," he said. "I just finished the test. I don't think she realized. . . ."

Gent didn't hear the rest. She spun away. Pregnant? Brightstoke was *pregnant*? Gent was filled with horror. It was illegal to execute a pregnant woman because, although she was guilty, the baby was not. And in this case, the baby would have been a member of the royal family!

Vermek looked at the men still standing by the rail. "Is she gone?" He moved past the captain and, summoning his nerve, peered over the side. "Dear grace." He drew back, shutting his eyes. "Oh, dear grace."

"You didn't tell us!" Gent snapped. "You didn't even tell us it was a *possibility,* Doctor."

Vermek didn't reply. He turned to the sea, while Gent, hot with anger and shame, stared at his back. She felt Besnett crawl out of her collar and take a position on her shoulder again, her skinny legs firm against the wind.

"Well, you know what they say," Vermek said, trying to steady himself by holding the rail. "Good pirates never die."

"What exactly is a good pirate, Doctor?" Gent snapped. He looked abashed.

She left him and marched to the foredeck, her cloak whipping at her back. "Murch, set a course for Rigel. We are still charged with finding the Pyxis."

"Yes, Captain, but uh . . ." His voice was polite, but his expression wasn't. It said: *How can we do that if Brightstoke is dead?*

"We'll find it ourselves," she growled. "Now get going."

The *Implacable* was anchored on a dark, lonely, windy Strand, one of millions of such Strands, which were like great tunnels as wide as oceans, flowing like rivers, filled with water and life and air, light and darkness, and all manner of majestic and dangerous creatures. These seas crisscrossed the galaxy, connecting the vast distances between stars. In fact, the *Implacable* was on the Eridanus Strand, a winding watercourse not known for its hospitality. The ship was hidden behind an enormous outcropping of rock, hoping to avoid the Queen's navy.

"Captain!" The *Implacable*'s second mate came running down the deck. "Captain, flotsam sighted on the starboard—"

Captain Sparks looked over the rail and saw it—a floating canvas sack. "Haul it up!" he ordered. "And be quick about it!"

His men scurried down a starboard ladder and hooked the sack. It rose slowly, dripping, out of the water. Once they'd laid it out, everyone stood back.

"All right, men, back away," Sparks said. He called for the cook. Mr. Muttycombe arrived with his leather pouch and began to open the sack. Slowly, he extracted the objects from their tomb. First he took out two bricks. (The captain and his men exchanged a look. This was very odd indeed—a bag full of bricks floating on the sea?) Then Muttycombe grabbed something much harder to maneuver. Two crew members yanked the canvas in the opposite direction, and the cook extracted a woman from the bag.

"It's *her,*" someone gasped. "It's the pirate Brightstoke!"

"Yes, the very one!" someone else added. "I saw her on Rigel, I did! The Queen's navy got 'er!"

Captain Sparks raised his hand. He knew his men were fearful. The captain himself felt uneasy. It was bad luck to have a dead pirate on board—not to mention what would happen if the navy found out that its bricks didn't sink.

She was a sad sight, bloated and blue, but the cook straightened her tunic and felt for vital signs anyway.

"She's dead," he pronounced.

Dry-mouthed, the captain stared at the sack. "What else is in the bag?"

After another struggle, the cook withdrew a dead lynx. The crew members looked at the dead woman's body with a new awe. How had she been sewn in a sack with a lynx and not received a single scratch? It was anyone's guess, and some terrible guessing was going on in the crew's minds.

Just then, Sparks saw the woman's hand twitch.

"Did you see that?" he asked. "Her hand gave a twitch. Are you sure she's dead?"

The cook inspected her body. "She's cold, sir," he said, "except here." He motioned to her belly. "It's a warm touch here. Captain, I don't know how to say it, but I think she's pregnant.

And by some miracle—I swear, sir, I've never seen anything like it—the baby might have a shred of life in it."

Sparks stared at the woman's flat belly. "Are you sure it's a baby? Could it not be some—some *fish* ate its way inside her belly? Maybe swam down her throat?"

"Beggin' your pardon, sir, I don't see how, with the canvas being shut so tight and all—"

"Of course," the captain snapped. "It would have been shut in *with* her, would it not? Now, in your opinion, Mr. Muttycombe, is it not possible that she swallowed a fish?"

"Well, sir, I'd need to cut her open to find out."

Sparks screwed his eyebrows together and thought. It was the damnedest thing he'd ever seen, but it had to be a fish—and the crew had to find out to put their minds at rest. He leaned closer to the cook and whispered, "If it is a baby, can it survive without its mother?"

Muttycombe shook his head. "Never heard of such a thing."

"So it won't hurt the baby if you cut open the belly. It's going to die anyway."

Muttycombe looked nervous. "Sir?" he said. "I don't—"

"Open the belly, then," Sparks said, loudly enough for his men to hear. "We'll find that fish."

Reluctantly, the men carried the woman's body to the kitchen below and laid her on the table. The cook leaned over her body, counted to three in his mind, and set the knife on the fabric of her tunic. Glancing over his shoulder, he saw the crew's terrified faces, but he steeled himself.

The knife was dull and it took some hard pressing. Just as he broke the fabric, the woman's eyelids fluttered. The men gasped and drew back. All at once, the woman jolted to life.

The cook and his men flew away, howling, crashing into tin pots and silverware. They gripped one another and stared in horror as Brightstoke coughed, spitting up a good pint of seawater. She rolled sideways off the table, falling to the floor. No one moved to help her. They were terrified of her powers.

After a moment, Brightstoke climbed onto her knees and coughed up the last of the seawater. Only then did the crew break for the stairs, shouting for the captain.

"It's not true, is it?" Sparks demanded. "She's not alive?"

"She is, Captain, by my life, she is. We spoke and she said: *'Good pirates never—'*"

"Nonsense!" Sparks interrupted. He ran a hand down his chest. "This is ridiculous. Mighty ridiculous. Two men—you there! Get your weapons and come with me."

Minutes later, they unlocked the door and crept down the stairs, their knives drawn and tuskets ready. They were surprised to find that the kitchen was empty and the woman was gone. They extended the search from every hidey-hole to the top of the masts, but no matter where they looked, they couldn't find the notorious Halifax Brightstoke, second-greatest pirate of the seas.

With an air of frustration, Captain Sparks called off the search and ordered his men to a long-awaited mess. As the captain finally lifted a fork to his own fine plate of ragoo'd rabbit, somebody topside began shouting again. Reluctantly, he tossed down his fork and went up to find the cook pointing to the spot where the lynx had been. The animal was gone, and two pairs of wet paw prints led right up to the starboard rail.

Sparks wasted no time drawing anchor and setting the ship hastily on a full-speed course for "anywhere but Eridanus."

TWELVE YEARS LATER

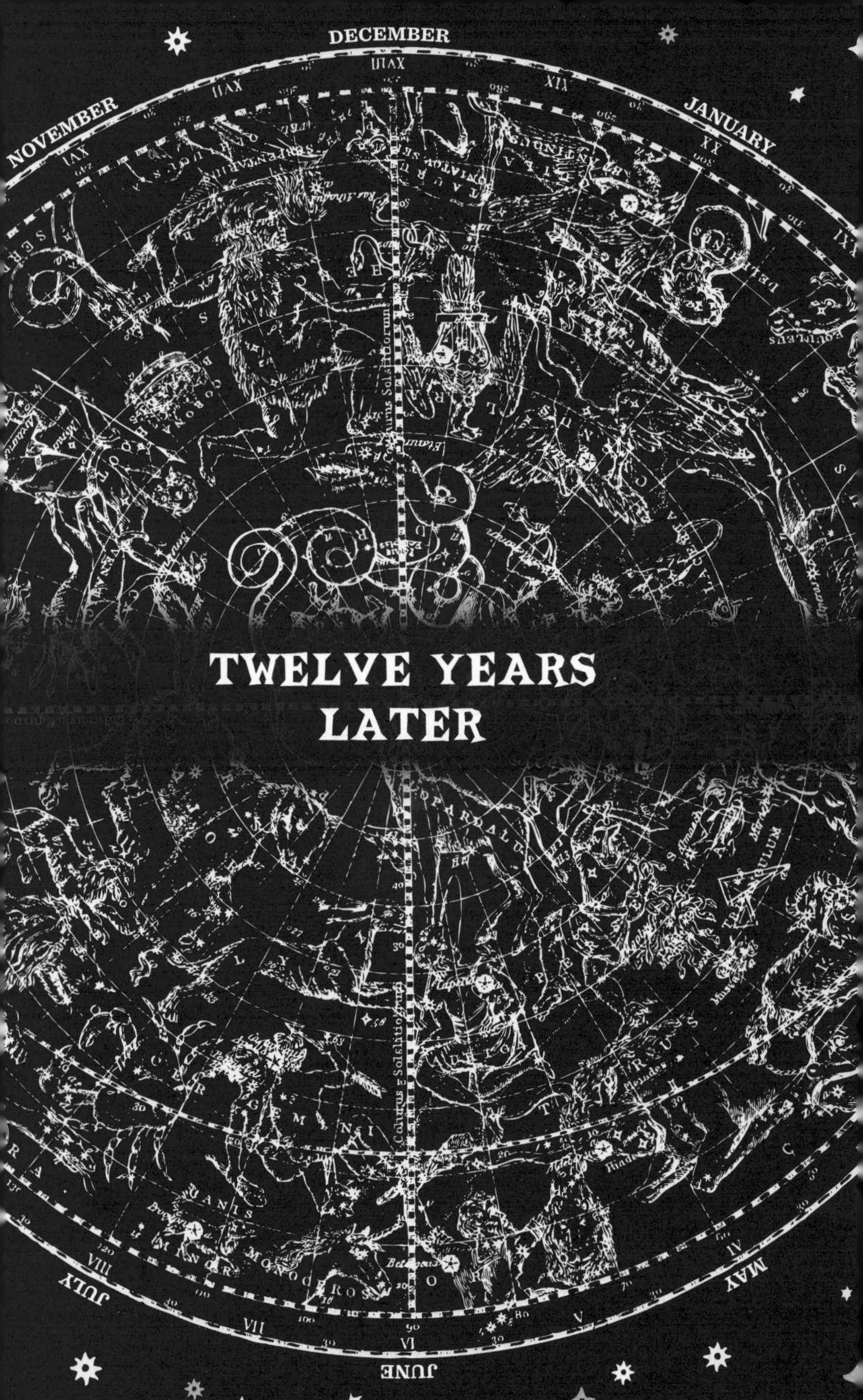

CHAPTER 2

The *Markab*

Shoes squeaking on the wooden planks, grocery bags landing with a thud on the deck floor, Emma and Herbie climbed on board the *Markab,* a single-masted thirty-foot yacht, just like they did every Saturday morning. Dad had been taking Emma out on the yacht and teaching her to sail since she was five. Herbie had only been coming for the past six months—it had taken years to convince his parents that he would be safe spending the night on the *Markab*—but he had taken to sailing like a natural.

"Don't forget your life jackets," Dad said from the pier.

Emma tossed one to Herbie and slid quickly into hers. Then she unlocked the cabin door and hustled Herbie down the stairs before he could put on his life jacket. She wanted to make sure that their charts were still there.

"You always act like someone's going to steal them," Herbie said.

They'd spent the past few weekends creating two very elaborate charts of the night sky, and if Dad hadn't insisted that they leave the charts on the boat where they belonged, she would have carried them in her backpack permanently and treated them with the same reverence that she used for her compass and sextant.

"I just want to make sure nothing happened to them," she said, unlocking the drawer in the captain's desk. The charts were there, scrolled up as they'd left them. "Whew. Okay, let's get them laid out straight. I hate it when they curl."

She noticed that Herbie was wiping his sweaty hands on his jeans. It was equally strange that he kept looking out the window. He was watching Dad pour gas into the fuel tank.

"What's wrong?" she asked.

"Nothing."

She had a bad feeling that this was about her dad again. Herbie was forever suspecting Dad of something. He was a spy. He was a thief. He was a Colombian drug lord. It made her further uncomfortable that Dad did nothing to improve his image: he changed jobs once a year, often leaving one and switching to another profession entirely. He traveled frequently, no matter what kind of job he had. He always seemed to have a lot of money, and he could afford to keep a nice yacht at one of the most expensive marinas—even when he wasn't working for months at a time. Whenever anyone asked about his job, he said it was boring and not worth talking about.

Emma had tried explaining that Dad changed jobs because his boss had been a jerk, or because he worked too many hours for too little pay. She explained how her grandparents had died before she was born and left her parents with an inheritance, which they used in those lean months when her dad didn't have a job. But Herbie never fully accepted these explanations. He was always hatching a new theory about her dad's "real" activities. As far as Emma was concerned, there was one thing that Dad was reliable, almost obsessive, about—he took her sailing whenever he could—and that was what mattered.

Normally when they were on the boat together, Herbie was so excited about sailing, and just as eager as she was to get out on the ocean, that he didn't mention his wild theories—and he certainly never talked about them while Dad was there. But right now his face was screwed up with a look of suspicion.

"Didn't he fill up the tank *last* weekend?" he asked.

"I don't know," Emma said. "Why do you care?"

"It's just . . . I know he filled it up last week."

"Maybe he didn't fill it all the way," she said. "Come on, it's not like he's rigging up a bomb." She unrolled the charts and laid them on the table. "Hand me the meteorites," she said, motioning to Dad's special black rocks that were lined up along a shelf.

"They're *not meteorites,*" Herbie said for the hundredth time, but he collected the four stones from the shelf and put them at the edges of the charts.

She checked her backpack to make sure her equipment was intact, then stowed it beneath the desk. She gave Herbie another look. He was wearing his favorite green windbreaker. He had short black hair, pink cheeks, and kind brown eyes behind his metal-rimmed glasses. He was a bit taller than Emma, and over the past few months he'd gotten kind of chubby. Mom said he would grow out of it.

"Aren't you going to put on your life jacket?" she asked.

He broke away from staring at Dad. "Oh. Yeah."

She and Herbie had met in fourth-grade Chess Club. They became friends because Emma was the only person Herbie had ever met who would agree to call him Ragnar, Master of the Dragon Lords. He'd grown out of that phase a long time ago, but if she wanted to tease him, she could still call him Ragnar to terrific effect.

Herbie's parents were very strict about homework, even though he got perfect grades. He had eight older brothers and sisters, and if he stayed home, his parents would force him to spend the whole day studying so he could become like his brothers, three of whom were doctors. (The fourth one was an architect, the fifth one a dentist.) Herbie was already busy enough with Chess Club, Mandarin lessons, Bible study, and tuba practice, but these days the only thing he really wanted to do was go sailing with Emma.

Maybe he'd had a change of heart?

"Dad said we can do nighttime navigation today," she said. She was excited about this and she had thought Herbie would be as well. "You're not worried about it, are you?"

"No," Herbie said defensively. "I like navigation." He set his backpack on the sofa, put on the life jacket, and went topside before she could ask any more questions.

Five minutes later, the engine was roaring and Emma and Herbie were standing by the captain's wheel. Behind them, a clink sounded: the mainsail's cords, which had little silver rings on them, were dangling from the mast. Herbie was staring at them in puzzlement.

"Herbie," Dad said, releasing the boat from the pier, "why don't you take her out of the harbor today?"

Herbie shot Emma a look that said *I can't!* She was surprised. Normally, they took turns guiding the boat—if Herbie sailed them out, then Emma would trim sails. Steering the ship was actually the easier job, but it meant standing closer to Dad.

Emma leaned in closer to Herbie and whispered, "What is going *on?*"

"Later," he whispered back.

"Fine." She turned to Dad. "I want to be at the wheel today," she said. Herbie looked embarrassed as he moved toward the sails. Emma had the distinct impression that he didn't want to stand close to Dad because he wouldn't be able to be his typical polite self.

Trying to ignore the whole thing, Emma focused on the boat. She put the engine into gear, gripped the wheel, and steered them deftly past the yachts and into the bay.

Every time they sailed out, she watched Dad closely. She had always wanted to be more like him. She stole jackets from his closet and wore them even though they were too large. She would have liked to have his jet-black hair and green eyes, or his tall, solid build. Maybe if she had, the kids at school wouldn't pick on her so much. As it was, she'd gotten nearly everything from her mom—dirty-blond hair, a smirking mouth, and the distinct blue eyes that were narrow and catlike, sometimes cunning. She also got her mom's small, delicate frame and all the fierce pride that seemed to go along with it.

Emma reminded herself constantly that she and her mom were different in one big respect: Mom never went sailing, while Emma loved the ocean and lived only for the weekend, when she could be on the water again.

Dad snatched the binoculars that were hanging from a hook near the wheel and went to the starboard rail. Emma found this strange. He didn't use the binoculars unless something particular caught his interest.

"Dad," she called over the groan of the engine, "what is it?"

He quickly lowered the binoculars. "Ah . . . I'm checking the current."

"Why?" she asked, puzzled.

He didn't reply. Emma steered dead ahead, awaiting his orders. She was determined to prove what an excellent sailor she was. Right now she and Herbie were just ordinary seamen, but Dad had promised her that once she became an *able* seaman, he would take her sailing around the world. It was all she ever thought about, and her bedroom was littered with books about sailing the Caribbean and the Pacific Islands, and navigation guides from ports as far-flung as Muscat. Emma desperately wanted Herbie to come too, and Dad had already said he would consider it, but Herbie was cynical. "Are you kidding? My parents barely let me come sailing on the weekends."

"Set the sails!" Dad cried.

Emma switched off the engine and Herbie let out the sails. The wind gave them a hard, immediate punch.

"You all right there, Herbie?" Dad shouted over the wind.

"Yes, skipper," came a feeble reply. Herbie looked anxious but managed to keep the sails double-reefed.

Dad lowered the binoculars, but instead of draping them back over the hook by the wheel, he hung them around his neck. Emma found this odd as well.

"Windward, then!" Dad cried. His standing policy was to leave the marina no matter what the wind and currents were like. So Herbie set the sails in tight and Emma turned the *Markab,* driving her hard to weather.

As they headed into the bay, fighting a twenty-knot wind and an aggressive current, it took no time at all to drench the jib to the masthead and send foamy green waves splashing onto everyone, soaking them to the bone. *Herbie was right to be nervous!* Emma thought wildly. *This is crazy!* She gripped the wheel with determination—no matter how many times she'd done it, it still made her heart pound to tackle a strong wind. Now it seemed to be coming after them personally, knocking them with repeated blows. Her arms were straining from holding the wheel. She imagined the boat capsizing. It frightened her so much that she felt the impulse to shout for Dad's help. She was too small for this! She resisted the urge to look at Herbie, who was no doubt gripping the boom with his own white-knuckled fear.

"You okay?" Dad called. It wasn't a question; it was a challenge. If she said no, he would take the wheel, but she knew what he would think: she was cowardly, just like her mom.

"I'm fine!" she said defiantly. She kept her eyes on the water.

The wind drove them quickly toward the entrance to the bay. The Golden Gate Bridge loomed above them, glowing a majestic orange against the morning's deep-blue sky. Beneath the bridge ran a busy shipping lane, but right now there were no large container ships in sight.

Emma guided them into the open expanse of the sea. As soon as they'd cleared the bridge's shadow, she dared a glance at Herbie and saw that he was looking a bit more confident.

"All right, kids," Dad said, clapping his hands. "We want to go north. Where's the wind?"

Emma rolled her eyes. It was annoying that after they had traversed some of the trickiest straits in the world, Dad still didn't seem to think they could handle the open ocean. Any ordinary seaman could do that!

"Northerly," she said.

"Excellent. Which course?"

"Three-ten," Emma said, giving him a zombie stare.

"And how are you going to do that with a northerly wind?"

"Tacking to port and beating to windward," she recited monotonously.

"Good. Herbie, can you handle the sails?"

"Dad," Emma said sharply, "I think we can handle the *sails.*"

"Very well," he said with a touch of mock asperity. "Then she's all yours, skipper."

"Thank you," Emma said sarcastically.

She turned to the wheel, feeling more confident and finally allowing herself to enjoy the wind rushing through her hair and the salty spray dappling her face. There were a few salmon fishing boats near the coast, but the *Markab* was quickly putting them behind it and heading into the ocean. She couldn't suppress a happy grin.

Then suddenly the *Markab* slammed to a halt.

The force of their sudden stop reverberated through every bone in Emma's body. It thundered to the top of the rigging and nearly sent Herbie and Dad flying into the sea. If it hadn't been for some quick ducking and grabbing, they would have toppled overboard.

"What was *that*?" Emma cried, feeling irrationally that this was her fault. Had she held the wheel too hard? Broken the rudder?

"We must have hit something," Herbie said breathlessly, climbing to his feet.

Everyone looked to the sails, which were still pillowed taut with the wind, yet the boat did not seem to be moving an inch in the water. Emma turned the wheel, but nothing happened.

"What *was* that?" she asked. Both she and Herbie turned to Dad. Strangely, he had run to the stern and was now staring at the bay behind them.

"Dad," Emma said.

He spun around, looking startled.

"What are we supposed to do?" she asked.

"You're in charge," he said. "You can handle this."

"But we're not moving!" she cried.

"Figure it out." He went back to scanning the coastline.

Emma was sweating, and a terrifying flutter was beating up from her chest. She left the wheel and circled the boat desperately, trying to imagine what could have stopped them so suddenly.

"I can't see anything!" she said. The water beneath them was choppy with foam. "Maybe we hit a bank?" she asked.

"There are no banks here," Herbie said. "Uh, Emma . . ." He pointed over her shoulder. "We've got a ship coming."

She turned to see a large container ship. It was about twenty miles out, driving a course into the bay. The *Markab* was right in its path.

"Dad! It's a ship!"

But Dad already had it in his sights. "I think you'd better hurry," he said. He was trying to play it cool, but his voice had a shaky quality.

"What do we *do?*" she squealed. "That ship's going to hit us!"

Herbie was paler than she'd ever seen him. "Maybe we should inflate the life raft?" he squeaked.

"Yep," Dad said, and with surprising alacrity hauled the life raft canister from beneath the bench. "Emma," he said, his voice strangely aggressive. *"What are you going to do?"*

Emma was having trouble breathing. The container ship seemed to be getting closer much too quickly. *Don't panic,* she thought. *Don't be a chicken.* She walked frantically around the deck, shoving a boat hook into the water and trying to understand what was holding them in place. Whatever it was, they had only a few minutes to break free of it. She spun on Herbie.

"Start the engine!" she shouted, kicking herself for not having thought of it until now. Herbie scrambled for the controls and fired them up. Emma raced back to the wheel. The engine roared to life and she revved it to its full horsepower, while Herbie ran to the stern to check the ripple.

"We're still not moving!" he cried.

True panic set in. Emma felt her legs weaken. She revved the engine even harder and looked again at the container ship, which was terrifyingly close now. Dad was fumbling with the lines to the raft, and she could see that he was alarmed. *Think, think,* she told herself ruthlessly. *We just have to break free.*

PFFFFFFF! The raft inflated. Dad hauled it over the side.

There's got to be a way! she thought wildly.

"Come on, kids!" Dad said. "Into the life raft!"

"No!" Emma cried. "The *Markab* can't sink!" It couldn't be that they'd lost the bottom of the boat—they'd be upside down by now. They must be *stuck* on something. And the only way to get free would be to try to jolt themselves loose.

"What's the plan?" Dad asked.

"We've got to break ourselves free. Herbie, sheet the mainsail in tight. I'm going to try to pivot!"

Herbie rushed to obey her.

As soon as the mainsail was sheeted tightly enough, she gunned the engine in reverse and turned ninety degrees to port. The *Markab* tipped with a sudden, rapid force. Terrified that they'd capsize, she turned quickly to starboard, tipping the boat to the other side.

"Keep going!" Dad shouted, staring at the container ship. "I think they've noticed us. They're changing course, but not fast enough."

"Emma, hurry!" Herbie cried.

"I am hurrying!" she cried back, steering wildly to port now and tipping them again. "Just one . . . more . . ."

SNAP! Abruptly the *Markab* broke free and found itself in full wind, tipping halfway to the water and sliding into an uncontrollably reckless course. Emma seized the wheel and steered them desperately to starboard, shouting at Herbie to reef them so she could regain some control. All the while the steel hull of the container ship grew larger, but every ounce of Emma's attention was focused on getting them clear of its path. With Herbie rushing about behind her, she finally got the *Markab* steadied, and she blasted it on a straight course away from the Goliath.

They heard a resounding *crack!* as the bow of the container ship hit whatever had stopped the *Markab.* An enormous piece of timber rose up into the water like a whale, broken in half against the hull of the great ship. It looked like the sunken remains of a fishing pier. It was covered in long spikes and kelp, and it flopped back into the water.

They plowed ahead for half a mile before anyone felt safe. Then the relief seemed to come over all of them at once. Dad hauled the life raft back over the railing and sat down, running a hand over his face. Herbie slumped onto the bench, his shoulders trembling. Emma lowered her head to the wheel, still shaking with adrenaline.

"We hit a piece of wood," Herbie said numbly.

"What was it even *doing* there?" she said.

But Dad looked relieved. "That was good work," he said. "You two handled it perfectly."

Despite her shaking hands, Emma felt a small burst of pride. They had saved the boat. They really did know what they were doing. Even Herbie's face brightened.

"Does this mean we're able seamen now?" she asked.

"Not yet," Dad replied. "You still have a lot of work to do. Unfortunately, it does mean we're going to have to cut this trip short."

"What? No!" Emma and Herbie protested at once.

"Whatever we hit may have damaged the hull. Just to be safe, we'd better take her back in."

There was no disputing the sense of that, and with heavy hearts, Emma turned the wheel and Herbie went to the sails, and they steered the *Markab* back into the bay.

CHAPTER 3

Spy, Alien, Drug Lord

Mom was delighted that they'd come back so soon. She offered to cook lunch, but by way of consolation to Emma and Herbie, Dad had insisted that they order a pizza.

Heading upstairs to Emma's room, Emma and Herbie couldn't stop talking about what had happened on the boat.

"I just can't believe we *hit* something," she said. "I've never heard of that happening."

"Yeah." He gave a nervous laugh. "Quick thinking with the whole pivot thing."

She swung her door open and they went inside. "You're not getting sick of sailing, are you?"

He shook his head quickly. "No way."

She was happy to hear that. Herbie had talked about becoming a navy captain ever since he was in fourth grade.

Herbie's phone alarm beeped. He sighed.

"I'd better start on the homework." He reached for their backpacks and took out their folders. The deal was that he did all their homework one day, and Emma would do it the next. They'd made the deal in fifth grade, and although Emma sometimes had to work harder than Herbie to get an equally good grade, it was better than having to do homework every night.

Herbie worked through their algebra problems, while Emma took out a book called *Everything You Ever Wanted to Know About Knots* and began reading.

She had just come to a chapter about reef knots when she realized that Herbie was strangely quiet. Usually he did all the talking, even while doing algebra, and if she didn't answer, he'd pester her with questions.

"Did you see Cad at school yesterday?" she asked.

"No," Herbie said. Cad was a burly seventh grader whose real name was Cadogan. Everyone called him "Cardigan" and he hated the word so much that whenever Herbie wore a sweater to school, Cad beat him up.

"Then what?" she asked.

Herbie set down his pencil and took a deep breath. "Okay. I wasn't going to tell you this, but . . . I think I should. I saw your dad on Tuesday."

"You couldn't have," she said. "He was in Phoenix until Thursday."

"I know he *said* that," Herbie replied, getting flustered. "But I saw him. Here!"

Emma stared at him witheringly, then rolled her eyes. "Is this what you didn't want to tell me on the boat?"

"Yeah. I swear I saw him at the marina," Herbie said. "I mean technically, he was on Marina Boulevard. I was going to my tuba lesson and he was just down the block. I actually recognized his voice before I saw him. He was talking on his phone."

"He was in *Arizona*."

"I know that's what he said." Herbie got a bullish expression on his face. "But I'm *sure* it was him. I got a good look at him, and like I said, I recognized his voice."

"Did you talk to him?"

"No."

"Then you don't know for sure." Emma resumed reading, but it was hard to concentrate when Herbie was staring at her so intently. "How far away were you?"

"Half a block. I was just going over to say hi, but he went into the marina really fast."

"So you didn't get a good look at him."

"No, I *did*. Then a few minutes later I saw him sail away on the *Markab*."

Emma felt her cheeks burn hot. Herbie had suspected Dad of many things. She always told herself that he had a hyperactive imagination, but this accusation was new and it brought a flush of anger. Dad *never* went on the boat without her. "Remember the time you thought you saw my dad on that TV show about the Mafia?"

"This is totally different!"

"I don't think so," she said. "You've mistaken him for someone else before. And now you're mistaking the *Markab* for a different boat—"

"No, I'm *not*."

"Anyway," she cut in, "my dad was gone this week."

Herbie pressed his lips together. "I'm *sure* it was him."

"How can you be sure when he was half a block away and—and it was probably getting dark anyway?"

"I think I'd recognize your dad," Herbie said coldly. "And I'm sorry I had to tell you this, but I thought you should know."

"Know *what*?"

Herbie's cheeks were red now too.

Emma closed her book and stood up. "I have an idea—why don't we just go downstairs and ask him about it?"

"No!" Herbie leapt up. "No, don't do that."

"Why not? He'll tell us the truth."

"Emma, that's a *really* bad idea."

She was out the door before Herbie could reach her. "Wait, wait," he whispered, struggling to get past her on the landing. "Don't tell him I said this, just in case—"

Aggravated, Emma shirked him and went downstairs.

Dad was in his study, a long, narrow room decorated with thick Persian carpets and old tea lamps. Tall bookshelves lined every wall, each overflowing with books. A grand mahogany desk stood at the end of the room, and Dad was sitting there, writing in a ledger.

"Hey, Dad," Emma said, plunking herself down in one of the overstuffed chairs. Herbie stood awkwardly beside a lamp.

"Hi, guys," Dad said.

"Where were you this week?" Emma asked.

He looked up. "In Phoenix. Why?"

"Just wondering how your week was." She gave Herbie a subtle I-told-you-so look. "You were at that conference, right?"

"Yes."

"And you were gone the whole week?"

"Well, yes," he said, looking at her oddly. "Why are you asking?"

"It just seems like a long time," she replied.

"It sure felt like forever," he said. "These things usually do."

As he pattered on with ridiculous details, like the way the hotel bar had served "southwestern peanuts" (whatever those were) and how Phoenix was as scorching hot as the bird it was named after, Emma felt a wave of satisfaction. Of course Herbie had seen someone else at the marina.

"Pizza's going to be here any minute!" Mom called from the kitchen. "Jack, do you have any cash?"

Dad stood up, reached for his wallet, and left the room.

The minute Dad was out of earshot, Herbie whispered, "He's lying."

Emma blew air out of her cheeks and reminded herself that Herbie had once dared to suggest that Dad was an alien.

"He went somewhere else this week," Herbie said in a very arch tone.

"What*ever* . . ."

"No, listen. I think he went out on the boat."

"You can't get to Phoenix on a *boat,*" she snapped, leaping out of the chair.

"I know." Herbie glared at her. "So I guess he didn't go to Phoenix."

A cold silence passed between them.

"I've been thinking about it," Herbie whispered. "The mainsail was untied—he *never* leaves it untied. And the fuel tank was empty. But I'm one hundred percent certain we filled it up last week. Remember he spilled gasoline on his foot and he drove all the way home with one shoe in the trunk?"

Emma felt a twinge of alarm. "I'm sure there's an explanation," she said flatly. "Why don't *you* ask him this time?" It was a mean thing to do, knowing Herbie would never ask her dad anything.

The doorbell rang.

Herbie pressed his lips together. "I think your dad might—" Seeing Emma's scowl, he hesitated and took a breath. "I think he might be smuggling things."

"Now you think my dad is a *drug lord*?" Emma blurted.

"No!" Herbie said.

"Listen, my dad is not a spy, not an alien, and not a drug lord," she hissed. "And there is *nothing weird going on.*"

CRACK!

The sound of breaking glass startled them both. Then came a shriek from the front of the house.

Emma and Herbie bolted for the door, but before they could reach it, Dad burst in, slamming the door behind him and lurching for a bookshelf.

"What's going on?" Emma cried.

Dad yanked a book from the shelf—she couldn't see which one—and with a loud *pop,* a lower section of the bookshelf snapped out of the wall, opening like a door.

"Get in!" he hissed.

"Wait, what's going on?" Emma demanded.

He pushed her head down and shoved her into the compartment. Herbie scrambled in behind her. "Stay in here no matter what. DO YOU UNDERSTAND ME?"

Emma had rarely heard this tone from him before, and it frightened her. "Yeah."

He shut the door with a final, disturbing *thunk,* cramming them into a hot, dark hidey-hole that, until two minutes ago, Emma hadn't even known existed. It smelled like dust and leather and wood. There was not much space, and they were forced to curl their knees into their chests, their shoulders touching. A bit of light came in through a long, narrow peephole at eye level. They could just see past the row of books and into the study. Only then did Emma realize that Mom was shouting and that heavy footsteps were thundering through the house.

CHAPTER 4
Caz Rastall Comes to Dinner

Dad rushed to his desk, but he had barely reached it before the study door was blown open and a man barreled in, a gun in his hand.

"Put your hands where I can see them!" he shouted.

The peephole gave Emma a limited view. She couldn't see the man's face, but she saw his black shirt, strangely billowing and open at the chest. His forearms were covered in horrible burn marks. Scarred, lumpy red skin went from the tops of his elbows all the way down to his fingertips. The fingers were odd too. They looked as if they'd been chopped off, chewed up, and then sewn back on. They moved crookedly, backward even, as he pointed the gun at Dad and said, "Now, get up."

A woman entered the room behind him, dragging Mom in a vise grip. Emma gasped and clapped a hand to her mouth.

"Oh no," Herbie whispered.

The woman was shorter, and Emma could see her face. Dressed in a pizza delivery uniform, she was a ragged woman with a mess of blond hair and a pair of narrow green eyes. Wiry and tough, her whole body seemed to give off an electrical impulse that might crackle at the slightest provocation. She threw Mom to the floor. Mom scrambled to her feet to find the woman pointing a gun at her.

When Mom stood up, the man let out a deep, rich laugh. "Well, well, Halifax Brightstoke!"

"He knows your mom?" Herbie whispered.

"Caz Rastall . . . ," Mom replied in a dark voice.

"And she knows *him*?" Emma squeaked.

"And Laine Night," Mom said coldly, staring at the woman. "I should have known."

To Emma's amazement, Mom looked not at all frightened. She gave Rastall a challenging gaze. "I almost didn't recognize you with all the burns."

"You thought you were clever hiding here, did you?" Rastall spat. "Well, there are others here too. You should never have left Draco, my girl."

"Draco?" Herbie whispered.

"How did you find me?" Mom asked.

"Why don't you ask your husband?"

They couldn't see Dad's face, but Mom's expression showed a hint of dismay.

"You're nothing but a petty thief," Mom said.

"Oh ho!" Rastall cried. "And you're not?" He gave a laugh.

Emma gaped.

Another man came into the room behind them. He was

short and thuggish, and his arms were just as burned as Caz's. He was carrying a gun.

"Did you find the Pyxis?" Caz asked him.

The man stepped forward and held out a necklace. "Was in a jewelry box upstairs," he said, his voice rough. Emma recognized one of Mom's necklaces, a rather large silver locket. It was circular, with gears and dials like an astrolabe.

Caz seized it with amazement.

"Unbelievable," he said, laughing wickedly. "Your jewelry box?"

"Give it back," Mom commanded coldly.

Rastall spun on her. "If you value your life, you'll tell me what I need to do to activate it." He held up the necklace. The amulet spun helplessly on its chain.

"There's something else," the man said. "They've got a kid. A girl, I'm thinking. She's got a bedroom upstairs."

Rastall looked alarmed. He pointed his gun at Dad. "Where is she?"

"She's out," he said. "At soccer practice."

"You're lying!" Rastall strode angrily toward the desk. "WHERE IS SHE?"

"I told you. She's at soccer pra—"

CRACK! Rastall knocked the butt of his pistol against Dad's head. Dad fell forward, unconscious. His body hit the carpet with a terrible *thud.*

"If she's gone for help," Rastall said bitterly to Mom, "so help me, I'll hunt her down and kill her too."

Mom didn't seem the slightest bit fazed. She was staring at the amulet. "If you don't give it back right now," she said, "I'll make sure you don't leave this room alive."

Emma was flabbergasted.

"You'll make it easier on yourself if you tell me what I need to know," Rastall said.

"I'll never tell you anything, you filth!" Mom said, lashing out with a kick. It sent Rastall sprawling backward and knocked the gun from his hand.

Laine fell on Mom, but she was ready. Emma watched in complete amazement as Mom aimed a square punch at the woman's face. Laine blocked it and struck back, but Mom caught her arm and twisted until something snapped. Laine howled in agony, and Mom punched her in the neck. She fell to the floor.

Emma couldn't believe what she was seeing. Her mother was fighting as if she did this every day! She spun just in time to fend off the second burned man, delivering a forceful kick that sent him sprawling onto a table and crashing to the floor. The gun flew out of his grip and slid across the carpet.

Mom made a dash for the gun. She was nearly there, but Rastall was up on his feet. He lunged for her. Mom raised her fists and it looked as if she might strike him again, but suddenly a spurt of blood sprayed from her nose, and she stumbled. It only lasted a few seconds, but it was enough for Rastall to seize his gun. He pointed it at her chest as Laine delivered a vicious punch to Mom's face. Mom fell backward, tumbling over the chair.

Rastall gave a wicked laugh. "I'm afraid, dear Halifax, that you may need some persuasion." He hauled her to her feet and nodded at Laine. "Tell me how to start the Pyxis or I'm going to shoot your husband."

Mom was shaking, but she stood there with a defiant gaze.

Laine aimed her pistol at Dad and fired. The noise of the explosion seemed to rip through the hidey-hole. Mom screamed.

Both of Emma's hands were clapped to her mouth. She was whimpering, her whole body shaking violently. Herbie grabbed her arm. They couldn't see enough of Dad to know where the bullet had struck, but they heard him groan. Laine raised her gun again.

"STOP!" Mom shrieked. "Stop! I'll tell you." Her face was so full of anguish that Emma began to cry.

Blood was pouring from Mom's nose and she looked woozy. Emma had the awful feeling that she couldn't tell them what they wanted to know. How did one "start" a necklace, anyway?

After a moment, Mom said, "All you must do is hold it and wish it to start."

Laine's eyes opened wide with something verging on horror and excitement. "Did ye hear that? Try it now! Go on! We've got to make sure she's not lying."

Rastall was gazing skeptically at Mom. "I know you too well, Halifax, to believe that answer. Do you think I'm a fool?"

Emma looked at her mother just in time to catch the wisp of a vicious smile. "Go ahead," Mom spat. "Try it if you don't believe me."

Rastall narrowed his eyes.

"Go on!" Laine cried. "Yer wastin' time!"

"We can't start it now!" he snapped.

"Give it to me, then." Laine lowered her gun. "I'll try it!"

"No!" he replied. His eyes never left Mom's face. "If we start it now, it'll send a signal, and the whole planet will know in an *instant*—"

"I know, I know," Laine said impatiently. "Like an invisible siren and everyone can hear 'cause they're always listenin' for it. But I don't care about that, do I? They ain't going to find us—we'll be halfway to Draco—"

"It *will* reveal its location," Rastall cut in. "No matter where we go."

"But she could be lying!" Laine said.

"Exactly right." Rastall's eyes gleamed. "And since we don't want the whole universe to descend on this wretched little city, I think we'll just have to take our dear Halifax along for the ride!"

Emma's heart leapt into her throat. Laine seized Mom. Her nose was bleeding profusely now, her head lolling forward.

"What about Mad Jack?" Laine asked.

"Bring him," Rastall intoned. "We'll need him later."

The burned man bent over and hauled Dad onto his shoulders.

Emma and Herbie listened as the kidnappers thundered through the kitchen and out the back door. They heard snatches of conversation—about a car parked in the alley and whether they should go back to look for Emma. They heard their own hearts racing, blood pounding in their heads, their breath magnificently loud in the confined space. Emma was crying silently, too stunned to speak.

It was Herbie who began feeling the walls around him, looking for a way to open the hidey-hole. "Don't worry, Emma," he said breathlessly. "We'll get out of here and call the police. They'll find them. We know exactly what they look like."

When his fingers finally struck the latch, the door sprang open and they both tumbled out.

Emma hit the carpet and lay there facedown, struck dumb with shock. Herbie sat up and rubbed his foot. Something had fallen out of the hidey-hole behind them—a wooden box about the size of a backpack had knocked into him. He pushed it aside and knelt over Emma.

"Just stay here. I'm gonna call the police."

CHAPTER 5

Sweetser and Wantling Join the Party

For the next hour, officers swarmed through the house. There were beat cops in uniform, plainclothes police, and even forensic techs in white bubble suits. Emma sat numbly at the kitchen table while Herbie hovered around her, bringing root beer and cookies because he thought she was in shock. She hadn't said much since they fell out of the hidey-hole.

Emma was desperately grappling with what she'd seen. Despite Herbie's many suspicions over the years, she'd never truly believed that her parents were involved in anything illegal or dangerous—or even that they could be. They were honest people, and they expected her to be honest too.

But they had recognized Rastall and Laine—and Laine had

recognized Dad, calling him "Mad Jack." It was bad enough that her father might actually have a criminal past, but now to discover that her mother did too—and that she wasn't afraid of a small punk like Rastall! She had stared that gun straight in the barrel and told Rastall she'd kill him if he didn't give her necklace back. Emma couldn't think of a single time when her mother had shown such bravado before. In fact, all she could think of were the times when a *little* courage would have been welcome. Like when their car had gotten a flat tire on the freeway, and Mom had waited two hours for the tow truck to come. (*"It's not safe to change your own tire,"* she'd said. *"You could get hit by a car!"*) Or the time in McDonald's when a distracted clerk had tried to charge them ten bucks for a hamburger, and Emma was the one who had to point out his mistake—Mom being too shy to correct him.

Emma simply couldn't believe that her parents were criminals. They hadn't done any kidnapping or shooting. They had been victims, actually—forced at gunpoint to cooperate with criminals. For all she knew, they were heroes, working undercover for the CIA. It would certainly explain why they hadn't told her anything.

But she had a horrible feeling that Herbie was right and her dad was involved in something shady.

Herbie sat down beside her. "You want more root beer?" he asked.

Emma shook her head. She noticed that the police were watching them. "I can't believe this is happening," she whispered.

Herbie seemed relieved that she was finally talking, and he leaned closer to whisper back. "Have you ever seen those kidnappers before?"

"No," Emma said. "It's totally weird that they were after my mom's necklace. They called it the Pyxis."

Herbie nodded. They had both heard the word before—they had even drawn a picture of it for their sailing chart. It was a small constellation in the southern sky. The Pyxis was supposed to be a compass and was part of the bigger constellation Argo Navis, which was a ship.

"They were also talking about Draco," he said. "Like it was a place. Like they'd been there."

"I don't get it," Emma said. "If this necklace is so important, then why did my mom leave it lying around?"

"Did she ever wear it?"

"Yeah, when they went out for fancy dinners. The rest of the time she just left it in the jewelry box on her dresser. But it was obviously really important to her; otherwise she wouldn't have threatened to kill Rastall just to keep it safe."

Herbie blew air out of his cheeks. "That was a shock."

"She was *fighting,*" Emma said.

"Totally not your mom."

"I know."

"Look, you have to tell this to the police," Herbie said. "The sooner they start looking for your parents, the better chance they have of finding them."

"I don't think they're going to help us."

"What do you mean?"

"They're not going to believe any of this."

Herbie was about to protest, but the investigator in charge came into the room. He was an enormously tall, soft-jowled man. Although the kitchen entryway was high enough for a giant to pass through, he ducked anyway as he entered. A petite woman hovered near his shoulder and gazed warily around the room.

"Hello there." The man spoke to them as if he were talking to a four-year-old. "I'm Lieutenant William Sweetser. I'm in charge of this case. This is my assistant, Sergeant Penelope Wantling."

Emma stared at them doubtfully.

"I'm sure the other officers have already told you that we'll be taking you to social services until we can find your parents," he said. "But first, I'd like to ask you some questions." He took a seat beside Emma. The chair gave an unhappy groan. "We're going to make this as easy as possible, all right?"

Emma glanced at Herbie. He was wearing his look of polite neutrality. It meant he thought the officer was an idiot.

Sweetser explained that he had heard their story from the other officers, but he wanted to go over the facts again. "There were three kidnappers," he said. "Two men and a woman?"

Emma nodded.

"They broke in through your front door, held your parents at gunpoint, and then took them away?"

"Um . . . they *shot* my dad and beat my mom bloody, then dragged them out of the house."

Sweetser cleared his throat uncomfortably. "And you two survived by hiding in a closet?"

"My dad shoved us in there," Emma said.

"That was resourceful," Sweetser said. "Now, at any point, did these kidnappers say what they wanted?"

"They took a necklace from my mom's jewelry box," Emma replied. "They called it the Pyxis."

Sweetser blinked. "The Pyxis?"

Emma stared at him. "That's what they said."

"And did they say what it was?"

"They wanted to activate it," Emma said darkly, "to make sure it worked, but they didn't, because it was going to send a signal that would alert everyone else to its location."

Behind him, Sergeant Wantling scribbled furiously in her notebook.

"Let me get this straight," Sweetser said. "They wanted to activate a necklace?"

"That's what they said."

Sweetser motioned to Wantling to stop writing. They exchanged a look, and she seemed to understand that Sweetser thought the story was ridiculous. A bit embarrassed, she lowered her pencil.

"Well," Sweetser said, "sometimes it's hard to remember things clearly when you've had a shock. Maybe we'd better talk to you again in the morning."

Emma gave him a deadly look. "I have to go to the bathroom," she said.

Sweetser nodded. Emma stood up, giving Herbie a meaningful stare on her way out.

She didn't go to the bathroom. She went straight to Dad's study. When she opened the door, a faint whiff of his cologne brought a choke to her throat, but she went inside anyway and locked the door. Peeking through the window, she saw that the police were loading up their vans, so she shut the blinds as well, all the while trying not to look at the bloodstain on the carpet.

Emma pulled a chair over to the special bookshelf, stood on the seat, and began sliding books off the shelf, each time looking to see if the compartment came open. Herbie had shut it again, and they had lied to the police and said they'd hidden in a closet. But something had fallen out of the hidey-hole with them. It was a box about as big as a dictionary, and it was made of a bright reddish wood. There had been a design on the front. She'd only caught a glimpse of it, but she thought it was a horse. Whatever it was, Herbie had noticed something about it that had made him hide it again. And it was obviously important, or her dad wouldn't have hidden it in the first place.

Finally, she grabbed the right book (*The Call of the Wild*). There was a *crunk* behind the wall, and the hidey-hole popped open.

She peered into the compartment. The wooden box was on the floor. She removed it and shut the hidey-hole again.

Bringing the box to the desk, she set it down. There was a flying horse carved on the top. It was a large, beautiful white animal, its body inlaid with emeralds and mother-of-pearl. Beneath it, the word *MARKAB* was spelled out in black onyx stones. Dad had said he'd named the boat after his favorite star on Pegasus, but he'd never said why. It seemed obvious that the box belonged on the boat. It was made of the same reddish-brown wood as the boat's desk and shelves.

She began feeling around the edges. *SNAP!* The lid popped open. She lifted it gently.

Inside she found a large book. Prying it free, she set it carefully on the desk. It was a thick, gleaming leather-bound book that crackled when she opened it. The pages were like onionskin. There was no title on the binding, but on the first page, she read:

A STONECIPHER'S Almagest
consisting of
Ninety-Five Chapters
in which one can discover
A VIEW OF THE INFINITE SKY
in finite points
and
A DEEPER UNDERSTANDING OF THE UNIVERSE
◈ DESIGNED BY A Gentlewoman ◈

Puzzled, she turned back to the box, which was much larger than the book. It appeared to be empty, but when she touched the bottom, the wood flipped over in her hand, revealing another compartment beneath it. Inside that was a smaller box.

It took a bit of prying before she could release this one. It was a wooden square the size of her fist. Once she removed it, she felt around the edges but couldn't find a way to open it. When she turned it over, something inside of it went *clunk.*

She heard a car door slam. Peeking out the front window, she saw Sergeant Wantling going down the stairs to welcome a new officer. Emma rushed to the closet, found one of Dad's old backpacks, and shoved everything inside—the book, the large Pegasus box, and the smaller box that she'd found inside it.

On her way out the door, she saw Herbie coming down the hallway. "You were right," he said. "They don't believe you. They thought you were totally making up your story."

"Come on," she whispered.

"Wait, what are you doing?" he asked, glancing at the backpack.

She took his arm and began dragging him down the hallway toward the bathroom. "I got the box that was in the hidey-hole," she whispered. "Let's go before they catch us."

"What? Go where? You can't just leave. They're taking you to social serv—"

"I'm going to the *Markab,*" she said. "I think there's something important in the box, something my dad doesn't want anyone to know about. If the police find out I have it, they're going to take it away."

"Emma, you can't live alone on a boat," he said.

"I won't. I just need to see what's inside this thing while there are no police around. And I need you to do me a favor."

"What?"

They had reached the bathroom and she pulled him inside, shutting the door and locking it. "I need some tools," she said. "A hammer and chisel."

"And you want me to get them."

"Doesn't your dad have them?"

"Yes, but if I go home, my parents will know I'm not sailing, and they'll make me stay and finish my homework."

"Then don't let them see you," she said. Giving the window a hard yank, she got it open. "Get the tools and meet me on the *Markab.* It'll look better if we split up anyway."

"Wait, what am I supposed to tell the police?"

"Nothing. Just sneak away." She lowered the backpack out the window. It landed on the grass with a gentle *thud,* and she crawled through the window frame, dropping silently into the yard.

CHAPTER 6

The Signal

The *Markab* gave a creak as Herbie stepped onto the deck.

Emma was nestled into the small sofa, the most comfortable spot on the boat. With shelves above and below her and desks on either side, she had spent the past hour inside her own private nook. She had piled a blanket onto her lap and was now curled into a warm ball, reading the *Almagest,* the book she'd found in the wooden box. It had a chapter for each of the constellations. At the very back of the book she'd found a pullout map of the night sky. She was just folding it up when Herbie stuck his head in the hatch.

He climbed down the ladder, his backpack clunking loudly.

"Did anyone see you?" she asked, climbing down from her nook.

"No," he said, scowling. He set the backpack on the floor

with a metal clang. "You would NOT believe how ridiculous it was after you left—"

"Did you bring the hammer and chisel?" she asked.

He looked at her warily. "Ye-e-es," he said. "Right after you left I had to—"

"I found this." Emma pulled the *Almagest* from the nook and handed it to him. "It was in the box that hit your leg."

He looked at the title page. "Uh . . . okay. Why did your dad hide this?"

"I don't know. And check this." She flipped to the back of the book and unfolded the map for him. "Hand me the meteorites."

"They're *not meteorites.*" Herbie collected the four stones from the shelf and put them at the edges of the chart Emma had placed on the kitchen table. An enormous map of the night sky sprawled before them—so big that one of them could have curled up on top of it and fit very nicely. But this chart was different from the ones they knew. Hand-drawn lines connected the stars of each constellation, but they also connected each constellation to its neighbors. The result was a vast network of lines stretching all across the galaxy.

"All right," Herbie said, looking baffled. "Why are all the stars connected?"

"That's what I can't understand," she said. "The book has a chapter for each constellation, but then there's all this weird writing." She flipped to a sample chapter to show him and landed on the page for the constellation Orion. A few pages gave a description of an ocean somewhere, followed by some strange symbols.

min dec 42 deg. Whl. Plcn. 99 sk. ≈ S: gry.

"What is that?" Herbie asked. "It looks like a code."

"I've been trying to figure it out, but it doesn't make any

sense. I just *know* this has something to do with my parents' kidnapping. It has to. Why else would they hide the book?"

"Emma," he said gravely, "you know what this is?"

She blinked.

"It's a game manual."

"No," she scoffed. "What?"

"Yes. I think it's pretty obvious that your mom and dad were involved in an elaborate role-playing game."

"Ro—" Emma snapped up. "Herbie, this is not a game. *They shot my dad!*"

"People take these things seriously," he said grimly. "I mean, look at this page. It's describing an imaginary place. And those weird numbers and letters are probably some sort of technical specs. If you were playing the game long enough, you would know what it means."

"This is not a game. I can't believe that *you* would be skeptical about that," she shot back. "Do you remember when you said my dad was an alien?"

"I didn't mean he was *actually* an alien—"

Angrily, she leaned over and grabbed his backpack, reaching for the hammer and chisel. But he stopped her.

"Listen," he said. "The police are looking for you. They flipped out when you left, and a dozen more cops showed up at the house."

Emma's hand dropped from the backpack. "Did they interrogate you?"

"No. I was watching from the bushes in the side yard. And I guess one of the cops finally called *my* parents because then MY MOM showed up."

"Oh."

"Yeah. And she thought I'd been kidnapped too." His face

was getting red. "And I couldn't let her think that. So I climbed back in through the bathroom window and went through the house and came outside and told everyone I was okay. The police were freaking out about you. I told them I'd been upstairs in the bathroom and I had no idea where you were."

"Did your mom say anything about the boat?"

"No. But once the police were gone, she told me to search the boat, and if I didn't bring you back, I'd be grounded for a *month.*"

"Seriously? Your mom didn't tell the police about the boat?"

"No. Which is why you have to come with me. Like, NOW."

"I *can't.*" She shut the book and stood up. Her body was trembling. "Look, this book has the answer—I'm sure of it! If I take it off the boat, the police will take it away from me. And *they're* not going to find my parents!"

Herbie was giving her a dubious look. She knew he wanted to disagree, but he had to admit the police seemed pretty lame.

"If I go to the group home," she said, "I'm not going to be able to find my parents. Some social worker's probably just going to make me do my homework."

"It *is* your turn."

"I know," she said, "but I think I should be given a hardship excuse."

He frowned at her. "What, just because your parents were kidnapped?"

She looked at him seriously.

"Fine," he said, sitting in a chair and pulling his backpack onto the table. "But I'm only giving you the hammer and chisel if you *promise* me two things."

"Thank you," she whispered.

"First," he said, "you have to come with me. My mom says we have to bring you to social services—or I'll be *grounded for a month.* And you know she's not kidding. Even though you're in a group home, we'll find a way to find your parents."

"And what's the second thing?"

"You have to say"—he pointed to the *Almagest*—"that this is a massive role-playing game, and that's all that it is."

She clenched her jaw. "Before I do that," she said, "I need the hammer and chisel."

"Why?" he asked. She stood and went to the sofa nook. From beneath the pillows she removed the smaller box she'd found, and brought it to the table.

"I just want it to go on record that I think this is the *worst* idea in the universe," Herbie said.

"Okay," Emma grunted, positioning the chisel at the edge of the wood.

"If it doesn't have a latch, then you shouldn't open it," Herbie said. "What if it's—" Emma brought down the hammer, and the wood split with a satisfying crack. Herbie cringed. Slowly he opened one eye. "Booby-trapped?"

"Clear!" she said, peeling away the wood as delicately as if it were an eggshell.

Herbie leaned forward. On the table was an amulet.

"The Pyxis," she said triumphantly.

"Okay." Herbie looked a little less skeptical. "It looks like the one the kidnappers stole."

"It's the real one," Emma said. "It has to be."

"It could be some thrift store astrolabe for all you know."

She rolled her eyes. "Why else would my parents keep it hidden like this?"

"Because they were taking the game seriously," Herbie said, but he didn't sound so certain anymore.

Emma held the Pyxis closer to the light. It was a silver object that looked very much like an astrolabe: a single flat disk with ornate wheel plates fastened on top. The disk and the plates were carved with strange symbols that Emma might have guessed were Arabic inscriptions, just like those on the astrolabes she'd seen in the maritime museum. The only difference was that this astrolabe had a pair of blue-white stones fastened to the center of the disk. The stones glimmered like twin stars.

"Remember what the kidnappers said about it?" she asked.

"Yeah, that it could send a signal all over the world in an instant," Herbie said. "But technically, that's not possible. I'm assuming it works with satellite positioning, but because of the shape of Earth, there will always be some kind of—"

"What I meant was that someone would be *listening* for it," she said. "That's why the kidnappers were afraid to activate it. They were afraid that everyone else would come after them. But my mom told them how to do it."

"Yeah," Herbie smirked, "but you're probably not going to be able to activate it *with your mind*."

Emma clenched the Pyxis in her palm and shut her eyes.

"Wait!" Herbie said. "If there's one thing we know, it's that these role-playing people take this stuff very seriously."

"So you think it might activate?"

"Noooo," he said. "It's just—you never know what it *will* do."

She shut her eyes again.

"Wait!" he cried. "Let's just pretend that it's possible, okay? If you activate it, then anyone could detect the signal, right?"

"Maybe," she said. "And actually . . . Herbie! This is how I can get my parents back! The kidnappers must have a way to detect the signal. If I switch it on, the kidnappers will come looking for it."

"Yeah, but they had *guns*?"

"Don't worry," she said. "According to you, this is not going to work."

She laid the Pyxis in her palm. Herbie sucked in his breath and shook his head. "Emma, I don't think this is a good . . ."

She stopped listening. She was hoping that what Mom had said was true: you only had to wish it to start it. Did you have to say it out loud, or did you just have to feel it? And what would it feel like—a curious wishing? Or, like now, a desperate wishing—

The Pyxis jumped. Emma's heart leapt violently into her throat. Herbie nearly fell down in his scramble to get away. The Pyxis was jerking as if there were an animal inside kicking to be born. The blue-white stones at the center began to glow like lightbulbs. Emma and Herbie watched in amazement as the stones' glow grew brighter—first shining on the silver disk, then lighting their faces, then pouring into the room.

Emma dropped the Pyxis on the table, and the shaking stopped.

Her chest was clunking, her whole body vibrating. She and Herbie stared at each other in shocked silence.

"I was wrong," he squeaked. "*That* was the worst idea in the universe!"

They looked down at the Pyxis. It was quiet and still, but the lights hadn't gone out. Now a faint blue sheen surrounded the amulet, and the light was pulsing like a heartbeat.

"That is *totally* radioactive," Herbie said.

"It's just a thrift store astrolabe, remember?" she whispered. "Put it back in the box."

But the box was lying in six pieces on the floor.

"Okay," Herbie said, his voice shaking. "Okay, we are totally overreacting. All that happened is a little light went on. And I know what it was."

"What?"

"Those stones must be filled with a thermotropic liquid crystal. Their colors respond to changes in temperature. All you have to do is get them warm enough and they'll switch on. It's basically an advanced type of mood ring."

Emma still couldn't catch her breath. "I don't think it's a mood ring," she said numbly. "I think this is real, and that's why my parents didn't want anyone to find it." Carefully, she hung the amulet around her neck and tucked it into her shirt.

"You really shouldn't do that," Herbie said.

She went to the table and flipped the map open again, replacing three of the meteorites. The fourth one she kept in her fist.

Herbie sat down at the table beside her. "Look, I'm sorry about your parents," he said, casting her a worried look. "I know the police are going to find them."

She squeezed the stone. "My dad could be dead by then."

"He won't be," he said. "But I think this might help the police. We should tell them about the game."

"It's not a game."

"Okay," he said carefully. "But we should tell them about it anyway."

"Do you smell that?" She tilted her head. "Something smells like chocolate. I think it's"—she opened her palm—"the stone."

Herbie frowned.

"Smell it."

He leaned forward and his expression changed. "Yeah, I think I've sort of smelled it before."

She lifted the stone to her mouth, sticking out her tongue for a probing taste.

"No! No, wait!" Herbie cried, leaping up. "What if it's toxic? You don't know what that is."

"It's not going to kill me. Why would it smell like chocolate if you're not supposed to eat it?"

"Look." Herbie was getting frantic, his cheeks reddening. "I believe you," he said. "You're right. There's probably something else going on with the Pyxis and this book and . . . I don't know what, but it's totally possible. One thing we do know is that these gaming dudes have some serious tech. And you don't know what that is."

"It's chocolate." Emma, still frowning, opened her mouth and lifted the rock, but Herbie leapt forward and grabbed her hand. For a moment their hands were locked in a tussle as each one struggled to gain control of the rock, but Herbie's hands were bigger and stronger. He managed to pry it out of her clenched fist. She shrieked and grabbed his wrist, determined to get it back. He very unfairly used his strength. Emma countered by raising her foot to the bench behind him. Herbie, realizing that he was about to lose the tug-of-war, could only manage to strain his head down and reach for the rock with his teeth. Emma shrieked. It startled him so much that the rock popped free and flew straight into his mouth—perhaps with a bit too much force. It seemed to hit the back of his throat and gag him. A look of surprise came over his face. Emma released him and fell back.

Spitting brown drool, Herbie gave a wincing, revulsed

swallow. He finished by executing his notorious "lizard hiss," which involved an open mouth, bared teeth, Jurassic-era sound effects, and a blitzkrieg of spittle.

Emma was flabbergasted.

"OH EM GEE GNARLY!" he spat. "It totally melted in my mouth!"

"It *melted?*"

"It wasn't a rock!"

"It was chocolate!"

"No! I mean, it tasted like chocolate, but it was texturally *ewwww.*"

"Uhhh, Herbie . . ." Emma fell back, feeling woozy, and pointed to his stomach, where a large, transparent blob was emerging from his shirt.

CHAPTER 7

Meteorites

Frantically, Herbie pulled up his shirt. A jellylike coating was pouring through the skin of his stomach, spreading up his chest and down his legs. Squealing, he stuck out his arms and backed up, knocking into the wall. He could hear Emma shouting, but muffled by the jelly skin, it sounded far away and added to the horrifying sense of being cocooned in sludge.

"HELP ME!" he shrieked.

She couldn't seem to hear him. He moved toward her, but she leapt desperately behind a chair to avoid touching him.

The sludge kept spreading, stopping only once it had covered every inch of his body. He was panting, squeaking, staring down at himself in horror.

All of a sudden the sounds around him grew a little louder.

Almost normal. It occurred to him that nothing hurt. In fact, his nose and mouth were filled with the flavor of chocolate. And it seemed that he could breathe, and the wacky goo wasn't spreading onto the rest of the boat. He tentatively lifted a shoe off the floor and noticed it wasn't sticky on the outside. It had only encased him.

COOL!

Emma looked stricken. He raised his arms, rolled back his eyes, gave a deep groan—*MAAAAAAAAH!*—and began lumbering toward her, just to see her completely freak out, her face an explosion of terror, her body a tangle of confused limbs as she launched herself, tripping, over the kitchen table and into the booth behind it with a *thunk.*

He broke into wicked laughter.

She was on her feet in an instant, heading for the hatch, when she saw him laughing. Her shoulders fell.

"Oh, *seriously?*" she cried.

He ran a hand over the skin of his jellylike coat. It was ever so slightly bouncy. In fact, he felt as if he could float.

She exhaled and made an effort to smooth her shirt.

"Emma," he said, looking a little surprised. "This is a serious game."

Emma watched Herbie carefully for a while. He didn't seem to be in pain.

"I'm going to try it too," she said. She leapt up and took one of the stones from the shelf. Surprisingly, Herbie didn't protest.

The stone was a deep, rich black, and she pressed it gently with her fingertip. It was hard at first, like a regular stone, but as she kept pressing, it began to feel softer, smoother. Finally her finger sank in with a squish like a spoon into a glob of jelly. The stone was oily and cold, and she jerked away.

"Does it hurt?" she asked.

He shook his head.

She lifted the stone tentatively to her mouth. It smelled cold and clean and vaguely metallic, but when it touched her tongue, a delicious flavor exploded—chocolate and raspberry and coconut cream.

She slid the stone gingerly onto her tongue. It dissolved at once into a hot, sugary substance as it slid down her throat, spreading its warmth through her chest and arms. When it reached her stomach, an intense flash of heat burst through her body. She felt tingly and numb, and, looking down, she saw the same jelly growing over her skin and clothing. Within seconds it had covered her completely. She touched it with her finger. No amount of poking was going to break it. Smooth and impenetrable, it was just like a second skin.

"Wow," she whispered. Thoughts were popping into her mind too fast for her to keep up, but one emerged quite suddenly: Dad would have known what this was. He'd probably used it before. In her mind's eye she saw both of her parents coated in this jelly skin just like she was now, and she felt a stab of betrayal.

She slumped onto the sofa. "They never told me any of this."

"Maybe it's an adults-only game," Herbie said.

"I can't believe you still think this is a game. My parents were kidnapped because of this thing." She held up the Pyxis. "My dad was *shot*."

"Yeah," he said. "We have to assume it's real enough for some people and that we just activated the Pyxis too."

"And the kidnappers are going to come back for it," she put in.

"We can't be here when they come," he said.

"They could be here in, like, ten minutes or something." She stood up. "We should assume they'll come soon. But we just want to talk to them, right? I'll tell them we'll give them the Pyxis in exchange for my parents."

"They have *guns,*" he said. "Remember?"

"Fine. So we'll hide the Pyxis somewhere else, in case they try to take it."

"We can't do that," he said. "If they're following the Pyxis's signal, then wherever we move it, that's where they're going to go. We don't know how specific their sensing devices are."

Emma exhaled. "Right. Okay, so we've got to rig up some way to trap them."

"I think we should call the police."

"No! They're not going to believe us."

Herbie raised his arms, motioning to the skin. "They're not going to believe this?"

"They'll probably accuse us of making things up. Besides, I don't want them to know where the boat is, in case they confiscate it or something."

"Emma, we *have* to call them." He reached for his phone. "At the very least we should go somewhere safer. A public place. Preferably the closest police station. I don't know where that is. . . ."

"This is the safest place," Emma said, heading for the ladder. "We can make a quick getaway if we need to."

"Wait—where are you going?"

"To get the harpoon gun."

✦ ✦ ✦

Herbie's phone would not stop ringing.

"Emma," he moaned. "It's my mom again."

"DO NOT ANSWER IT."

"We are in so much trouble."

They couldn't leave the boat looking like this. The skin had not worn off—they didn't know if it ever would. They had waited for over an hour. Emma figured it was only a matter of time before Herbie's mom realized he was still there and came looking for him. She hoped that the jelly skin would be gone by then.

Anxiously, they stood side by side on the ladder, peering out the hatch and watching the marina. It was dark, and the air was bracingly cold. Emma could feel it through her jelly skin. Even though sounds were slightly muffled, she could hear the familiar clanking of metal rings against the ship's masts as they bobbed in the water. She scanned the marina, her breathing louder now, amplified within the gooey coat.

"If the kidnappers get here before my parents do," Herbie said, "I think we should just start the boat and get away."

"But I have to talk to them."

"The harpoon gun isn't going to scare them," he said. "They'll shoot us both."

The clatter of wood sounded near the harbormaster's office. Emma and Herbie craned their necks to see. Gradually, they made out the silhouette of two men on a pier to the right. They seemed to be climbing to their feet.

"Is that them?" Emma whispered.

"No. Those guys are bigger," Herbie whispered back.

The men began moving silently down the pier, heading in their direction. As they came closer they passed beneath a streetlight, and Emma and Herbie saw their clothing. They wore long wool coats and dark-blue breeches with scuffed white boots. On each man's head was a tricornered hat plumed with feathers that resembled ears of wheat.

"Okay, what's with the Revolutionary War costumes . . . ?" Herbie said.

But Emma could just make out a logo on their chest pockets. It looked like stars in the pattern of a constellation. The stars were outlined to show the shape of a woman with wings. *Virgo.*

"I don't think those are Revolutionary War . . . Oh no," she whispered, gripping the harpoon gun in her hands. "They have guns."

They could see them now—long rifles with white bayonets at the end.

One of the men stopped and fished a small trinket from his collar. When he turned in their direction, the trinket began glowing blue.

"It looks like they're tracking a signal," Herbie said.

"Shhhhh!"

The men looked up. They motioned to the *Markab.* "Pyxis," one of them whispered. "It's over here."

Emma figured that the men were part of the . . . game? She didn't know what to call it. But she did know that they were coming straight for the *Markab,* and that they had guns, and that if she didn't do something—anything—they'd both be in more serious danger than they'd been in all night. Making up her mind, she scrambled onto the deck. Herbie looked surprised and leapt up behind her. She raised the harpoon gun, but her hands were shaking.

"Stop where you are!" she cried.

The men stopped. One of them held up the blue amulet, realized that she was the source of the transmission, and motioned to his partner. They started running toward her.

"Don't come any closer!" she shouted. "I'm warning you!"

Herbie rushed to the wheel and started the engine.

Emma dropped the gun and made a leap for the pier. She tore the rope free, releasing the boat, and leapt back onto deck just as Herbie put the engine in gear, jerking forward so hard that she fell on her rear.

Behind them, the men dove for the boat but missed, splashing into the water. Herbie gunned the engine and headed straight for the marina gates.

"Who were those guys?" he shouted.

"I don't know!" Emma shrieked.

The men scrambled back onto the pier and went racing down the walkway. They were tall and fast and managed to catch up, running alongside the boat.

"They're heading for the end of the walkway!" Emma said.

Up ahead, they had to turn left to get out of the marina and into the bay. It was a narrow channel. If the men made it to the end of the walkway in time, they would easily be able to leap onto the *Markab.*

"Hurry!" Emma cried.

Herbie gunned it harder, and the *Markab* shot forward.

CHAPTER 8

Arcturus Venture

Emma watched the men run, their long legs pumping furiously. She could already tell that they were going to reach the *Markab.* She lifted the harpoon gun, hoping it would scare them—she already knew she couldn't bring herself to shoot them. She braced herself against the railing, but her arms were trembling as the *Markab* approached the turn.

The men had almost reached the walkway's end. Three more steps and they'd launch themselves over the short gap from the pier to the boat. Emma tried to steady the gun.

"Emma, hold on—!"

Herbie's words were cut off by a tremendous boom that sent thunder through their bodies. Emma fell to the deck. It hit the two men like an explosion, throwing them onto their faces. The *Markab* groaned against the force.

"What was that?" Emma cried, scrambling to her feet.

Herbie was up just as quickly, grabbing the wheel and righting the boat's course.

He revved the engine again and steered out of the marina, heading straight into the bay. Emma looked around frantically but saw no sign of an explosion.

"Did we lose them?" Herbie asked.

"I think so!"

They reached the spot where they usually stopped the engine and let out the sails. Emma switched off the stern lantern just as Herbie shut the engine down.

"The engine's too loud," he explained. "They'll hear us."

"Yeah."

"But don't let the sails out yet."

"We can't sit here," she said. "The currents will drag us out to sea." Already the tides were pushing them so that the *Markab* was facing the Golden Gate Bridge. The great structure rose ahead of them, glowing reddish orange in the night.

"We'd better put our life jackets on," he said.

"Yeah."

As they did, Emma's mind was racing. "Those guys had logos on their coats. I think they showed the constellation Virgo. I'm getting the idea that everyone belongs to a constellation."

"Well," Herbie said, "it would explain why the kidnappers were talking about Draco."

She took Dad's binoculars and went to the railing. "Those men must have come in on a boat," she said. "Where is it?" Looking around, they saw no other boats on the bay.

"And I don't understand where that explosion came from," Herbie said. "Uh . . . actually, Emma?" He pointed over her shoulder, and she spun around.

Beneath the bridge, there was a green flash of light. Slowly, more flashes appeared, like sparklers flickering. They seemed to be rising up from the water.

"What is that?" she asked.

"Some kind of luminescent kelp?" Herbie offered.

"Um, no . . . look up there." She pointed upward, where the same green flashes began flickering on the lower part of the bridge's towers and beneath its roadway. The sparklers grew more numerous and brighter until there were thousands of them. The tiny lights appeared to be forming a massive circle beneath the bridge.

"Okay," he said, "maybe not kelp."

Emma ran to the mast.

"What are you doing?" Herbie asked.

"I want to get closer!" She let the mainsail out and the wind gave a kick.

Ahead, the lights were growing brighter. There were no other ships nearby—nobody else was foolish enough to navigate the outgoing tides in such a bitter wind. But Emma and Herbie barely noticed. They were gaping at the great circle of lights.

As they watched, something seemed to form in the top edges of the circle. It wiggled like the same jelly that was covering their bodies, and it spread slowly downward like a rippling wall until it reached the bay waters. The wall was tinged a faint green, trembling with energy and motion. Behind the wall, they could just make out the silhouette of a giant ship.

Emma was dumbstruck. "Herbie, do you see that?" she cried. "Is that . . . ?"

"Yeah," Herbie said. "It's a ship. And it's coming in!"

They watched in amazement. The ship was an outline, blurry around the edges, but they could see her great masts and wide, square rigging. She was enormous, and with every yard they drew closer, she became larger still.

The ship cut through the jelly wall with surprising majesty. First her bowsprit sliced through like a knife tip, and then the crisply edged bow with a magnificent figurehead trailing down both sides—a pair of hunting dogs, carved with such artistry that they seemed to be coursing alongside the ship. On the starboard side, the wood beneath the railing was painted red and carved with images of fighting dogs. The name *Arcturus Venture* stood out in bold white on her bow. She rode high in the water and sailed ahead with fierce determination—yet she must have been a hundred years old. When her mast came into view, with its old-fashioned ratlines hanging down from solid timber, they saw sailors on board scrambling about to reef the sails and slow the great vessel before she went crashing into Alcatraz.

"Herbie," Emma said, "I don't think this is a game!"

Herbie grabbed the wheel and began to take the *Markab* around, but when Emma looked behind them, she saw the two men from the pier. They were flying across the waves as if they were windsurfing. Each man was standing on some sort of flat object, but neither was holding a sail.

"They're behind us!" she cried.

"Where do we go?" he shouted.

If they made to starboard, the great ship would cut them off. To port were shallow waters where the *Markab* would be grounded. Herbie had no choice but to keep them sailing straight ahead.

"I think that's some kind of portal or bridge!" Emma said, pointing to the massive wall of jelly beneath the Golden Gate.

"I know it's a bridge!" he snapped back.

"No, not the *bridge.* The other thing—the goo! If we keep going straight, we're going to have to go through it!"

"We can't!" he cried. "We don't know what that is! We should head to Sausalito. I'm going to try to cut behind the big ship and—"

But the *Arcturus* was bearing down on them. As if to shake any misconception that the ship was too old-fashioned to pose a threat, twelve wooden panels slid open on her bow, like a dog baring its teeth, and a quartet of sleek silver cannons slid out of each with a screech of metal.

"Look out!" Emma screamed.

The frontmost cannons fired in symphony, making four loud *ka-booms*. Emma and Herbie ducked as the projectiles tore low overhead, blowing ruthlessly into the marina behind them. Boats and buildings erupted in massive explosions that sent thirty-foot fireballs into the sky.

"Those weren't cannonballs!" Herbie cried. "They were *missiles*! Who are these guys—the navy?"

Emma focused on the water. Their only hope was to skim past the ship's starboard side. If they stayed low and close enough to avoid the cannons, they might stand a chance.

"Herbie, we have to—"

"I know, I know!" He crouched by the wheel, steering closer to the *Arcturus*'s side.

CRACK-CRACK-CRACK! The shots gave them a terrible jolt. Emma gripped Herbie's sleeve. "Are they *shooting* at us?"

"Yes!" he screamed. "They probably fired their missiles to force us into the range of their rifles!"

Emma couldn't make out the sailors, but she saw their white rifles glinting near the railings, tiny flashes of light exploding with each shot. When a bullet whizzed past, she yelped and crouched lower.

CRACK-CRACK-CRACK!

Emma turned just in time to see a flash of green light hit Herbie square in the chest. He went skidding wildly backward and crashed into the mast as the air around him erupted in a ball of smoke. The wind blew the smoke away, and incredibly, in the space where he'd been stood a large green iguana.

"HERBIE!" Emma shrieked. The lizard gave no indication that it recognized her. It darted in a quick circle, looking baffled.

CRACK-CRACK-CRACK! The shots all happened at once. She ducked behind the mast, but she could have sworn she saw dozens of bright-green bullets flying out of the sky. One of them hit the iguana in the rear, and with another loud *pop* and a poof of smoke, Herbie was kneeling on the deck, wet and cold and shaking violently.

"Herbie!" She pulled him down. He was still covered in the glistening skin. "Are you okay?" He didn't seem able to speak.

She scrambled back to the wheel and saw that they were fifty yards from the bridge.

Herbie was staring at his hands in mild shock. Emma looked at the *Arcturus* again. It was heading rapidly toward Alcatraz. In a minute or two, once the big ship was farther away, it would be easy to swing the *Markab* toward Sausalito. They could dock at Fort Baker and make a run for the guard station there.

Then she looked back at the space beneath the Golden Gate Bridge, still glittering with green luminescence. What on earth was that glowing green jelly? She had never seen a ship like the *Arcturus* sail in from the open sea like that. She had a strong feeling that it had come from somewhere else—some kind of portal into another dimension. It was probably foolish to plow straight into a giant wall of jelly, but the *Arcturus* had just done it with no ill effects. The closer she sailed to the wall, the more certain she was that something extraordinary lay beyond it. Through the jelly screen she could make out a strange tunnel-like place. The waves were higher on the other side, and it looked like it was raining. She squinted, trying to get a better look, but the jelly wall was rippling and she couldn't be sure what she was seeing. Maybe she was imagining it. . . .

But what if I'm right? she thought. *What if this is not a game, and beyond that wall is some other place? Some sort of answer to why my parents were kidnapped?*

Shouts came from the deck of the *Arcturus,* men calling to bring the ship about.

Emma glanced at Herbie, who was still staring at his hands. Gripping the wheel, she made a decision. She aimed the *Markab* straight for the center of the bridge. Thirty yards later, the world began to bend into a narrow tunnel that went straight from the *Markab*'s bow to the water. The sky seemed to be caving in. The front of the boat slipped away, into a thread of light that was not a thread anymore but a giant black hole sucking them into its darkness. Emma tried to resist, but everything fell away—the railing, the benches, the captain's wheel. There was nothing to grab on to, and before she knew it, she was falling.

She fell helplessly, her eyes wide open, her body protected by the gooey skin. An unbearable pressure was squeezing her from all sides. She wanted to scream, but it felt as if her whole body were being pressed flat. Then the light disappeared altogether, and they plunged into blackness.

✦ ✦ ✦

With a violent jolt, Emma was back on her feet, her hands still gripping the *Markab*'s wheel. The ship was flying forward at incredible speed. Everything seemed louder now. She heard the wind whipping the sails, the crash of water on the hull, and a mysterious clattering. Looking down, she saw that her jelly skin was slipping away. She had the strangest sensation of lightness, as if she could have floated right up into the sky.

Tipping at thirty degrees, the *Markab* was getting battered by towering swells. She had to fight to stay on course. The air was icy cold, and rain whipped down like hail. It was hard to see, but from what she could tell, they were in an ocean, fighting gales and high waves.

Well, I was right, she thought. *This is not the Pacific!*

Looking back, she saw a sheer wall of jelly suspended oddly above the sea. It was the bridge back to Earth. Through the wall she could just make out the fires burning at the marina, and the lights of the city beyond. There was no sign of the *Arcturus*—it must have been turning around.

SNAP! One of the ropes holding the boom burst free. The boom swung wildly and the *Markab* slowed, coming down from its tilt.

"Herbie!" she cried. He was lying on the deck, staring blankly at the sky. She noticed his jelly coat was gone too. "Are you okay? Can you talk?"

"Y-y-yeah." He looked pale and scared, and his jaw was shaking with cold. "Where are we?"

"We went through the jelly bridge," she said.

"That w-w-was amazing. Did we just go through some k-k-kind of space-time warp?"

"I don't know. Can you get up?"

He gazed up at her wearily. "I'm not sure, I—"

"The boom is loose!" she said.

At that he leapt up, racing aft to grab the lines. She left the wheel to help him, for the boom—the arm beneath the mainsail—was such a heavy, dangerous thing that it took both of them to wrestle it still and secure it.

"How long were we in that tunnel thing?" Herbie asked.

"It felt like a few seconds," she said. "Are you sure you're okay?"

"Yeah. Something hit me. It felt really weird. . . ."

"I know. You turned into an *iguana,*" she said.

He was horrified. "I did not!"

"Okay, maybe it was a gecko."

He looked back at the jelly bridge. "Where *are* we?" he asked.

"I don't know," Emma said. "But I don't think we're on the ocean. It doesn't look the same."

"No, no, we're not," Herbie said. "I mean, we went *through* something. I think we're in a different dimension."

"Whatever it is, we can't go back," she said.

"What? Why not?" Herbie spun around.

"That ship will blow us apart," she said. Pulling open her collar, she looked down at the Pyxis hanging there. It was still glowing a faint blue. "They're going to know where we are—if they have those detector things. We can't hide. We have to try to outrun them."

CHAPTER 9

The Butt End of Monkey

The rain was pouring down so hard now that she could barely see. Emma was more deeply tired than she'd ever been. She clutched her jacket to her chest and nearly choked as the wind lashed her hair into her mouth.

Herbie was below, icing the large bruise on his chest where the strange green bullet had hit him. Emma had to remain topside to keep the *Markab* safe.

The boat raced forward, desperately trying to outrun the navy. It was a brutal journey of pounding through waves, wiping rain from her face, and trying not to freeze up from the cold wind and water. She kept checking her collar. The sight of the Pyxis's light glowing faint blue made her feel all the more urgent.

As the minutes ticked by and the navy failed to materialize, she slowed the boat a bit. She had no idea where they were. All her attention was focused on the waters, but the rain had turned into a solid sheet, and she couldn't see what was ahead. She didn't know, for example, if this body of water had an edge—a bank of some kind—and if she was going to go nailing right into it. What if it had sharp rocks, or reefs, or cliffs? Anything could come looming out of the darkness.

It seemed to take forever, but eventually the rain stopped. The air turned bitterly cold. Around her, she could see nothing but a great expanse of sea, its waters rippling a deep, dark black with whitecaps combing the currents. There were no islands or rocks, just choppy seas and leagues of water spread to every horizon.

As the clouds cleared, she saw that the starlight was incredible—flickering lights crowded every inch of the sky. In some places it was so clotted that it looked like spilled milk. But when she looked directly upward, she got a shock. The stars were tearing off behind her in long white and blue streaks, their tails like meteorites. It made her think that they were traveling at warp speed.

"Uh . . . Herbie!" She looked into the cabin. "HERBIE!"

He came topside, looking frantic.

"Look up," she said.

He gaped at the stars, but when he noticed the ones zooming away behind them, he stumbled in amazement. "OH! What is that?"

"Herbie . . ." She could barely talk. "Are we in *space*?"

It surprised her that he didn't object—that instead he turned to her, looking stunned. "I think we're in a wormhole," he said. "I mean, it would explain all those lines on the chart . . . why all the stars are connected like that . . . but that would mean we're on our way to another planet. . . ." He winced, shut his eyes, and shook his head. "No. No, that's crazy. You don't just sail into a wormhole."

"Why not?"

"Because you'd get ripped apart by the forces of gravity and space-time."

"Well, we were wearing that gooey meteorite stuff."

He stared at her for a moment.

"And it's gone now," she pointed out. "And the bridge we went through was made of the same stuff. Maybe it was there to protect us or something."

She had never seen Herbie looking quite this intimidated, and it worried her a bit.

He went below into the cabin again. She watched him root around for more ice.

Turning back to the water, she suddenly felt a small burst of excitement. This wasn't the Pacific Ocean—this was outer space! And every crazy thing she'd seen might not have been crazy after all. The jelly skin and the strange sailors and the Pyxis glowing blue, not to mention Herbie turning into an iguana. These things belonged to a world she'd never believe existed had she not seen it for herself. She thought about the *Arcturus*—not about the sailors, but the ship: a grand, old, glorious ship that had come from outer space. As she was silently marveling at a sky shot through with billions of stars, it thrilled her to realize that the universe was immense.

Then, with a pang, she thought about her parents and wondered why they hadn't told her anything.

✦ ✦ ✦

For the first time all evening, she spotted something ahead. She aimed the *Markab* for it, and as they got closer, she saw an old sign attached to the top of a wooden buoy. It said:

ALPHA DELPHINI, IF YER LUCKY.

100 NICKS.

"Herbie!" she cried. "Come see this!"

He came topside. He was carrying the *Almagest.*

"The sign said we're coming to Alpha Delphini. That's a star," Emma said excitedly. "Can you tell where we are from the map?"

He quickly unfolded it and laid it on the bench, studying it with a flashlight. After a few minutes he said, "Okay, I think I figured this out. There's a constellation on here I've never heard of before, but I think it's where we just came from. It's called . . . Monkey. And that's because it's shaped like a monkey. Almost like it's"—he tilted his head—"squatting or something."

"We live on *Monkey*?"

"Well, no, we would be from a *star* on the Monkey constellation," he said. "It's the only constellation with a line attached to Alpha Delphini that's long enough to have more than one hundred nicks. I guess those are like miles. There's a legend here on the map showing distance in nicks. . . ." He scratched his head. "But if we're only a hundred nicks from Alpha Delphini, we've come really far from Monkey."

"Is that really where we're from?"

"It makes sense," Herbie said. "We did evolve from monkeys. Apparently we just came from a star called Solacious."

"Our sun is called Sol," Emma said.

"Well, it says 'Solacious' here and it's right at the monkey's butt."

"We're from the monkey's *butt*?" she squawked.

He nodded grimly.

"Okay," she said. "Go to the chapter on Monkey. Or Alpha Delphini. Tell me if you can make any sense of it. I mean, what if there are hazards we should know about?"

He began reading. After a few minutes, he said, "It says this is a pretty empty sea. Otherwise, there's nothing useful." He shut the book and looked up at her. "Is the Pyxis's light still on?"

"Yes," she said. "We have to assume that the *Arcturus* is still behind us. And by the way"—she motioned to the mast behind her—"the mainsail has a tear."

He got up to inspect the damage.

"It must have happened when we went through the jelly bridge," she said.

"We can't go much farther with that," he said. "It's going to rip in half."

"I know," she said. "I think we should go to Alpha Delphini. It looks like it's the only star that's connected to ours, and we're halfway there already. . . ."

This clearly upset him. Frowning, he stood up and marched to the railing. "But we *can't*. We should just find somewhere to hide and let them pass us by."

"But there's nowhere *to* hide. And the Pyxis is still glowing. They'll find us if we stop."

"I think it'll stop glowing eventually."

"Right, but when?" she asked.

"Let's just find somewhere to hide," he said.

"There isn't anywhere."

Shaking his head, he slumped onto the bench and heaved a sigh. "We are in so much trouble."

✦ ✦ ✦

Herbie spent some time studying the torn mainsail. Emma looked back at it sympathetically, which was when she noticed the gouges in the mast and the cabin roof.

"Herbie," she said. "Those are bullet holes from when they were shooting at us."

He took a closer look.

"You're lucky you didn't get hit by a bullet," she said. "It must have been a ricochet."

"The bullets are still inside the holes," he said, standing up with a baffled expression. "And they're *glowing*."

"Don't touch them," she said. "In case they turn you into an iguana again."

He seemed a little more willing to accept this idea now.

"Seriously," she said. "I thought you were going to be poisonous."

"It's not funny," he said. "It was scary. It felt like cold water went through my whole body, and then my arms and legs were all different. . . ."

"Greener?" she asked.

He shuddered. "Was I green?"

"It was hard to tell."

"I was probably some kind of small Komodo dragon."

She snorted. "You were totally an iguana!"

"I never want that to happen again."

"It's good another one hit you and you turned back into yourself because I didn't bring a cage."

"Funny." He opened the bench seat by the wheel. Inside were Dad's tools. Herbie took out a pair of tweezers and an old bait jar. "I'm going to get these bullets out of the mast," he said.

"Be careful," she said solemnly. "But . . . do you want to pick an animal name in case it happens again?"

He shot her a look. It alarmed her a bit that she couldn't lighten his mood. He must have been really affected by turning into a lizard.

Once he'd pried the bullet free, he dropped it in the jar and showed it to Emma. It was shaped like a bullet (albeit smashed by the impact with the mast). It appeared to be made of metal, but Herbie was right—it was glowing a dark, murky green. As they watched, a tiny bit of water seeped out of it, pooling in the bottom of the jar.

After collecting seven more bullets, Herbie sealed the jar and brought it below. Emma peeked once through the cabin windows and saw him rooting through the galley.

A few minutes later, he came topside with two ham sandwiches, some chips, and a Coke. Dad had left the food from their failed weekend trip on the boat. Emma accepted a sandwich gratefully.

Herbie sat on the bench. "I can't even begin to explain this," he said. "I mean, I can't wrap my head around it. A bullet turned me into a dragon. The Pyxis glowed when you touched it. And we are in outer space?"

"Yeah." Emma was eating a little too voraciously. Herbie watched her.

"I have the feeling your parents would know all the answers to this."

She didn't reply.

"I'm sorry they didn't tell you," he said.

"It's fine," she said through a mouthful of food. "They're going to be fine. I'm going to get them back."

Herbie looked at her warily. "Yeah."

"I know they didn't tell me anything," she said, swallowing. "But I'm sure they had their reasons. And they were wrong reasons. But it doesn't matter. I'm getting them back. That's what's important."

He wisely remained quiet.

"What?" she asked. "You think I'm going crazy."

"You are a little woo-woo."

"I'm okay," she said. "It's just . . . if we really are in space, and I think of all the things they didn't tell me, I have a really hard time believing that these are the same people who grounded me for three weeks for lying about that bar of chocolate that went missing from the kitchen."

Herbie smiled. "Yeah. The same people who failed to mention that *Draco* is *real*."

Emma gave a grim laugh. "And that those meteorites weren't really meteorites!"

Herbie sat up. "Wasn't I saying that for years?"

"Yes!" She took another huge bite of sandwich. "And that whole your-dad-is-an-alien thing—you were totally right!"

"You know, we could have both been turned into animals tonight," he said. "We have no idea what this place is like."

"We didn't even know it was *real*," she said.

They looked at each other, and Herbie said gravely, "I was SO not prepared for an iguana."

They finished the rest of their sandwiches, gazing worriedly about. After a while, Herbie said, "I think we should wait until the Pyxis's light turns off and then go back to Earth."

"What? No." Emma was shocked. "I know my parents are out here somewhere. You heard the kidnappers. They were from Draco. Of course they would take my parents out here. It's where they're from."

Herbie shook his head. "We have NO idea where your parents are. They could still be on Earth."

"They're probably not," she said. "Don't you remember? The lady kidnapper—"

"Laine," Herbie said.

"Laine said they were heading to Draco," she finished. Herbie seemed skeptical. "She wanted to activate the Pyxis, but the guy—"

"Caz."

"Right. Caz didn't want to activate it on Earth. And Laine said no one would catch them because they'd be halfway to Draco."

Herbie sighed. "Yeah, you're right. But that doesn't mean they actually made it to space. We don't know where they are."

He was right, and there was no disputing it.

"Okay," Emma said, "but obviously we can't keep running forever. If we really are in space, and that sign was right, then there's going to be another star up ahead. Maybe it has a planet. That would give us a place to hide until the Pyxis's light goes off."

Herbie shook his head. "Say this planet really exists. We have no idea what it's like. I mean, is there AIR?"

"Check it out," Emma said, pointing. To starboard, a giant star was emerging on the horizon. It was glowing bright blue. A few seconds later, a companion star emerged some distance to the left. It was smaller and less bright.

"That must be Alpha Delphini," she said.

"It is a binary star system," he agreed.

Thanks to studying nighttime navigation with Emma's dad, they both knew a bit about the constellations. They knew that Delphinus resided in a region of the sky known as the Sea. It was a tiny constellation that kept company with its bigger brothers Pisces, the fish; Capricorn, the sea goat; and even Cetus, the monstrous whale. Their celestial navigation books made it sound almost charming, and of all the sea creatures, the little dolphin did seem the friendliest.

The stars were growing larger. It seemed they were approaching the system quite rapidly. A shadowy form appeared on the horizon. Backlit by Delphinus's muted blue lights, it looked at first like a flotilla of ships. They quickly brought the *Markab* to a nervous crawl.

As they sailed closer, they saw that their "flotilla" was just a collection of rotted ships moored to buoys. There were maybe twenty of them, all knocking against one another in their small, forgotten graveyard.

Emma drew the *Markab* right up to the edge. They saw a caravel that had once been shiny and blue like a dolphin but that now looked more like a walrus with rigging. Two of its three masts were missing. It was dripping with seaweed and pocked with barnacles. The hull was so neglected that it ought to have sunk from the rot long ago. The ship's name had faded and then been sloppily painted over with a new one: the *Mereswine.*

"Do you think they got stuck here?" Herbie asked.

"No," Emma said, trying to sound calm. "They probably just got dumped."

Curious and a bit anxious, they navigated slowly around the dead boats, seeing no signs of life. On the graveyard's opposite side, they spotted two buoys in the water some hundred yards to starboard.

"Let's check out those buoys," Emma said. She steered the boat in that direction. They were halfway there when the sea was shaken by another explosion. Now they recognized the sound. On each of the buoys, green lights were sparkling.

"It's that jelly bridge thing again," Herbie said.

"We'd better hide," Emma said. She switched on the engine and they made a quick turn just as the green lights began to illuminate the ocean floor between the buoys. The bridge was opening.

They managed to get the *Markab* hidden just in time. A large man-of-war came plunging through the bridge, followed by two schooners. All the vessels were much higher than the *Markab,* so Emma and Herbie climbed into the cabin, hiding while the ships passed nearby.

They could make out the bowsprits—all three were shaped like crows. The name *Nero Kraz* was painted on the escutcheon of the nearest ship. It was a stout craft, lying heavy in the water, its hull painted pitch. Above that were two sets of black sails, their edges fringed like feathers.

Flocks of crows were flying everywhere. They were large black birds with bright-red eyes. A dozen or more of them were circling the masts. Others were perched on the rigging, but most were situated on the deck, clumped like hungry beetles around the masts. Their shrieks filled the air with ghostly cries.

"Do you think they'll see us?" Herbie whispered.

Emma didn't reply; her heart was thumping so furiously in her throat. If the sailors on those ships had a way to detect the Pyxis's signal, it would take no time at all for them to realize exactly where it was. She peeked down her collar.

"Is it out?" Herbie whispered.

"Yes," she said, slumping in relief.

It only took a few minutes for the ships to pass.

"They're heading for Earth," Herbie said.

"I hope the navy nukes their asses."

"We could follow them," he said. "They'll probably open a bridge back to Earth."

"Are you crazy? What if they catch us?"

"Oh, come on," Herbie said. "You just don't want to go back. Don't you at least want to see what the Coast Guard does when three huge galleons appear out of nowhere?"

"I've got to find my *parents,*" she replied. "And they're in space. This bridge is the only way to get to Draco."

He sighed. "Okay. But wait—we might need to eat those meteorites again to go through this bridge. I mean, we should do it just to be safe."

"Yeah, you're right."

"But we've only got two left," he pointed out. "Which means if we go through this bridge, we'll be stuck on Alpha Delphini."

"No. I'm sure we can find a way to get more meteorites while we're there." At this, Herbie scoffed.

Once the ships were out of sight, she leapt up and grabbed the last two meteorites.

"We can't stay here forever," she said. "And we've got to get through the bridge before it closes."

"My mom is going to kill me."

They hurried topside. Emma switched on the engine and steered them away from the graveyard.

Once they were clear of the other boats, they each ate their stone and watched as the coat materialized over their bodies. Satisfied that the strange substance was working, Emma killed the engine, Herbie set the sails, and the wind pushed them quietly into the current that led to the bridge.

CHAPTER 10

Porta Amphitrite

Going through the jelly bridge was less difficult this time. Once again Emma felt herself falling into blackness. A moment of silence went by, and she couldn't feel anything. She thought she'd let go of the *Markab*'s wheel and that she was falling down the same deep, dark well, but with a jolt she was back on the water, Herbie standing safely beside her. For all they knew, it might have been a trick of the mind, this passing from outer space to a planet.

They were not in space anymore. They were on a planet bursting with orange-golden sunlight. A buoy announced that they were entering Porta Amphitrite, and a brilliant blue sea shimmered all around them. In the distance were land and a large harbor crowded with ships. A small village lined the coastline, its dockside houses tall, colorful, and ornamented with richly carved facades.

They gaped at the ships that were passing by—great squat catamarans and slender, brightly rigged ketches. A massive wooden caravel was sailing out of the harbor. It was painted blue, its crisp white sails neatly rolled up. On the ship's bowsprit, the figure of a woman was painted to resemble Virgo in her white peasant dress and bare feet. She was holding an ear of wheat. As the ship drew closer, they saw merchants on board.

Herbie shook his head. "We are out of meteorites, we have a hole in the hull because we're taking in more water than we should, and now we're entering Mos Eisley."

Emma gave a shriek of delight as one of the ships in the harbor before them rose up into the air. "Look!" Two great masts on its sides were spread open like wings, pumping steadily as the small ship gained altitude.

"How are they—what the—is that even possible?" Herbie gaped.

A huge grin spread across Emma's face. "Herbie, we are on ANOTHER PLANET!" She punched his arm gleefully. "Can you *believe this*?" He was still gawking at the flying ship, so she grabbed his shoulders, shook them, and said, "Duuuuuuuude! Herbie! We're in outer space!"

"Yeah," he said, letting himself smile. "That is pretty cool. Look at that one!"

Emma turned just in time to see the tail end of a ship slipping under the water. It seemed to be covered in iridescent scales.

"So many ships . . . ," Herbie said.

"Every constellation must have its own," she said excitedly. "Look!" She pointed to a large ketch made of sleek black wood. Its bow was pointed like a pair of joined pincers, and its mainmast curled upward like an insect tail.

"Scorpio," Herbie said.

"No, Cancer," she said.

"But then it should have more masts, only that wouldn't be practical . . ."

They continued chattering as Emma navigated through the traffic that was swelling around them. It seemed not to matter where they docked the ship, so Emma chose a small pier at the farthest end of the harbor and pulled the *Markab* into an empty slot.

They tied the yacht to the pier. Making sure the cabin was locked, they grabbed their things, climbed onto the pier, and looked around.

Emma's first impression was that a zoo had docked there. Two sloops that appeared to be from Aries were unloading herds of goats and flocks of sheep, and the animals' bleating competed with the frustrated cawing of toucans in cages. From another set of cages, dogs—from Canis Major?—were letting out an energetic yelping of their own, confronted with a skulk of foxes. ("Vulpecula," Herbie whispered. "There's only one fox constellation.") All the foxes were tied to leashes and being led down the pier by a thin, nervous-looking merchant in spectacles. The occasional shadow fluttering in the water below appeared to be a school of dolphins.

Emma and Herbie picked their way through the creature crowd, stopping only once to avoid two burly men who were chasing a runaway hare. ("Lepus!" Herbie said.) From all sides came the calls of eager buyers—"Ho, sir! You there! Is that your ship?" and "Sell me the little craft and I'll make you the king of Indus!"

"They speak English here?" Herbie asked, looking amazed.

"I guess so."

They walked a few more feet, and indeed they could understand what everyone was saying, but their voices, although clear, didn't always match the movement of their mouths. Herbie stopped to puzzle about this.

"It's like . . . their voices are being translated," he said. "How is that possible?"

"Maybe something in the meteorites?" Emma suggested. "Look, I don't see a harbormaster, but we should ask someone about docking permission."

"Yeah," Herbie said. "We don't want to get a fine."

She laughed. "Yeah, since we don't have any money."

"Oh!" His face fell. "We don't even know what the currency is here. How are we going to get more meteorites?"

"Don't worry," she said nervously. "I'm sure we'll find something."

She knew that Herbie would start to argue that they should go back to Earth, so she strode quickly into the crowd and Herbie jogged to catch up, his backpack clinking at his shoulder. It had the *Almagest* inside, along with the boat keys and two more sandwiches just in case.

They approached a harbor gate, two great wooden doors bleached gray by the salty air. On either side, a narrow cobblestone street lined the wharf like a frill on the ocean's bright-blue bonnet. The road was crowded with shops, taverns, and inns. Emma headed to the left, where the dock was busiest. They walked for a while, but there was no sign of a harbormaster.

"Do you think anyone's going to notice we're not from here?" Herbie asked.

Emma shook her head. "Everyone looks weird."

They wandered down the street, glancing in shopwindows and staring at the surprising variety of people. Many of them looked very much like the humans on Earth, but when a pair of lanky creatures stepped out of a tavern right in front of them, Herbie grabbed Emma's arm. She stopped in her tracks. The two creatures had wicked lizard faces, goatlike torsos, and long green fish tails that could cut brutal slashes in anything standing behind them. Sauntering confidently onto the sidewalk, one of them threw back his cloak, revealing a row of pistols and deadly knives dangling from his belt.

"What. Is. It?" Herbie whispered.

"Just keep walking," she whispered back. They forced themselves past the creatures, who were eyeing them aggressively.

At the end of the block, Herbie let out his breath. "I have seen a lot of weird things today, but that was—that—the most—I can't even believe—"

He only stuttered when he was really upset, but Emma couldn't suppress her excitement.

"I think they were Capricorns," she said. "You know, part goat, part fish. What if that map was right, and all the stars are connected? Forget traveling around the world—we could travel the galaxy. Think about it, Herbie. With the *Markab,* we could go *anywhere*!"

"But we're going back to Earth, right? I mean, after we find your parents."

She hesitated. "Yeah. Don't worry. I'll get you home—I promise." He glared at her. "I'm just saying, we *could* go anywhere. If we wanted to."

They kept walking. A man was coming down the sidewalk toward them. He was carrying a stack of papers, a hammer, and a bag of nails. He stopped at a lamppost ahead and posted a few notices there.

"You would think with all this jelly technology," Herbie said, "they could do better than a hammer and nails."

Emma and Herbie went closer.

"Oh wow . . . ," Herbie whispered. "Is that your . . . ?"

Emma froze. At the top of each notice was a photograph of Mom! She looked much younger. And her clothing! Emma had never seen Mom in such attire. She wore a flowing white shirt held down by a dark-red corset. Her long black skirt was slit on both sides, revealing high leather boots and quite a lot of leg. Black gloves reached to her elbows, and a huge captain's hat dwarfed her delicate face. From her belt hung two enormous pistols. She was standing in a pose—one hand on her hip, the other holding a sword over her shoulder—that suggested she was as comfortable wielding that sword as she was chopping carrots in the kitchen. There was a vicious, cunning look on her face.

"Whoa," Herbie whispered. "Your mom's totally a pirate."

Then Emma got another shock. Standing behind Mom was a group of men, all wearing doublets and breeches. Dad was just behind her left shoulder, and the cold look on his face was equally foreign to her. She gulped.

The notice read:

THIS MORNING A PYXIS SIGNAL WAS TRANSMITTED ACROSS THE GALAXY. EVERY SHIP IN THE FLEET WENT SAILING AFTER IT, BUT MOST LOST THE SIGNAL.

THE NAVY DOESN'T WANT TO TELL YOU THAT HALIFAX BRIGHTSTOKE, THE SECOND-GREATEST PIRATE OF THE SEAS, IS STILL ALIVE!

THE REWARD FOR FINDING HER WILL BE YOUR FREEDOM FROM SLAVERY AND PRIVATION AND A RETURN TO THE IDEALS OF JUSTICE FOR ALL.

HELP US FIND HALIFAX! LONG LIVE THE REBELLION!

Emma and Herbie stood gaping at the picture.

"Yep," she managed. "The same mom who grounded me for borrowing change from her purse."

Herbie was shaking his head. "I was so wrong about your dad. Your mom is the badass."

Emma's jaw dropped. "What. The. Hell with my parents?"

"I think your dad knew this was going to happen," Herbie said. "Remember how, when the kidnappers broke into your house, he reacted right away? He shoved us into that closet *fast.* I mean, the fact that he had a secret closet at all. He was prepared for it."

Emma felt queasy about this, but he was right: her parents must have been waiting for the day when their past would catch up with them, and Dad had been surprisingly well prepared. . . .

She peeled the notice free, revealing another one beneath it.

Executed for treason on the Eridanus Strand twelve years ago, the notorious Halifax Brightstoke is lying dead at the bottom of the sea.

Queen Elemin Marchpane of Virgo offers a reward of 1,000,000 gold ducats to the man or woman who should find the source of the Pyxis transmission that has sparked rumors of Halifax's rise from the grave.

Halifax is dead, but the Pyxis is not.

PIRATES DON'T DIE!! was scrawled over it.

"Your mom was *executed?*" Herbie said.

Emma was stunned. She felt a weird tingling, as if at any moment the sidewalks might turn into rivers, the lampposts into ships. And if she looked out at the harbor, she might not see water, but stars and planets and the blackness of space. It was not exciting anymore to feel that the whole world could change in an instant, because now the deepest and most fundamental part of it had changed.

Her parents, who had always just been her parents, were people she never knew.

CHAPTER 11
Scuttlebutt

It felt as if all the humor had been sucked out of the world. Emma and Herbie walked quietly down the sidewalk. Herbie watched her worriedly, uncertain of what to say, but Emma said nothing. She still held the notice, crumpled in her hand.

Suddenly, Herbie jerked to a halt.

Ahead of them, a group of men were climbing from rowboats onto a pier. They were dressed in blue breeches and white hats, just like the sailors they had seen at the marina on Earth. Behind them, docked in the harbor, was the great ship *Arcturus Venture,* its red hull glinting in the bright noon light.

The vendors noticed that the navy had arrived, and quietly they began closing up their stalls, hastily tucking away their wares and moving back from the pier.

Emma and Herbie slid silently into the crowd, hurrying to

get away. They turned into a narrow alley that was crowded with fish vendors and pushed their way to a massive water plaza. It was filled with small dinghies and dolphins. They skirted the edges and turned down another alley, burrowing deeper into the city.

Yet every road seemed to lead them back to the harbor. Again and again they'd hurry down a street, only to find themselves facing the sea.

In frustration, they cut into a dark alley and walked to the end. They had arrived on a derelict-looking road. There were few people in sight. Halfway down the street, they heard laughter ahead, and a group of navy sailors came around the corner. Herbie grabbed Emma and pulled her into the nearest tavern. A faded sign above the door said JOB'S COFFIN.

The Coffin was dark and buzzing with voices. They stopped in the doorway. It took them a moment to realize that the tavern was shaped like the inside of a whale. The walls were sloped and painted dark red. A cavernous set of ribs dangled above the bar, and just above the door hung a frightful row of teeth. There were only two windows in the room, circular portholes that were covered in grime.

"Scary dive," Herbie said. "And somebody should tell them that most whales don't have teeth."

There was only one free table at the very back of the room, so they made their way there. Many of the tavern guests were human, but among them was a pair of black bears sitting at a table and drinking from steins. Just beyond the bears was a booth full of monkeys. They wore bandoliers and carried pistols, and their skinny legs were practically swimming in oversized black boots. Beneath another table was a pack of dogs, all sleek and gray, sitting at their master's feet.

Herbie blinked. "I don't think my brain was built to handle alcoholic animals."

Emma and Herbie sat on two old casks beside a thick wooden table. Their waitress, a scrawny bald woman who was being called this way and that ("Oy, Berenice! What's takin' so long?") came to their table, looking irritated.

"Show me yer money," she said.

Herbie shot Emma a nervous look. He slung his backpack onto his lap and unzipped the outer compartment, where he kept his wallet. But before he could reach it, Berenice spotted the jar full of bullets, half sunken in their mysterious water. She seized it, her eyes widening with excitement.

"I'll take the scuppers," she said, eyeing them warily as if they might protest. Both Emma and Herbie looked at her in surprise. Berenice glanced nervously over her shoulder and then hunched over the jar, swishing the water around and inspecting it carefully.

"Scuppers?" Herbie asked.

Berenice jiggled the jar. "Where did ye get them?" she whispered suspiciously.

"Er . . . someone was shooting at us," Herbie said. "Out in space."

"On a Strand?" Berenice asked. "Musta been the navy."

"Wait, a *Strand* . . . ?" Herbie said. "Is that the ocean thing in outer space?"

Berenice snorted. "You don't know nothin', do you? Yes, it's called a Strand. And I'll take your scuppers," she said smugly. "Since they're no use to you."

"Um . . . no." Emma snatched the jar. "You can have *one,* but only if we can eat and drink and . . . and you can give us ten of those black meteorite thingies that turn your skin into jelly."

"You mean vostok?" Berenice smirked. "And you don't know what that is either. Where exactly are ye from?"

"Yes, uh . . . vostok. We knew that. We need ten pieces. And you can have *one scupper.*"

She gave a sneer. "Two," she said grudgingly.

Emma hesitated. "Fine. We'll give you one now," she said. "And one more when we're done here—but only if we like the food."

Berenice gave the jar one last look—as if she couldn't quite believe her luck—and huffing, she hustled off.

"Why would she want a bunch of smashed bullets?" Herbie remarked.

"I think she was more interested in the water," Emma said. "Did you see how she was swishing it around?"

"So let me get this straight," he said. "First we ate vostok. Then someone shot at us with scuppers. Then we got on a Strand and came here."

"I guess so," Emma said.

Getting a better look at the creatures around them, they were beginning to realize that the animals here looked much worse than the ones they'd seen outside. The bears were too thin and missing large patches of fur. There was a Capricorn, but he was sickly and green. He had lost all his scales, and some sort of slime was oozing from his ears.

When Berenice came back, she was carrying a tray with an empty bottle, a bag full of vostok, and two small glasses of a greenish-brown substance. She set the glasses on the table. "Yer starters," she said. "Food's comin' up."

Herbie recoiled in disgust.

She shot him a frown. "It ain't the best memory water, but it's what we serve here. Ye don't like it, ye leave."

"More memory water here!" one of the monkeys called out, motioning to Emma's and Herbie's glasses. "Same size as those!"

Herbie's eyes narrowed. "Memory water?"

Berenice made a fuss about getting her scupper and a teaspoon full of water to go with it. In her desperation, she spilled a drop on her arm and cursed at her carelessness. Emma quickly realized that the water in the jar was much cleaner and purer than the water in the glass on the table. She took the jar from Berenice and insisted on doling out the payment herself. She put only a few drops of the water into Berenice's bottle.

"Stingy," Berenice grumbled as she stuffed the small bottle into her skirts.

Herbie put the vostok in his backpack. "At least that's taken care of. And now we know what it's called."

Emma reached for her glass of memory water out of curiosity, but Herbie stopped her.

"I've been watching the critters," he said. "Nobody's actually drinking this stuff. They're just sticking their fingers in it."

Indeed he was right. Across the room, the two bears each held a paw in their glass. They looked quite relaxed, sitting there with closed eyes and peaceful faces.

Emma stared at her glass. It was small, with just an inch of liquid. But whatever was in that glass seemed to have turned a bullet into a transmogrifying device. While the fluid looked revolting, it was obviously not poison, because everyone was touching it. *Why?* she wondered, looking around. Did it give the customers some magical qualities too?

Herbie looked uneasy. Emma stuck her finger in the glass.

"I guess we're drinking the Kool-Aid," he said. Using the very tip of his pinkie, he touched the water too.

Emma didn't allow her finger to remain in the glass; she simply swiped the water and pulled her finger out. A powerful smell filled her nose—the strange scent of wood and old rope. She felt a strange shifting. Around her, the air became very quiet, as if someone had turned down the sound. Slowly she heard a song from inside the glass, the echo of an old sea chanty. She drew the glass closer. It was as if the song was lingering inside the rim. It seemed to flow into her ears and take root inside her skull, where it grew louder and clearer. She could make out the words and hear the creaking of wood, the strange shuffle of footsteps.

Staring into the glass, she saw a picture forming beneath the water, like figures in a snow globe. Six men were sitting on cargo boxes, two of them singing, the others harmonizing. She stared with fascination and amazement as the men sang.

Where do our precious waters go?
Down to the Queen Virgo, oh-ho!
The tyrant, boys, she breaks our backs,
But now we have her Halifax.
Oh-ho! The revolution, oh-ho!

Suddenly the vision frightened her, and she gave a jolt, sloshing the water onto the table. She set the glass down and saw that Berenice was eyeing her with a seductive grin.

Herbie was looking at Emma in confusion.

"Did you hear that?" she asked. "The song about my mom?"

He shook his head. "But I got a whole lot of whispering."

Emma listened as the last notes of the song died away. Was that a memory? How could she possibly hear a memory that belonged to someone else? And why was it about her mom?

She had the dreadful feeling that her parents were slipping farther away. Not only might she never see them again, but she hadn't known the most basic things about them in the first place, like how they came to space and where they were really from. The song seemed to suggest that her mom was from Virgo. Mom must have known about memory water. Did she drink it? Was that *Mom's* memory in the water? How did memories end up in the water in the first place? Emma bet her parents would know the answer to that—and to a good many other things besides. Those vostok, for example, had been sitting so innocently on the *Markab,* right under her nose all those years. She and Herbie had argued over the origin of those stones for months, which practically begged Dad to tell them the truth. And yet he'd said nothing. Like one of the stones, he had sat there just as dumbly. He had gone out of his way to hide the truth. She figured he had to have a very good reason.

Voices began to trickle into her skull, much like memories from the glass, only these ones seemed to be coming from the tables around her. They came in whispers that penetrated the bar babble. She could suddenly hear the bears in the corner.

"They say Halifax drank from the seas back then, just like the pirates did," one bear said. "It gave her the powers she had."

"She weren't magic," his friend replied. "She were beautiful, that's all. And that's why they followed her."

"Then what about the gloves she wore? You don't wear gloves like that until ye're one of them."

"Anyone can wear gloves, you idiot."

"Not like those. And people said she had powers. It's what you get from drinking the waters."

"Ye been drinkin' 'em yerself these many years," he said with a laugh. "Ye got any magic powers yet?"

"This water's corrupted—you know that."

Then the conversation stopped. Emma glanced at the bears. They were still talking, their lips moving, but she couldn't hear a word they were saying, only the chatter of the bar folk around her.

A minute later, another voice seemed to leap out of the crowd.

"Halifax was executed for a good reason, I say!"

She couldn't tell who was talking, but individual voices continued to rise out of the clamor and head straight to her ears. *Halifax. Treason. Pirates and Mad Jack. The Pyxis.* It seemed like magic, the way the voices became clear just long enough for her to hear them before they disappeared again. It gave her the idea that something was controlling it—perhaps the memory water.

Another conversation came to her—this one from the monkeys huddled in the booth in the corner.

"And apparently Halifax is being transferred to a ship called the *Eel,*" one monkey said.

"The *Newton Eel*? That's captained by Gent—the same woman who executed her twelve years ago!"

"Now that's poetic justice."

"What do you think they'll do to her?"

"They'll take her straight to Hydra. I don't think the Queen will risk letting her survive *another* execution."

"Think they'll chop her head off?"

"Nah, they'll throw her into the Whirl."

"You're sure it was Halifax?"

"Sure as suns! Everyone saw her being dragged up the

gangplank. And she looked terrible. Sick and skinny, her hair was wild . . . she was screaming about slibbernuts and cocklies."

"What are those?"

"Nothing. It's nonsense. She's lost her mind."

The conversation vanished abruptly, and Emma looked at Herbie. He could tell from the look on her face that something was very wrong. Quietly, they gathered their things and left.

CHAPTER 12

Scuppered

Are you . . . tripping the light fantastic?” Herbie asked.

Emma shook her head. “It was weird,” she said. Her voice was shaking. “I heard things people were saying across the room. I’m pretty sure it was because of the water.”

“Dude, that is so not fair. I just heard a bunch of sailors talking about rope.”

“It was bad.”

“What did you hear?” he asked.

She told him about her mom supposedly having special powers, and that she was being brought to Hydra on a ship called the *Newton Eel,* which was run by the same woman who had executed her, Captain Gent. When she got to the description of her mom walking up the gangplank and shouting out nonsense, Emma choked on the words and fought back tears.

"They're going to kill her," Emma squeaked.

Herbie stopped walking. He looked chagrined.

"I know it sounds crazy," she said quickly, "but I think I really was hearing their conversations and they were telling the truth—"

Herbie cut her off. "So what's our plan for getting them back?"

"My parents?" She wiped away a tear. "Wait, you're okay with that? I thought you wanted to go home."

"We have to find your parents first. You can't do it alone. And you can't do it without the *Markab*."

A faint smile broke through her gloom. "You rock," she said.

"So do we have a plan?" he asked.

"No."

"I think we should ask around at the harbor," he said. "Someone might know where the ship holding your mom went . . . but first I think we'd better check on the *Markab*."

"Good idea."

The town was considerably busier now. It seemed that they had to push their way through crowds on nearly every street. When they reached the harbor road, they stopped to scan for navy sailors. Walking carefully alongside the water, keeping a sharp eye out, they headed for the pier where the *Markab* was docked.

The navy sailors seemed to have vanished, and the pier was even more crowded with animals. Emma and Herbie had to pick their way past a tangle of sheep. They managed to get within twenty feet of the *Markab* before spotting a navy sailor. He was sitting on a cask—a young man, maybe twenty. His uniform was brand-new, and he was almost completely hidden by a bevy of swans. The birds, which were tied together by their necks, were tugging one another and squawking loudly. The man was shooing them away halfheartedly.

He was sitting right next to the *Markab.*

Emma and Herbie quickly ducked behind a row of cages that were filled with chameleons and other lizards. One of the animals hissed at them.

"They found us," Herbie said.

"We can still get to the boat," Emma replied. "We just need to sneak around behind those swans and wait until the sailor looks the other way." Even *she* thought this was risky, but they didn't have a choice.

They slipped around the side of the lizard cages and scurried across the walkway, crouching low to stay hidden beside the swans. The birds had stopped squawking and were trumpeting angrily, putting up such a loud honking that the sailor, who was now supremely annoyed, stood up and began pushing them. They shrieked in protest. *HONK HONK!* The sailor didn't notice Emma sneaking down the narrow pier and crawling silently over the *Markab*'s side. Herbie, who was following her, swiftly untied the *Markab*'s rope and climbed onto the yacht.

"Now what?" he whispered. "He's going to notice when we start the engine!"

Emma bit her lip. He was right, and she couldn't think of a quiet way to get free of the slip. "Not if we hurry. Those birds are loud."

HONK HONK HONK!

"We're going to have to make a run for it," she said. "How are we on gas?"

Herbie shook his head. "We maybe have enough to get out of the harbor, but that's it!"

"That's all we need." Emma went to the wheel. Herbie stayed crouched by the mast.

HONK HONK!

Emma started the engine, and it gave a roar. Suddenly, the swans' trumpeting stopped.

"Oh no . . ." Herbie peeked over the railing. The sailor had stopped shooing the swans away and was staring at the *Markab.*

"Hey!" he shouted. "You there! *Stop!"* He started running toward the boat, but Emma quickly put it into gear and backed out of the slip. With a quick turn, she set them on a course for the harbor and hit the throttle hard, driving the boat forward with a jolt.

"Emma!" Herbie shouted, pointing at a group of sailors running down the pier. "They're coming after us!"

Rifle fire rang out as the *Markab* fled toward the open sea. Emma killed the engine with practiced hands, Herbie let out the sails, and the *Markab* shot forward. But they weren't clear yet. Behind them, the navy had set off in a group of cutters, and the boats were gaining speed. Two more cutters were approaching from the side. The small ships were light and swift on the water. Their sails were much larger than the *Markab*'s, and they were moving twice as fast. As they approached, Emma could see the sailors on their decks. They were wearing the same uniforms that she'd seen on the Strand, and the men were aiming their rifles at the *Markab.*

"Herbie, duck!" she yelled. They both crouched as a round of rifle shots tore into the *Markab*'s mast and sides.

Ahead of them, the harbor was packed with ships. Emma was sure there were lanes of traffic, but they were impossible to make out. She turned the yacht to avoid a large, brightly colored ship, but just behind it were two freighters passing each other. She aimed the *Markab* alongside one of the freighters, but then gave a shriek. To port and ahead, three more navy cutters appeared.

"They're surrounding us!" she cried.

Just ahead, a massive galleon came into view. It was sailing straight for them, approaching rapidly. It was much too wide for the narrow channels between the other ships, and as it came closer, its hull scraped at the smaller ships and sent sailors screaming for cover.

The wind was pushing the *Markab* right into its path.

"Herbie!"

He didn't need prodding. He reefed the sails with lightning speed, and Emma started the engine. It roared to life, and she steered them desperately out of the monster's path.

"Emma, hurry!"

She drove the *Markab* farther to port, watching as the navy cutters scrambled for safety.

They stared up at the ship. They had never seen one so large. Its upper hull was painted bright red and covered with wood carvings, gothic windows, and gun ports. There was a great lion carved on the bowsprit, and on the starboard side an escutcheon showed the name ARGH in white letters. Aside from the mainmast, mizzenmast, and foremast, there were two great masts folded against its sides like wings. Metal cannons lined the top deck from the bow to the gallery deck, and far above those, towering masts butted into the sky. The square rigging carried ratlines, and humans and monkeys were clinging there. The whole ship must have been twenty stories high.

As the great ship drew closer, another odd detail became apparent: just above the waterline, the wooden hull was covered in iridescent scales. The scales glimmered and wiggled exactly like a fish's as it swims through the water. It was the strangest ship Emma had ever seen, and despite her pounding heart, she felt a flicker of terrified awe.

"I don't see any navy on their deck!" she said.

The ship was nearly upon them now, its bow moving past them. If they had been closer, it would have crushed them like a giant, oblivious foot. It cut a massive seam in the water, and the waves sent the *Markab* juddering sideways. Herbie and Emma stared upward to a deck they couldn't see, and all they could hear were the splashes of the waves and the strange, humanlike groaning of the wooden monstrosity.

"Come on, Emma, let's head back to the bridge."

"No, we have to—"

"Look out!" Herbie shouted. They looked up just as a humongous net fell over them, trapping them like fish. The net was attached to the big ship. The fibers of the net seemed to be wriggling of their own accord. They grabbed the *Markab* like hundreds of tentacles, attaching to its hull and sails and yanking it upward. Emma and Herbie fell to the deck. The yacht gave a lurch as it rose out of the water. The *Markab* hit the side of the *Argh,* and something crunched.

Emma scrambled to her feet just in time to see a massive door on the *Argh*'s side slide open. She looked around desperately for something to use to defend herself, but when her arm touched the netting, it grabbed ahold of her. She struggled to get free, but the fibers took her other arm, and she was trapped.

"Herbie!" she shouted. Straining to look over her shoulder, she caught sight of Herbie also tangled in the netting. Like a fast-growing vine, it had him by the neck and was wrapping slowly around his chest. His face turned red as he gasped for breath.

CHAPTER 13

The Great *Argh*

With a crunch, the *Markab* hit the floor and tipped, crashing onto its side. The fibers of the giant net fell away, sending Herbie falling with a clatter and dropping Emma to her knees. She scrambled to Herbie, who was struggling to catch his breath.

"You okay?" she gasped.

He nodded.

The *Markab* was lying on its side like a wounded whale. They were inside a large cargo hold filled with rows of boxes and stacks of wood. From all around came the squawks of busy monkeys. Emma scrabbled over the wheel and climbed off the yacht, landing on the wooden floor with an angry *thunk.* She raced around the *Markab*'s side, looking for whoever had freed them. The netting lay around them like a giant octopus.

She was horrified to see just how much damage had been done to the yacht: its sleek hull was torn to pieces, and bits of it were lying scattered all over the floor. The mast had somehow broken in half and the sails were ripped to shreds. Angry tears welled in her eyes.

Ahead of her, a group of monkeys were closing the cargo doors.

Herbie climbed down from the boat, his face flushed with anger. "What happened?"

"They destroyed our ship!"

Two monkeys approached them, motioning them to a staircase and squawking urgently.

"So what?" Herbie said. "These monkeys don't talk?"

One monkey hooted and shook a fist at Herbie. He turned to Emma. "They destroyed our boat!"

"I know!"

Fuming, they followed the monkeys to the stairs, climbing up five long flights. When they reached the top deck, they were plunged into chaos. The deck was teeming with kids. There were hundreds of them, all wearing identical beige trousers and shirts with red woolen vests over the top. Monkeys scampered everywhere and dangled from the masts above, where they were unfurling sails. The ship groaned and lurched forward as the wind hit the sails with a *crack*. The *Argh* sped up, coursing into the open sea.

A young man's voice shouted, "Swing guns, on my count! Captain says vostok now!" A whistle blew, and a passing monkey tossed vostok to Emma and Herbie. Emma noticed that everyone was hurriedly eating their stones.

"Vostok bridge ahead!" someone cried. "Fire the cannons!"

Emma and Herbie swallowed their vostok and waited for it to slide its silky safety over their bodies. The skin was just beginning to appear when—*crack!*—cannon shots filled the sky with a flash of light. Emma pushed her way to the railing, Herbie tailing her. The ship rattled and lurched, resisting the massive force that was drawing it through the bridge. The whole wooden structure let out a deep, coarse rumbling that sounded very much like an *AAAAARGHHHHH* of complaint. As a crushing force threw them to the ground, everything around them disappeared.

Emma's first sight of the new Strand was the sky. When she opened her eyes, she saw its dark chaos towering above her, crackling and rippling between the masts and the dozens of sails pulled taut in the wind. This was nothing like the gray Strand that had brought them from Earth. This one loomed with roiling black thunderclouds and flashes of lightning. Loud cracks and groans seemed to swell from a greater place, and she had the sense that not only were the clouds churning and tossing, but the very fabric of the Strand itself was coming apart.

She was lying on the top deck, feeling light-headed. Beside her, Herbie was staring fearfully at the sky.

"You okay?" she asked.

"Yeah," he grumbled.

She helped him up.

Now that the crowd had cleared, they had a better view of the top deck. It was enormous. The journey from stem to stern almost required a car. On each side, the wooden railings were as high as Emma's shoulders, their slats as thick around as her waist. And above, the three masts reached so high that their tips were scarcely to be seen.

A gallery deck took up most of the back of the ship. It was two stories above the main deck, shaped like a square house. Through the rain, Emma saw carved window frames and ornate scrollwork hemming the roof. A bank of windows ran around all four sides of the upper floor. She thought the deck was probably a navigation room.

Herbie was still gaping at the ship. "Did you see the lion on the bow?" he said. His anger seemed to be fading as he looked around with curiosity. "It was huge."

"Yeah," Emma grouched.

"This must be a Leo ship. But it doesn't look like we're going back to Earth. This is a totally different Strand." He turned to her. "I know they damaged the boat," he said, "but I think they were trying to rescue us."

"Yeah." Emma was frowning. "But they *ruined* the *Markab.*"

They looked around at the crew—or Arghs, as they called themselves. A young girl was shouting orders. Dozens of other kids were climbing the ratlines. A rigging rope flew free, wriggling and thrashing like an angry snake until two boys grabbed it and tied it down. The Arghs were so relaxed at their work that Emma wanted to shout at them, "*HEY, IDIOTS, YOU DESTROYED MY YACHT!*"

"Sure, Santher, no problem," someone said loudly and sarcastically. "Let me just go ask the captain if you can hubble back there to conquer the navy all by yourself."

They turned to see a tall boy, a bit older than everyone else. He had a crown of black hair, pretty green eyes that peered out from behind silver wire-rimmed glasses, and a nose that was permanently turned up to the world.

"Okay, *Mouncey,*" Santher snapped. "So you're saying we should just run like a bunch of scared mice?"

"Of course we shouldn't." Mouncey patted down his vest. "Except that we're saving our asses!"

"That's *stupid*!"

"Well, you are welcome to bring that up with the captain. I'm quite certain he's going to want a full explanation for how this whole fiasco started in the first place."

"It wasn't a fiasco!" Santher said.

"Then what was it?" The voice was deep and loud, with a rumbling quality that brought silence to the deck. Emma and Herbie turned to see a man—the only adult they'd seen so far on the ship—coming up from the stern.

"Captain Lovesey," Mouncey said, snapping to attention, which caused everyone else to roll their eyes.

"Mouncey, Santher," the captain said. "Someone care to tell me what's going on?"

"Well, sir, Santher here has proposed sailing back to Delphinus to take up a fight with the navy." Mouncey gave him a wry look. "And he would like to go back himself, since the rest of us are cowards."

The captain looked around at his crew. He cut a strange figure. It looked as if half of his body had been burned. The right side of his face was scarred and mottled, his shoulder hung oddly, and his right arm was thin and withered, held to his side by a sling. The other half of him showed a powerful, rippling form, with sun-darkened skin, whiskers, and a great shag of hair that was matted from wearing a hat. He wore a beige linen shirt and the red waistcoat of an old uniform. It bore no insignia, only a dark spot on the chest where it looked as if he'd torn off a patch—in the shape of a lion.

In the air beside his head hung a floating spyglass. At least it seemed to be floating, since no one stood behind it, and when it spoke, its great bloodshot eye blinked cruelly.

"Well!" the spyglass cried in a scornful voice. "Somebody get the boy a hubble!"

"Nelson," the captain growled, raising his hand to silence the spyglass. "Would someone care to tell me what happened back there?"

Three kids started talking at once, but Santher stepped forward. He was slender, with fuzzy light-brown hair and a pair of sharp blue eyes. He couldn't have been older than thirteen, and yet two streaks of gray hair ran back from each temple.

"The navy was chasing these two on their cutter!" he said, pointing at Emma and Herbie. All eyes turned to them. "We saw they were kids, and we weren't going to let the navy get 'em!"

"It's not a cutter," Emma said sharply. "It's a *yacht,* and you've destroyed it!"

"Oh, do pardon us," Mouncey said highly. "For saving your butts!"

The captain's eyebrows shot up and he turned to Santher, who looked sheepish. "Well," Santher exclaimed, "we had to bring 'em into the cargo hold—we couldn't leave 'em on the water!"

"You brought a *yacht* into the *hold?*" the captain asked.

"It's only temporary, sir. I promise I'll take care of it—"

Clearly upset now, the captain studied his crew. Some of the Arghs were shaking their heads, but Santher shrugged innocently. "The navy was after 'em!"

Just then, a girl came up the stairs near the gallery deck. She was younger than most—probably about eleven—with a pile of short, mousy hair and great blinking brown eyes that were partially hidden behind a pair of floppy bangs. There was a hawk on her arm.

"Laika," the captain said by way of greeting. "What's the report?"

"The navy's behind us, sir. Three ships. Men-of-war."

This caused some murmuring in the crowd, but the captain nodded. "Mouncey, I want another head count to make sure we didn't leave anyone behind. Once that's done, we'll go up to full speed."

"Yes, sir," Mouncey said, scurrying off.

"You two." The captain motioned to Emma and Herbie. "Who are you?"

Emma glanced nervously at Herbie. "I'm Emma," she said. "And this is Herbie."

"Emma and Herbie who?"

"Emma Garton and Herbert Yee."

Lovesey's one good eye was focused on Emma's face. "Nelson," he said, "would you be so kind?" The spyglass floated over, positioning himself in front of Lovesey's ruined eye. Now Nelson's great bloodshot eye stared down at them while Lovesey gave an odd harrumph. There was an intensity in the gaze that made Emma shrink.

Lovesey nudged the spyglass away, looking thoughtful.

"Are you from Delphinus?" he inquired.

"Uh, no . . . we're from Monkey," Emma said.

"That's a long way," the captain replied. "Where are your parents?"

"Actually, I'm looking for them," she said. "They were kidnapped."

Lovesey turned to Herbie. "And you?"

"I'm with her?" he squeaked.

"And why was the navy chasing you?"

Emma's mind fumbled about for an explanation, but she was so nervous and angry, and the crew was staring at her so intently, that she couldn't think of a single good lie. All she knew was that she wouldn't tell them about the Pyxis.

"I don't know," she said. But the moment the words left her mouth, she realized that Lovesey didn't believe them any more than she did.

"It's very odd," he replied. "You see, the navy doesn't usually send so many ships to chase down two small children. Now, they *might* consider stealing a whole ship full of children, but to go to all that trouble just to find two? In all my years I have never seen the navy go to such lengths, and most certainly not in a busy port like Amphitrite. Why, there are plenty of children there, if children were what they were after."

Emma swallowed hard.

"Do you care to elaborate on your explanation?" Lovesey asked. It wasn't really a question so much as a threat. Emma looked to Herbie, but he had nothing to say.

"Very well," Lovesey replied coolly. "The navy's after you, which means that you're outlaws, and unfortunately, I can't afford to harbor you on my ship. It will only endanger everyone else on board. For that reason, we'll be letting you off on the Cygnus system. Albireo, to be exact. That's our next port of call."

Emma fought the impulse to tell him the truth—that they were hiding the Pyxis, which was pretty important. But she knew that it was dangerous to reveal that secret. And anyway, from the jut of Lovesey's chin, she could see that he was as firm as old mutton. She felt the sudden, dead weight of disappointment. Someone with a ship full of children ought to be more sympathetic.

"Santher," the captain said, "have someone show them to the dining hall and then to their rooms. Tomorrow, I want them put to work in the aerie."

"The aerie, sir?" Santher seemed a bit surprised.

"Yes, you heard me." Lovesey looked at the two of them, but particularly at Emma. "And get that damned ship out of my cargo hold."

CHAPTER 14
The Aerie

The *Argh*'s dining hall was fit for the great kings of Leo. Tables filled the large space, each surrounded by many high-backed chairs, most of which were big enough to be thrones. Two or three children could sit in each. Arghs were everywhere, standing in groups. Some of them were even sitting on the tables. Everyone wore red vests and beige tunics and trousers, which looked remarkably like old military uniforms. Most of the tunics were much too large for the children's small frames, and many had the same worn spot on the chest where it looked as if a lion-shaped patch had been removed.

The ship's cook, Nisba, came out of the kitchen with a group of Arghs. They all carried plates of food on each arm. Nisba didn't look like the sort of woman you would find serving hundreds of loud children. She was slender, but her tall black boots gave the impression of toughness, as did the pile of electric-red hair that framed her face with its own sort of wildness. Barking orders to the servers, she moved through the crowd and made sure plates were set on every table.

When Emma and Herbie entered the room, it grew considerably quieter. Even Nisba turned to stare. Word had already spread that there were guests on board, and dozens of curious eyes took in Emma's blue puffer jacket and Herbie's green windbreaker. The younger kids in the room began puzzling out which system Herbie was from, and whispers of "Perseus" and "Orion" floated about. Emma, they figured, was just a Monkey, because the monkeys had a strong feeling about these things, and they had already said so, but Herbie—well, he was another matter.

"Perhaps he's Draco royalty," someone whispered.

Emma overheard this remark and snorted. *"Ragnar."*

But Herbie had noticed Laika, the young girl they'd seen on deck. She was sitting at a table with Mouncey and Santher.

"Let's sit there," Herbie said.

"Okay. Why?"

"Didn't you see her before? She was holding a hawk."

They made their way to the table. Herbie took the seat beside Laika, leaving Emma with a seat facing the boys.

"Hi," Laika said brightly. "I'm Laika. I'm from Canis Minor. And that's—"

Mouncey cut her off. "Actually," he said, pointing at Emma, "we want to know where *you're* from."

"I told you already," she said a bit stiffly. "We're from Monkey." She wished she'd chosen a seat farther from Mouncey. He was giving her the evil eye.

Another Argh arrived at their table with plates of hot food—

chicken pies and potatoes—and everyone began eating except Laika, who leaned forward conspiratorially.

"SO," she whispered, "tell us everything you know."

"What do you mean?" Emma asked.

"About the *pirates*."

There was such a look of eager anticipation in Laika's eyes that Emma hated to say her next words. "I don't know anything about the pirates."

"Good grace, Laika," Mouncey snapped. "Would you please stop with that pirate nonsense?"

"Shut up!" she said. "You know they're out there. They *have* to be." She turned to Emma. "We know they're very secretive."

"Or maybe they just *don't exist,*" Mouncey said.

"Uh, well, we saw a notice on Delphinus . . . ," Herbie offered.

Laika's face fell.

"I'm sorry," Emma said. "I really don't know any pirates. We're from a remote star on Monkey, and—"

"But you must know *something,*" Laika said. "Why else would the navy be chasing you?"

"Really," Emma said. "We don't know anything. We've never been to space before this."

"Why are you looking for pirates?" Herbie asked.

"Because they're the only ones who stand up to the Queen," Laika said, seeming surprised that he didn't know this already.

"We don't know anything about that," Herbie admitted.

"You can see that he means it," Mouncey remarked, leaning into Laika's ear. "Nobody knows about the pirates, because they don't exist. The Queen killed them all. Now stop asking everyone!"

Slowly, Laika picked up her fork and started eating, glancing up occasionally to regard Emma and Herbie with disappointment.

✦ ✦ ✦

Down a series of long, carpeted hallways, they passed a clock and a wooden statue of Leo's King, Cor Leonis, whose sword was held aloft in a heroic aspect. However, the king's right leg had been sawed off and was speared like a sausage at the end of his sword.

Taking a right at the statue, their guide, Wardle, led Emma and Herbie down a dead-end hallway. Wardle had small brown eyes, a thick snub nose, and a terrifically large jaw. Taken separately, his features might have been ugly, but together they were strangely handsome. Wardle came from the Cetus system, named after a terrible sea monster with gaping jaws, goatlike forelegs, and a serpent's tail. He showed them the slight webbing between his fingers and explained that he could hold his breath underwater for twenty-eight minutes.

"Do you have gills?" Herbie asked.

"No." Wardle looked offended. "Gills are for *fish*."

They stopped at a door at the very end of the hallway. It was narrower than the others, and it took some effort to turn the key in the disused lock.

"This is your room," he said to Emma, his voice deep and rumbly. "A bit out of the way of things, but I guess it's only temporary."

She entered a cavelike chamber. It had thinning red carpets and a single bright candle flickering on the wall.

Emma turned to Wardle. "Aren't there beds?" she asked.

Wardle pointed a thick finger at three doors in the wall. "Bedrooms's in there," he said. "It's a Leo ship, you know!"

"Oh. Okay."

Wardle motioned to Herbie. "Your room's down the hall. Follow me."

Emma said goodnight to Herbie and opened the first door in the wall. It looked to be a passageway into a deeper compartment. She ducked into the passage and approached an even smaller arched door. It was old and wooden, but elegantly carved with regal lions that glimmered in the candlelight.

Opening the door, she was pleased to find a small room that smelled of wood. To the left was a bed draped in a velvet quilt. To the right, a row of candles protruded from the wall, filling the room with a golden light. Three portholes above the bed were splattered with rain.

Emma sat heavily on the bed. She was trying not to think about all the things she'd lost, but remembering the *Markab* filled her with a sense that some malicious force in the universe was trying very hard to take every last thing away from her. First her parents, then, well . . . Earth. Then the *Markab.* And it was all because of the Pyxis.

Suddenly remembering that it was around her neck, she fumbled to unzip her jacket, felt the bump it made in her shirt, and let out a tremendous sigh of relief.

She stripped her shoes and jacket off, tossed them at the end of the bed, and climbed under the covers, where it was at least partially warm. Her eyelids felt as if they were made of lead. She hadn't slept for at least twenty-four hours, and before that she'd only slept fitfully. She wanted to keep thinking about every crazy thing she'd seen since coming to space, but as she lay in the large, cozy bed, she felt her eyes shutting, felt the delicious sensation of falling into a deep, warm, well-deserved sleep. . . .

The crab watch clanged its way through the Strand's chilly night, but Emma heard nothing of it. Nestled deep inside the *Argh,* she was aware of the occasional patter of rain on her windows and the strange creakings and groanings of the ship—which in her dreams she mistook for a pile of snoring bears, or the wooden chuckling of a carriage on a cobblestone street. She did, however, hear the breakfast bell jangle, and the distant slamming of doors, and the thundering of feet on the carpet in the hall, but she was so exhausted and so comfortable in her bed that she simply rolled over and went back to sleep. It was only when she heard her own door open and close that she forced her eyes open and grudgingly sat up.

There was no one in the room, but a uniform was lying on the trunk by the door. It was the same beige tunic and trousers that all the Arghs wore. Beside it was a red vest and a pair of boots.

Emma was sore from all the sailing they'd done, so it was a slow, painful task to slip out of her dirty jeans and T-shirt and into the clean trousers and tunic. As she was folding up her clothes, she heard a crinkling sound and remembered the notice she'd taken from the lamppost on Amphitrite. She removed it from the pocket of her jeans.

The sight of her mother brought a wave of sadness and grudging pride. Mom looked cocky, tough, and beautiful—not Mom at all. For the first time, Emma wasn't so embarrassed that she looked so much like her.

Then her eyes fell on her dad in the photograph. Seeing him brought a different feeling. His expression was cold in a way she'd never seen. It was easy to imagine the man in the photograph telling a blatant lie. *"I was in Phoenix."* She felt a jolt of betrayal. That didn't feel like the same Dad who'd taken her on the *Markab* all those years.

He must have had a good reason for lying to her. He'd been hiding the Pyxis all this time, and Emma was certain there was much more to the story than she knew. After seeing him get shot, she could believe that he'd been keeping a deadly secret—perhaps dangerous enough that he had needed to hide it from her as well. She was suddenly filled with a new burst of fear that the gunshot had killed him, that he was dead now, and that she would never see him or Mom again. Quickly folding the notice and stuffing it into her pocket, she left the room.

✦ ✦ ✦

Emma and Herbie met in the corridor and went to the dining hall.

"I need to do *something* to find out where my parents are," Emma said. "Maybe the captain can help."

"Let's ask around at breakfast," Herbie said.

In the dining hall, which was nearly empty, they sat at a table. A monkey came out of the kitchen and brought them food. They had barely downed two biscuits and a glass of juice each before Santher and Laika arrived to take them to their post in the aerie. Apparently, they were late.

"First I want to talk to the captain," Emma said.

"You can't," Laika replied. "Unless it's an emergency."

"I need some help finding my parents," Emma said.

Laika and Santher exchanged a look. "Maybe later," Laika said. "Right now you have to work."

Reluctantly, Emma and Herbie followed the others through the ship's carpeted corridors and up two flights of stairs to the top deck. They crossed the deck and stopped at the mainmast. Herbie looked like he was getting a bit seasick. "Errr . . . what exactly is the aerie?" he asked.

"It's the top of the main," Santher said, pointing upward. A cold, harsh wind lashed at their faces as Emma and Herbie stared up and up, considering their fate. The mainmast was as thick around as a dozen oak trees tied together. There were Arghs up there already, but they were far enough away that it was impossible to tell if they were humans or monkeys. And the wind, although certainly not stormy, had an abrupt, whipping quality that seemed more deadly by the moment.

"I can't go with you," Santher said. "I have to be on the bridge. But Laika will show you the ropes."

Surprised, Emma watched as he sauntered off. He turned once and winked at her over his shoulder.

"He really is cocky," Herbie said, frowning.

Laika didn't explain anything, and the look on her face suggested that she was still brooding over their conversation at dinner. She took hold of the ropes and began climbing.

"Uh . . ." Herbie cleared his throat. "Wait, we're actually climbing to the *crow's* nest?"

"Don't say that!" Laika said. "We never call it that. It's the *aerie*."

"Why don't you call it a crow's—?" Herbie asked.

"*Crow* is a dirty word around here," she said. "Corvans, ye see. They're from the Crow system and they're the ones who kidnap kids. Now hurry up."

Emma saw that Herbie was terrifically nervous. The one time they'd gone walking on the Golden Gate Bridge, he'd gotten queasy and had muttered something about being afraid of heights.

"Are you okay with this?" she asked.

"I can handle it," he said, setting his chin in a determined way.

Emma went first, grabbing the rope and stepping onto the ratline. It whipped in the wind, and she felt her whole body whip along with it. Although the ropes were wet, they weren't too slippery and she found that climbing was easier than she'd thought. When she'd gone ten notches, she felt a slight yank and saw Herbie begin his ascent below.

She continued easily. Every ten feet or so, she stopped to check on Herbie's progress. He kept pausing to wipe his hands on his pants, but otherwise he seemed to be doing all right.

It took ten more minutes to reach the wooden platform where the ratline ended, and when she crawled up into the small circular space, she was grateful for the break. Her arms were sore and she was breathing hard.

Looking around, she got a thrill. The storm clouds were behind them now, and the vast Strand spread before them, its dark-blue waters churning with foamy waves. The air was salty and fresh, and an exhilarating feeling swept through her.

When Herbie came over the side, she helped him up. He looked pale and shaken.

"Pretty good for someone who's afraid of heights," Emma said.

Herbie gave a wan smile.

Laika opened a small door in the side of the mast, revealing a circular staircase inside. "This way," she said brusquely.

They followed her up a narrow passageway that smelled of wet wood and ocean and the musty odor of a birdcage. At the top was another door. They opened it and went inside.

The aerie was a spacious, circular room built around the mast. There were twelve wooden perches, six of which held eagles and hawks. Behind each perch was a window with shutters to keep out the fierce winds.

"Cool," Herbie said, shutting the door behind him. "Are those eagles?"

Laika didn't reply, so the three of them stood staring at one another. She didn't seem interested in putting them to work. Instead, there was a new fierceness in her eyes.

"I think you owe us an explanation," she said. "The navy's after you, and you could be endangering the whole crew."

"Okaaaay," Emma said. She could understand that she might be putting the Arghs in danger, but the *Argh* itself seemed big enough to handle any foes. "Look, I'm sorry we don't know anything about pirates. I wish we could help you but—"

"Everyone knows you're lying about why the navy's after you," Laika said.

Herbie opened his mouth to answer, but Emma kicked his foot. "Like I said before, I'm looking for my parents. They were kidnapped on the Monkey system and probably brought to space. *I'm trying to find them.*"

The force of Emma's words seemed to convince Laika, but she still looked dissatisfied. "Well, you're going to have a problem doing that on the *Argh,*" she said. "We don't have any way of communicating with the outside world. We're fugitives from the navy, so it's too dangerous to use mesmers."

"What's a mesmer?" Herbie asked.

"You've never seen a *mesmer*? What part of Monkey are you from? Mesmers—gosh, they're everywhere. . . ."

Herbie shrugged.

"It's a talking glass," Laika said. "And trust me, they're too dangerous. They all talk to each other, and we can't risk anyone finding out where we are."

"Why?" Emma asked.

"Well," Laika said, taking up a broom and sweeping the floor, "because Lovesey stole the *Argh,* didn't he? And he saved our lives. If he hadn't stolen it, the Queen would have killed us like she killed our parents." Laika's cheeks were flushed. Emma and Herbie exchanged a guilty look.

"I'm sorry," Herbie said. "I kinda figured you were orphans, but I didn't know the Queen killed your parents."

"She killed them all when she destroyed our planets." Laika's sweeping began to intensify. Behind her, one of the eagles gave a startled flap of wings. Clouds of dust from the bird droppings rose in the air, making Emma's eyes water. "And Lovesey saved us. So if he says we shouldn't use a mesmer, then we shouldn't. He gave up everything to protect us."

"Is that why he's burned?" Emma asked.

Laika looked disapproving as she said, "Yes, he got burned. He used to be one of the greatest admirals of the Leo fleet, but when he saw that the Queen destroyed a whole bunch of rebel systems and was about to kill all the orphans who were fleeing from the planets, he stole the *Argh* and helped us escape. The galaxy's a big place, and we can avoid the navy most of the time, but there are bounty hunters who are searching for us, and they're allowed to do whatever they can to reclaim the ship—even if it means killing us. So no, you can't communicate with anyone outside, and we can't help you figure out where your parents are."

Emma was chagrined. She hadn't fully realized until now that the *Argh* was full of fugitives and that they were hiding from the navy. Quietly, she had to admit that having the Pyxis on board might very well put the whole crew in greater danger. The entire navy might be coming after them now. It further disturbed her that the Arghs were orphans, and that the Queen had destroyed their planets. It was no wonder Laika was hoping the pirates would show up to fight the navy. Emma wanted to ask how the Queen could destroy a planet in the first place, but she sensed that Laika was uncomfortable talking about it.

"You're going to have to figure out where your parents are when you get to the next port," Laika said. "That's Cygnus. And it's going to take at least a week to get there."

"That's a long time," Herbie said.

"I'm sorry," Laika replied, "but there's nothing we can do."

Diffidently, she gave each of them a broom and put them to work. They spent the rest of the morning sweeping the floors and changing the bedding and doing every bit of grunt work she asked them to do. Herbie seemed to feel bad that Laika was upset, and he asked a few questions about the birds and the aerie. He was genuinely curious, but Laika gave only terse replies. Finally, he said, "Well, I can see why you like working up here. You've got the best view on the *Argh*."

Laika seemed to soften a bit. "Yeah, you can see all kinds of things that you can't see from the main deck."

"Like what?" Herbie asked.

"Well, the dragons are the best."

Herbie nearly dropped his broom. "You mean, real dragons?"

Laika snorted. "Of course. What other kinds are there?"

"I didn't think they were real."

"Oh, they're real. You should see them on Draco," Laika said, her voice picking up a little more enthusiasm now. "We sail there sometimes. We sneak into the edges of the system because we're not technically allowed in, but the dragons flock really high up, so you can only see them from the aerie. It's amazing. And they're not really *flocks*—maybe just two or three at a time, but that's a lot for dragons."

Herbie was wide-eyed. "Are they only on Draco?"

"Aw, no, they're all over," Laika said. "We saw one last month on Regulus. . . ."

They kept talking. Emma was relieved that Laika was warming up to them. And she had to admit it was pretty cool that there were dragons in space. But she couldn't stop thinking about what she'd learned: there was no way to find out what was happening to her parents. It seemed pointless now to talk to the captain—if he couldn't communicate with the outside world, then he certainly couldn't tell her anything either. They had lost any trail they might have had, and now they were stuck on the ship until they landed on Cygnus. There had to be something else she could do. . . .

At the end of the day, they climbed down from the aerie. It was even more difficult than going up, and when they reached the bottom, Herbie looked rattled.

"Maybe we should ask Santher to give us some other work," Emma said.

"Like what, swab the deck?" Herbie said. "I'm not going to do that. Besides, I want to keep working in the aerie."

"I thought you were afraid of heights," Emma said.

"Not really," he said. "I just don't think it's a good idea to put your life in danger unless there's a really good reason."

"Like dragons," Emma said.

He smirked. "I just have to find a safer way to climb these ropes."

✦ ✦ ✦

The next morning, Emma was surprised that Herbie wasn't waiting for her outside her room. She searched for him in the corridors and the dining hall, but he wasn't there. Midway through breakfast, he came into the dining hall with a long coil of rope slung over his shoulder.

"I woke up early so I could rig up a safety cord for climbing to the aerie," he said. "A couple of the monkeys helped me, and I think we worked it out."

"Wow," Emma said. "How did you get the monkeys to help you?"

"They just came up to me and started helping. They're really smart and they seem to understand what I'm saying. Anyway, you can use the safety line too. But we have to go one at a time."

At the ratlines, she saw what Herbie and the monkeys had done: they had tied ropes to the lines at twenty-foot intervals. Now, as he climbed up, he would be able to tie a line around his waist, climb twenty feet, and switch to another line. This way, he could be secured the entire way.

Herbie went first. He was still a little nervous when he grabbed the first line, but as he got higher, she saw that he was moving with more confidence. He even waved to one of the monkeys dangling near the mast. The monkey replied with a happy hoot.

They spent the next two days working in the aerie. Twice a day they sent the birds on scouting missions, and Emma and Herbie both became quite good at handling the hawks. The rest of the time was spent cleaning and talking.

As the days passed, Emma grew more frustrated being stuck on the *Argh,* and she spent more time staring out the aerie's windows, scanning the Strand for stars or planets or even navy ships. She wasn't sure what she would do if she did see a ship, but it kept her hopes up to see that the *Argh* was making good progress down the Strand.

Laika had become more friendly, but she wasn't ready to give up her quest for the truth, and she continued to sneak in questions about why the navy was after them while Herbie tried to answer without revealing who Emma's parents were. Emma began to notice just how attentive he was becoming to Laika. Every time she gave them a new assignment, Herbie jumped to do it. And every time she talked about the ship, Herbie asked a dozen questions, which Laika answered enthusiastically.

On the third afternoon, they were waiting for the hawks to return when the room grew suddenly darker.

"Uh-oh," Laika said, rushing to the window. "I think those are screech bats. They flock this high up."

Herbie and Emma both dropped their brooms and went to the window. About fifty yards ahead, they could see a dark shape in the sky above them.

"What are screech bats?" Herbie asked.

"They're like regular bats," Laika said. "But they make this horrible screeching sound that will knock you out. We'd better get earplugs." She went to a cupboard near the door and began rooting around.

"They're not making any noise right now," Herbie said.

"They will if the mast disturbs them," Laika replied. She came back to the window with a handful of cloth scraps. "We usually sail below the colonies, but this one is pretty low. We might hit them. And the babies are the worst. They're louder than the adults. One time a baby knocked out the whole ship. . . ."

A terrific thump shook one side of the room. Laika quickly handed them the cloth scraps. "Here, put these in your ears."

"I thought bats had good navigational abilities," Herbie said. "Why are they hitting the wall?"

"They must be babies."

Emma and Herbie pushed the cloth into their ears just as bats began fluttering into the room. Emma shrieked. They didn't look like bats—they were more like large insects. Laika motioned to the windows and mouthed: *We'd better shut them!* The three of them raced around, closing the shutters while the bats fluttered around them. The thumping continued outside.

Herbie was saying something. Emma had to pull the cloth from one ear to hear him, but the moment she did that, she was jolted with pain. It felt as if someone had stuck a Taser in her ear. A horrific *SCREEEEEEEEEEEEEE* filled her head, and she fainted.

When she came to, she was lying on the floor of the aerie. The air reeked of dung and feathers, and Herbie and Laika were standing by the window, arguing.

"We can't kill it!" Laika said. "It's just a baby!"

"It's a *killer* baby," Herbie said. "Look what it did to Emma."

They noticed that she was awake.

"Are you okay?" Herbie bent over and helped her to her feet. "Why did you take the cloth out of your ear?"

"Because it looked like you were saying something important," she groaned. Feeling ridiculously woozy, she sat back down.

"Oh. Sorry. When you fell, you landed on one of the babies." He held up a small glass jar filled with water. There was a bat inside. It looked dead.

"You *saved* it?"

"It's not dead," Herbie said. "Its wing is broken."

"Why is it in water?"

"Apparently this is the only way to get it to stop screeching."

"They like being underwater," Laika explained. "It's where they sleep."

Emma took another look at the creature—it was tiny indeed, no bigger than her thumb, and she thought she detected a grimace of pain on its little face. "I'm sorry I hurt it," she said.

"He'll be okay," Laika said. "We're going to let him heal. Then we should keep him as a pet."

Herbie remained silent.

Once Emma stopped feeling dizzy, they left the aerie for dinner. Emma climbed down more slowly than usual, watching Herbie and Laika joking around below her. Emma didn't mind that Herbie was becoming such good friends with Laika, but it bothered her that they seemed to be having such a great time when all Emma could think about was where her parents were and how to find them.

By the time they got to the dining hall, Emma realized that she wasn't hungry. In fact, the only thing she wanted was to *do something.* She couldn't stand waiting anymore. Telling Herbie and Laika that she had to go to the bathroom, she turned on her heel and walked out.

CHAPTER 15

The Protector from Lynx

It took quite a while to find it, but after getting lost down a dozen dead-end hallways and stumbling into the shipwright's workshop, Emma finally found a staircase that took her to the cargo hold.

The *Markab* was still near the cargo door, and still lying in pieces. She spotted a few monkeys working along the many rows of stacked cartons and barrels, but otherwise the room was quiet. It brought tears to her eyes to see the *Markab* so damaged. She walked around the broken yacht, picking up shrapnel and loose bits of plastic and trying her hardest not to cry. She had come here thinking she might be able to repair it, but seeing it now, she realized it was going to be impossible. She simply had no idea how to fix it.

Overwhelmed, she sat down on the floor, pulled her knees

to her chin, and stared at the boat. Her dad had bought the yacht when she was five years old. It was the only boat they'd ever owned, and it had never been damaged before. What would he say if he saw it now? *"The one time you and Herbie take the boat yourselves, and you've destroyed it!"* At the very least, they'd lose their "ordinary seaman" status.

But if he were here now, he'd also have a lot of explaining to do. He'd have to tell her where he and Mom were really from, and why they were pirates, and why they never told her about the Pyxis or outer space. The *Markab* looked like any other ship on Earth, but what if Dad had bought it on the Strands? Maybe he'd even used it to travel to space. . . .

He and Mom had been hiding out for years without getting caught, so how did the kidnappers find them? This question had been bothering Emma, and now, after everything that had happened in the past four days, she figured that Herbie was right: Dad had lied about going to Phoenix. He'd probably gone to space instead. That was when Caz and Laine had seen him. They must have followed him home. Even though she didn't want him to see the *Markab* like this, she desperately wished he were here to explain himself, because if felt like she didn't know him at all anymore.

She also needed him right now. He would know how to repair the boat. He would be able to explain everything about space. He would find a way to communicate with the outside world and get them off this big ship. But he wasn't here. With a frightened flutter in her throat, Emma wondered if she'd ever see him again.

She wasn't sure how long she'd been sitting there, but the sound of someone coming brought her out of her gloom. Santher was making his way down one of the aisles. He seemed to be looking for something, and when he saw her, he came over.

"There you are," he said. "Herbie and Laika were getting worried."

"Oh." She looked at the *Markab.* "I wanted to check on the boat. I thought maybe there was some way I could fix it. . . ." Her voice cracked and trailed off.

Santher regarded her with catlike interest. "That astrolabe you're carrying around . . . it's not really an astrolabe, is it?"

She was surprised. "How did you know I have an astrolabe?"

"I didn't," he said, flashing her a grin. "You just told me. I saw the outline in your shirt at dinner last night and it looked like an astrolabe." Seeing that she wasn't going to reply, he motioned to the *Markab.* "We could try to repair your boat. But we'd have to rebuild the hull. It might take a few days."

"Wait." She stood up. "That's it—just a few days?"

"Yeah. We have a lot of monkeys. They're really good at this kind of thing."

"Could you do it?"

"Sure."

"How much will it cost?" she asked warily.

"Cost? Well, let's see . . . how about this: I fix your boat, and in exchange, you tell me more about your astrolabe?" His eyes were bright with curiosity.

"That's it?" she asked. "You only want to know about my necklace?"

"Yep." He was holding back a grin. "That's it."

"You don't actually *want* my necklace," she said. "You just want me to tell you about it?"

"Right."

"What if there's nothing to tell?"

"Oh, I have a feeling there is."

She knew it was dangerous to tell anyone about the Pyxis, but she was so desperate to restore the *Markab* that his offer seemed like a very good deal. A sneaky part of her figured she didn't have to tell him the truth anyway. She would just make up a story.

"Okay," she said. "I'll tell you about my necklace. But you have to fix the *Markab* first."

"Fair enough," he said. And with that, he was off. He marched down to the other end of the hold and came back with a chest of tools and a dozen monkeys. They swept over the boat at once, eagerly pulling and prodding every broken part, while Santher unloaded tools from the chest.

Emma still couldn't believe this was happening. "Are you serious about this?" she asked. "You can really fix my boat?"

"I can," he said.

"Have you ever worked on a boat before?"

He stopped unloading and threw his head back with a laugh. "Have I ever worked on a boat before! Don't you know I'm the shipwright's first assistant? I've been repairing boats for three years. I fix the *Argh*! I think I can handle a little scrap like this one." Still shaking his head, he ordered Emma to fetch some wood from one of the cargo aisles. She went off in vague disbelief to find the wood.

Santher appeared confident enough, but she still thought he was too young to know so much about boats and tools. The monkeys helped her carry back the great slabs of wood, and the boxes of nails and scrap metal, and the miscellaneous tools, and anything else that Santher needed. Emma stood watching uncertainly. Before long he put her to work as well, sanding down beams and sawing off chipped corners, all while keeping a close eye on her progress.

"Do you think this is going to be okay with the captain?" she asked.

"I don't see why not," Santher replied. "We came across a Delphinian corsar a few months ago. It was stranded, as they say, on a Strand near Lyra. We put them back in good form, and they didn't have anything to pay us with. The captain's pretty generous, you see. He's a good man, Lovesey."

Nevertheless, Emma began to feel guilty about their "deal." Santher was doing all this work in exchange for what—the truth about the Pyxis? But why would he care, unless he already knew what the Pyxis was? And if he did, then why would he want her to tell him what he already knew? She watched him work, instructing the monkeys in fitting a strip of wood to the hull, and saw that he was happy. Maybe he only wanted to do this because he liked it.

Santher and the monkeys worked tirelessly for the next two days. Emma spent most of the time in the cargo hold, pounding nails and sawing wood alongside the monkeys. It improved her mood enormously to see the *Markab* returning to life. Maybe by the time they got to Cygnus, she and Herbie would be able to take the boat with them instead of leaving it here in pieces. It would mean they could set off to find her parents. This thought did so much to restore her hope that she worked with a new, boundless energy.

She'd told Herbie what she was doing, and he was delighted

that the *Markab* wouldn't be lost. He promised to come and see the boat, but because Emma was no longer working in the aerie, Herbie was doing twice as much work.

Although they ate meals together in the dining hall three times a day, Laika was usually there and Emma didn't get much chance to talk to Herbie alone. She finally got an opportunity at breakfast one day.

"You've got to come down soon," she said. "We've totally remade the hull with wood!"

"Okay," Herbie said a bit smugly. "But I'm learning stuff in the aerie."

"Like what—how to pick up poop?" She was so happy that she couldn't help teasing him. "You're still crushing on Laika. Oh no . . . is she your *girlfriend* now?"

"No." He was blushing and fumbling with something in his pocket. Emma noticed that his pocket seemed to be moving.

"What is that?"

"Nothing. It's just . . ." He drew out the vial with the screech bat inside. The bat was awake now and struggling violently against its confines. The minute it hit the light, it shrank away. "Laika had to stay in the aerie and wait for some of the birds to come back. She asked me to bring Chester down so I could change his water. It's getting kind of green."

"Chester?"

"Laika named him."

"So she's got you on daddy duty."

He looked bored when he said, "She—is—not—my—girlfriend." The bat had stopped jerking, so Herbie set the vial gently on the table. Slowly, the bat looked around with interest. "There are other cool things about the aerie, you know."

"A nice view?" she deadpanned.

He pursed his lips, looking smug.

"What?" Emma said.

"We saw a dragon."

"WHAT?" She practically leapt out of her seat.

Herbie looked around with embarrassment. "Chill OUT," he said. "It was at night, and we weren't totally sure it was a dragon."

"Wait, wait. You were up there at *night*?"

"No! It was just getting dark. Right before dinner."

"Uh-huh."

He frowned. "Laika thought it was a dragon because she sees them every few weeks, but they like to stay out of sight. They're really quite stealthy."

"Ragnar, you saw a dragon!"

"Shut. Up."

She kicked his chair gleefully and laughed.

After breakfast, Emma went straight down to the cargo hold. As usual, Santher was already there, and he and the monkeys were in full swing, hammering and sawing and drilling. They woke up at dawn every morning and went straight to the hold, working until late at night. The result was rapid progress. They had almost finished replacing the boat's hull, and the *Markab* was sitting upright now, propped on giant beams. The new mast—also made of wood—had been erected the night before, and although it looked very different, the *Markab* was finally a proper boat again.

Emma went over to where Santher was working.

"I've been thinking about our deal," she said. "It seems a little unfair. You've done a *lot* of work. . . ."

"You know," he said, "when I first saw you, I had this crazy idea—I thought you looked just like Halifax Brightstoke." He smiled, and she forced herself to smile back. "And then, when I saw that astrolabe around your neck . . ."

"You thought it was the Pyxis?" Emma said, trying to sound as if this were the most ridiculous thing she could imagine. "You know that's crazy."

"Not really," Santher said. "There were all kinds of rumors flying around Porta Amphitrite. And the navy was chasing you like the hounds of hell. It kind of made sense."

"Okay," she said, trying to stay cool. "So you think I look like Halifax Brightstoke."

He shrugged. "I always thought she was a hero. She joined the pirates and started a rebellion and stood up to the Queen all those years."

Emma wanted more details about Mom standing up to the Queen, but she didn't want to sound completely ignorant. "So is that why you're fixing my boat—because you think I look like Halifax Brightstoke?"

"Well, yeah."

"Why do you care about her so much?" Emma asked.

"You mean, aside from the fact that she's the galaxy's most famous pirate?"

"Okay," Emma said. "I get that. But this is an awful lot of work."

Santher seemed a little embarrassed. "Well, she's a hero to everyone, really, but being from Lynx, I feel a particular connection to her. You know how they executed her, right? With the lynx?" Emma looked perplexed. "They sewed her inside a canvas sack with one of our cats and threw her over the side of a ship. We believe that lynxes are . . . well, they're special.

People like to say that this one helped Halifax survive. Maybe he clawed his way out of the bag. Maybe he dragged her to the surface. Anyway, they believe that he was her protector." His cheeks reddened slightly.

Emma was overcome with the sickening image of Mom being sewn inside a canvas sack. If the Queen captured her mother, she could easily do the same thing again.

Santher noticed her discomfort. "Okay, I guess it's silly to think that Halifax might still be alive, but nobody ever believed she was dead. It's been this unanswered question for twelve years: did she die? The navy says she did, but ever since that Pyxis transmission happened, everyone has been saying, *'See, I told you! She's not really dead! She's still out there!'* Everyone believes it. It's not just me."

"Yeah." Emma was relieved that she wasn't the only one hoping that her mom was alive. "So even though she was a pirate, she was a hero for standing up to the Queen?"

"Yes," Santher said. "When she died, the pirate armies fell apart. I mean, it *destroyed* the rebellion. That was really when the Queen won the war."

"And this is why Laika is looking for the rebellion. She's hoping that Halifax will come back."

He hung his head. "Laika's just . . . I don't know. Normally she doesn't talk about it that much, but yeah, when the Pyxis transmission happened, she started going on about pirates again. She really believes that if they come back, they'll overthrow the Queen."

"You don't think that will happen?"

"I wish it would!" he said. "But it's not going to happen—not without Halifax."

Emma was stricken by a sudden thought: if her parents were

so heroic, why would they hide out for so long? Surely the rebellion needed them this whole time. The Pyxis must have been more important than anything else. But why?

She had so many unanswered questions. They had been pounding around her head for days now, and the frustration was only growing.

Santher had fallen quiet. He kept glancing at the boat and back at Emma. "I'm probably an idiot for thinking you're Halifax's daughter," he said. "It's just . . . the Pyxis transmission got everyone excited. Only for a day. We really thought Halifax was going to come back. It's why Laika started nagging people, and I guess it's why I thought you were, well, related to her. But obviously it's not going to happen."

Emma hadn't realized that her mother's return would mean so much. She knew it was a terrible idea to tell anyone who she was, but Santher had given her hope when she had none, and after all the work he'd done on the *Markab,* she felt he deserved to know the truth now.

"If I tell you something, will you promise never to tell anyone else?" she asked.

He was watching her strangely. "Ye-e-es," he said.

Shaking from nerves, Emma sat down beside him. "My mom *is* Halifax Brightstoke," she said. "And my necklace—it really is the Pyxis. So . . . you were right."

Santher regarded her for a long moment. "You're not joking, are you?"

"No."

"You're telling me that Halifax Brightstoke is still alive?"

"I think so," Emma said. "I didn't know who she was—I mean, she was just my mom until I saw a notice on Delphinus.

She never told me anything about space. Neither did my dad. But then they were kidnapped. And my dad was shot. And I don't know where they are, but I think they're still alive. . . ." Her voice was too pinched to keep talking, so she paused to take a breath. "I'm going to find them. Once the boat is fixed."

Santher's face was flushed. She couldn't tell what he was thinking, but he hadn't moved a muscle since she'd said the words *Halifax Brightstoke.* Clearly the news was a shock, but she thought she detected a look of disbelief.

"You think I'm making this up," she said.

"No," he said. "I'm surprised. I think I believe you. Like I said, you look just like her. And you showed up on Delphinus right around the time of the Pyxis transmission. And the navy was chasing you. . . ."

"Are you going to stop working on the boat now that I've told you the truth?" she asked.

"No." He gave her the hint of a smile. "Don't worry, we're going to fix it up. It's going to be the best boat you've ever seen." He picked up a hammer, but his expression had changed to awe. "You have to admit, this is really big news. People should know—"

"You promised never to tell anyone," she put in quickly.

"I know." He shook his head in amazement. "I promise. But shoot, this is huge. Halifax Brightstoke is still *alive.*"

"I hope so," Emma said quietly.

"Why didn't she tell you anything about space?"

"I don't know." She fingered the Pyxis through her shirt. "Maybe she was afraid I would tell people who she really was?"

"Can I see it?" Santher asked.

She looked around to make sure that no monkeys were

watching before drawing the Pyxis out of her shirt. He dropped the hammer and took it in his hands, gaping in excitement.

"No wonder the navy was after you!" he laughed.

"They chased us all the way from Monkey." Emma gave a dispirited laugh. "The stupid thing is, I don't even know what the Pyxis is supposed to *do*."

Santher was stunned. "It's the key to the Shroud!" he said.

She gave him a blank look.

"Your parents really didn't tell you *anything*?" He let go of the Pyxis, and she tucked it inside her shirt. "Well, okay . . ." He looked around, still amazed. "First of all, the pirates went to war with the Queen because she was stealing all their memory water."

"I stuck my finger in some memory water on Delphinus," Emma said. He seemed surprised by this. "But I don't really know what it is."

"Did it make you sick?" he asked.

"No. I heard some guys singing inside the glass, and then later I could hear the people around me talking."

"That's weird. But it *is* pretty weird stuff. Nobody actually knows what it is." He leapt up suddenly and went to his tool chest. After rooting around for a few seconds, he drew out a parchment and brought it back to Emma. Sitting down again, he unscrolled it. Emma leaned closer. It was a very long map. At the top the words *Fluvius Eridanus* were spelled out in gold letters. The stars of Eridanus sat like bright-yellow wasps on a background of surprising blackness. Connecting the stars were the constellation's Strands, marked in silver ink.

"Cool chart," she whispered.

Santher ran his finger along the constellation. "All the

Strands of Eridanus are called the memory seas," he said. "They're the most dangerous waters in the galaxy. They have deadly currents and they're full of rocks and reefs. They also used to be infested with pirates, but now the navy has blockaded the system, so nobody goes there.

"They're called memory seas," he went on, "because so many ships have gone down in the Strands—thousands of them—and the souls of dead pirates and sailors are trapped in the waters. No one understands why, but people think that the Strands contain the memories of all the people who have passed through here—even the living ones."

He looked up at Emma. "But memory water has magical properties. The Queen started using it to make things. Her doctors made medical cures. The navy used it to make scuppers. It's all over the galaxy now—like in that net we used to bring you guys on board. It's the stuff inside wing masts that gives them their lift.

"Anyway, the Queen took it too far. She started making weapons that could destroy whole planets. And she did that a few times. The whole galaxy was terrified of her.

"When the pirates of Eridanus realized that she was using their water to destroy other planets, they went to war to stop her. But the rebellion wasn't that strong. The pirates started to realize that they couldn't win, so they began to drain their own system. They sabotaged the Queen's pumps, stole their own water, and put it on giant ships. And that's where the Shroud comes in." He rolled up the chart, searching for a good way to explain. "The Shroud is a hidden cave at the edges of the galaxy."

Emma pursed her lips. "If it's hidden, then how do you know where it is?"

He rolled his eyes. "Of course no one knows where it is," he said. "You need the Pyxis to find it. The Pyxis is the navigational device that Cascabel created to locate the hidden water."

"Who's Cascabel?"

"He was the pirate leader."

"I thought my mom was the pirate leader."

"She was his . . . girlfriend maybe? They used to call her the 'second-greatest pirate of the seas,' but that was a joke. She was way more important than him!"

"What about my dad, Jack Garton? Was he in this too?"

"He's your . . ." Santher smacked his head. "Of course—your name is Emma Garton! I completely missed that. Wow. Yeah, Jack Garton was the first mate on Cascabel's ship. They used to call him Mad Jack. I heard that he was executed by Cascabel." Santher looked at her warily.

"What?" she said.

"I'm not sure you'll want to hear this, but they said that Cascabel chopped off his head and placed it on the prow of his ship. But obviously that's not true."

"Why would Cascabel want to kill him?"

Santher shrugged. "Maybe he knew that Jack was going to run off with your mom."

Emma nodded, trying to imagine her parents running away from an evil pirate captain.

"What happened to Cascabel?" she asked.

"He's in exile on Eridanus. Nobody's seen or heard from him in twelve years."

"So doesn't he know where the Shroud is?"

"No. See, it's easy to put things inside—there are doorways all over the galaxy—but no one has ever opened the Shroud and taken things out."

"So what—it's like a black hole?"

"Yeah, except with the Shroud, there's supposed to be a way to open it again. That's what the Pyxis does. Cascabel commissioned the sorcerers of Eridanus to make it. He sailed all these giant ships into the doorways of the Shroud so that the Queen wouldn't get the memory water."

"Did he really drain an entire Strand?" Emma asked.

"No, he just took so much water that it killed the Strand. If you go to Eridanus today, all that's left is this mucky green sea. That's probably the memory water you had on Delphinus. But it's good that he did that because ever since Cascabel stole the water, the Queen's power has dropped. She doesn't have enough good water left to destroy a whole planet."

"So my mom was one of the good pirates."

"Yeah. But the thing is, if the Queen got her hands on the Pyxis now, it would lead her to the hidden memory water and she'd become powerful again. She'd go back to blowing up planets." He said this with a sudden sadness. "One of those planets she destroyed was mine. It was near the star Elvashak. My parents got me out on a ship just in time."

"What happened to your parents?" Emma asked.

"They died," he said. "There wasn't enough room on the ship for us all."

This information shocked her. Santher stood up and returned the chart to his tool chest. She watched him, mindlessly fingering the Pyxis and feeling more and more amazed. Her parents had given up their whole lives to protect the Pyxis and keep the Queen from becoming more evil. They had been heroes, and even though it bothered her that they hadn't told her the truth about space, she was secretly proud that they'd done so much to keep the Pyxis away from the Queen.

And here she was, carrying the Pyxis around. She had even activated it on Earth! And now the navy was after them. Now the Queen knew that the Pyxis wasn't lost forever. She realized suddenly that, by her own ignorance, she'd set something horrible in motion, something her parents had spent a very long time trying to prevent. It was why they had hidden on Earth all those years.

Emma suddenly felt very lost and overwhelmed. She could only think of one thing: she had to get her parents back, and until then, she had to protect the Pyxis like they did.

"Santher," she said, "promise me again you won't tell *anyone* about the Pyxis."

He nodded. "You have my word."

CHAPTER 16

A Baby Dragon-of-War

Santher worked for the rest of the day. He didn't even stop to eat. The monkeys worked tirelessly too, but ever since the conversation with Santher, Emma had been feeling restless, so she excused herself and went down to the dining hall for dinner.

She found Herbie sitting alone at a table.

"What's up?" he said.

"Nothing."

"You're fixing up the *Markab.* You should be happy."

She sat down. "I told Santher about my mom and dad," she said.

"What?"

"I know. It's crazy. But his parents died because of the Queen. And even though he's not talking about the rebellion all the time like Laika, when he heard that the Pyxis transmission happened, he got really excited too. And when he told me, I . . ." Herbie was giving her a terrible scowl. She tried not to quail when she said, "I felt like I owed him the truth."

"I can't believe you did that."

"He's not going to tell anyone."

"He might!"

She wasn't hungry, so between looking out the window and twiddling her spoon in her soup, she explained everything that Santher had told her about the Pyxis. Herbie listened, half interested, half fuming.

"So basically," he said, "by starting the Pyxis, you set a galactic war in motion."

"It wasn't my fault my parents were pirates and didn't tell me about it," Emma said.

"You didn't have to tell Santher the truth just to get this information," Herbie said. "There are other ways you could have found out."

"Yeah, like my parents?"

Herbie sat back and blew the air from his cheeks. "Okay, the bottom line is that the Pyxis is putting everyone in danger."

"Yeah," Emma said. "But if it's that important, why didn't my parents just destroy it?"

"Laika said it's protected by some enchantment or something."

"Wait . . . you've been talking to *Laika* about this?"

"No!" he said quickly. "She's been talking about it. In fact, everyone's been talking about it ever since they saw the notices on Delphinus. And there's something else I learned. It turns out . . ." He blushed. "Well, it turns out that before she was a pirate, your mom was a princess."

Emma got a shock. Her mom was a *princess*? She should have been used to it by now—hearing wildly improbable things about her parents. But it stung to think that the whole galaxy knew more about her mom than she did. "A princess," she said.

"Yeah, I was going to tell you—"

"What kind of princess?"

"Uh . . . a princess from Virgo. She was next in line for the throne."

"She was the Queen's *daughter*?"

"Not exactly," Herbie said, looking uncomfortable now. "She was her niece or something. Apparently Virgo queens aren't allowed to have children."

"So . . . that means . . . I'm a princess too?" Emma couldn't help grinning.

"I don't think you should go around—"

She cut him off. "That's 'Her Royal Highness' to you."

Herbie gave her a massive roll of the eyes. "Will Her Royal Highness Emma Brightstoke Garton of Monkey Butt please sign in for a reality check?"

"Okay, what?"

"What I was *going* to say," he went on, "is that this might be good news. I've been thinking about it, and I know the navy has your mom, but now that we know she's a *princess,* it makes me think it's not going to be that easy for the Queen to execute her again. She's probably going to have to bring her to trial. And everybody will want to hear where she was all this time. But we won't let it get that far. Once the *Markab*'s finished, we're going to find her. And until then, she has a good chance of staying alive. Laika said she was a badass. Remember how she fought with the kidnappers?"

Emma nodded, hoping frantically that Herbie was right. "I know," she said. "But we don't know where she is." *And anything could happen,* she thought.

"We'll find her," he said.

"The *Markab*'s almost finished," she said. "You should come and see."

A few hours later, as she and Santher were sanding the wood panels on the *Markab*'s new railing, they heard a monkey's angry squawk and turned to see Herbie coming down one of the aisles.

"Sorry!" he said, his hands in the air. "You came around the corner really fast. I didn't see you. . . ."

The monkey gave an indignant hoot and marched off.

Herbie approached the *Markab.* "Hi," he said a bit defensively.

"Check it out!" Emma stood on the new deck and motioned proudly to the boat. Herbie's eyes roamed over the work they had done. "Isn't it cool?" she said. "It's like a real boat now."

"It was always a real boat." Herbie sniffed. "Are you sure it's seaworthy?"

Emma stared at him. He wasn't usually this grouchy.

"Sure, she's seaworthy!" Santher exclaimed brightly, his head popping over the railing. "I work on the *Argh*; I've got plenty of experience with—"

"The *Markab* is a different kind of boat than the *Argh,*" Herbie said.

"Sure, but—"

Herbie ignored Santher and wandered critically around the boat. Emma leapt down and went after him.

"You're not mad at Santher, are you?" she asked.

Herbie spun on her. "No. I just want to make sure that the *Markab* won't sink when it hits the water."

When Herbie had done a full circle around the boat, he stopped and crossed his arms.

"So what do you think?" Emma asked.

"I suppose they didn't have any better materials than this old wood?"

Santher came down from the deck with a smile. "Well, actually," he said, "this is the best wood on the seas. I chose it for that reason, but I also figured that since the navy was coming after you and all, you'd want a new look for the boat, you know. . . ." He motioned to the hull. Now instead of sleek, white, industrial fiberglass, it was a rough-hewn dark-brown wood.

"I personally prefer the way it used to look," Herbie said.

". . . and I don't think the look is quite there yet," Santher was prattling on. "I really think we need to go for a full disguise, so I've been talking to the monkeys and we've come up with a plan." He turned and gave a loud whistle. In the distance, a few monkeys hooted in response. Moments later, a dozen monkeys came down the aisle, carrying two large but light and shapely objects made of wood.

"What are those?" Herbie asked.

"Wing masts," Santher said with a grin. "Dragon wings."

Herbie's expression went neutral. "Dragon wings?" he asked.

"Yeah, like they have on a dragon-of-war," Santher said. "I know what you're thinking: how can a ship fly? But I tell you, if a big, old galleon like the *Argh* can fly, then a little spit like the *Markab* will have no problem at all." Santher patted Herbie on the back. "We've got it worked out. We've got the wing masts, the propeller system, and the sails. We're going all out here. I know it'll just be a baby dragon-of-war, but she'll be pretty fierce anyway. I was even thinking of a dragon carapace for the hull. It's really not that hard to do. And do you know how the Draconi ships set their sails?"

Herbie shook his head.

"They do this incredible thing with triangular sails. I could sketch it. Come here, I'll show you."

Herbie and Emma followed Santher to the worktable.

Herbie turned to Emma. "Laika wanted me to tell you that we're probably going to reach Cygnus tomorrow."

"I thought it was in two days!"

"Don't worry," Santher said. "She'll be ready by tomorrow, even if we have to work all night." He and Herbie exchanged a look. "We could use an extra pair of hands. Do you feel like joining us?"

Herbie glanced at Emma. "Well, I guess I could," he said. "Just for a while."

After showing him the sails, Santher put Herbie to work immediately, and while Emma coughed up a "Ragnar" and Herbie shot her a scowl, she couldn't seem to wipe the huge grin from her face.

It took another whole day of hard sailing before the *Argh* found itself at the cusp of the star Albireo on Cygnus. The ship had made excellent time with storm winds behind them.

They were still a few hours from the vostok bridge when one of the eagles returned with a warning cry that signaled a navy fleet ahead. Just to be absolutely sure, they sent the eagle back out with Nelson, the spyglass, attached to its collar. Nelson returned to report that a navy fleet had taken up position in front of the bridge to Albireo and was inspecting every vessel that wanted to pass through.

Lovesey was troubled. The Queen's navy had no reason to put up such a blockade at the edge of a quiet star like this one. And this was a whole fleet! He turned the *Argh* hard to starboard and sailed in a wide arc to avoid the navy's detection, heading back up the Strand to the section where it split off to a connecting Strand toward Lyra and one of its smaller stars.

It took another two days of sailing to reach Lyra. Yet to everyone's dismay, the Strands around Sulafat were heavily patrolled by navy ships as well.

"Is she posting fleets in every vostok zone in the galaxy?" Lovesey cried.

Over the next week, the *Argh* cut a crazy course across the Strands. The Queen's navy was everywhere. The *Argh* was forced to avoid Lyra completely, dipping instead into Hercules, then sailing through Corona Borealis, and then being routed upward into Boötes waters before hitting a long stretch of Strand outside Alcaid, which would take them to the relatively quieter Strands of Ursa Major.

It took nearly a week before they reached the Strand to Ursa Major, and by then their food and water supplies had run dangerously low. Because they couldn't dock on any systems, they were unable to stock up on the necessities. The captain ordered water rations, and the crew was served two meals a day—breakfast and supper, which were always the same: a bowl of porridge and a slice of dried sausage.

Emma felt a gnawing anxiety—this was all happening

because of her, and the crew suspected as much. Santher assured her that he hadn't told anyone about her mother being Halifax Brightstoke. The *Argh* always avoided the navy when it could. But Emma heard people talking and felt their stares at her back in the dining hall. The Arghs knew there was *something* unusual about her. Maybe, like Santher, they had already guessed who she was—she arrived shortly after the first Pyxis transmission in twelve years. And she did look like the notorious Halifax Brightstoke. Now that the navy was everywhere, the Arghs were fairly certain that the Queen had posted ships all over the galaxy to catch Emma. What would they do if they found out that she was on the *Argh*?

By the time they reached Ursa Major, the crew was disappointed again. There were simply too many navy ships at the port zone of Alcaid, the tail star, and Lovesey was worried that the navy would soon surround them.

Unfortunately, they were in a bad position. To one side of them was Draco—an unfriendly, dangerous system that was patrolled by the mighty Draconi fleets. Although Draco was loyal to the Queen, it was also an independent system. When unwelcome ships sailed down its Strands, they had a habit of getting sunk.

On the other side of them were the sweeping Strands of Leo. Going there would risk drawing the attention of some of Lovesey's worst enemies, captains of the Leo navy who would give anything to capture the *Argh* and return the precious ship to King Cor Leonis. They couldn't go back the way they'd come. The *Argh* had no choice but to head off down a great connector Strand that led to Cepheus, a very remote system.

The journey was going to be a long one, and there was

doubt that they could even make it that far before running out of food and water, but Lovesey and Nisba took careful inventory of the cargo hold and determined that they stood a good chance of reaching Cepheus without losing anyone to starvation or misery—as long as they stuck to their rations. So the *Argh* headed off before more time was wasted.

CHAPTER 17

Markabs

The *Markab* no longer looked like a yacht. Santher and Herbie had outfitted it with the makings of an authentic dragon-of-war: now her hull wore spiked wooden beams that jutted forward from the bow like claws. Her mainsail was trimmed with two black sails and three smaller red ones, which were sharp and triangular and tilted rearward like spikes. The wing masts had been attached to her sides, and they were enormous. Stretched out fully, they dwarfed the small boat. According to Santher, they would lift her into the sky with lethal speed. The hull had been painted black and red in true Draco colors. The finishing touch was a pair of long-snouted cannons that protruded from two forward holes in her bow.

Emma arrived at the hold early that morning to find Santher waiting for her. She gaped at the ship in amazement, unable to stop smiling. They had done it! They had actually fixed the *Markab.* She hadn't thought it was possible, but it looked even better than before.

Feeling giddy, she let Santher help her onto the deck. There she noticed that someone had polished the cannons. Beside them, two stacks of cannonballs were fixed in wooden casks. They were glittery and black.

"Cannonballs?" she said, turning on Santher.

"Vostok cannons," he said. "Every ship needs them. They're for opening a bridge from a Strand to a planet. I'm going to show you how to load them, but first I want to make sure you know where everything is." He'd already done this, and she already knew where everything was, but she could tell he was nervous, so she didn't protest as he flipped up one of the benches to reveal the chest beneath it. "Here's where the tools are. And you remember how to repair a leak, right? Here's cork. Here's extra wood—"

He was never going to finish, so she interrupted him. "Thanks again for doing all this work," she said. "I really don't know how I'm supposed to thank you."

He grew quiet then. "I believe what you said—I mean, that your mom really is Halifax Brightstoke. And because of that . . . well, I guess . . . I just think it's important that you find her."

"Yeah," Emma said. "Thanks."

"Anyway, there's just one more thing I want to show you. . . ."

Emma was relieved when Herbie finally came down from breakfast. Santher immediately started from the top, taking Herbie through the entire inventory again. Gratefully, Emma crept into the cabin and looked around in silent awe.

It was beautiful. Santher had pulled out all the old wood paneling and replaced it with real wood. He'd kept the same design with the kitchenette, the booth table, and the large nook with the sofa. He'd also kept the bedroom intact. But now everything was made of solid, dark wood. It gave her the feeling of being inside the captain's office on an old pirate ship. She sat down at the desk and ran her fingers over the grains in the wood. She could have sat there all day, but she heard a noise above.

Going topside, she was startled to see Captain Lovesey standing by the *Markab*'s side. He was frowning, and Nelson was bobbing at his side, giving small harrumphs. Herbie stood frozen by the mast, and even Santher looked nervous.

"Uh, sir, thanks for coming by," Santher said awkwardly.

"Did he know you were fixing us up?" Herbie whispered.

"Yes, Yee," Lovesey called up to the deck. "I have known about Santher's generosity for some time." His eyes fell on Emma and rested there a moment. "But you are aware that we have been unable to land the *Argh* for more than a week now, and it looks like we're not going to be setting down anytime soon. So I'm afraid your expedition on this lovely little dragon-of-war is going to have to wait."

Emma came forward. "But, sir . . ." She glanced at Herbie. "I was under the impression that the navy is after us because of me and Herbie. So wouldn't it be better to let us go? I mean, we're only causing trouble."

Lovesey blinked. "Garton, while that is very true, I believe that it's not any safer for you to be out on the Strands by yourselves, especially on a small boat like this one." He motioned to the *Markab* with his good arm, and Nelson nodded vehemently.

"The truth is, this may look like a dragon-of-war, but it is much too small to take on a whole fleet, and if you are going after your mother like I think you are, then you will have to take on a whole fleet."

Emma and Herbie exchanged a look, and Herbie mouthed: *He knows?*

"Yes, Yee," Lovesey intoned. "I know."

"Then you know this is an important mission," Santher interjected. "They could find Halifax!" He breathed this last word with a kind of desperate secrecy.

"Yes, it's noble," Lovesey said, "but it's not worth the risk. Even with the *Argh,* I wouldn't dare take on the navy. My primary goal is to protect the children on this ship. I cannot endanger their lives, and so I can't let you endanger yours either. If you leave on this boat, you will only get captured by the navy"—he broke off and gave Emma a significant glance—"and that, Miss Garton, is something I'm quite sure you do not want."

Slowly, as if his leg was paining him, Lovesey motioned to Nelson and began walking away. He paused by the door and said over his shoulder, "Santher."

"Yes, Captain."

"I expect you to get back to the shipwright's workshop this afternoon. Shucks has been asking for you."

"Yes, sir," Santher said, trying not to sound dejected.

They waited for Lovesey to leave the room before turning to one another in disappointment.

"And here I thought I was keeping a secret," Emma said.

"Lovesey's very sharp," Santher replied bitterly. "I guess we have to wait."

"No," Emma said. "I'm not going to wait."

Santher looked at her keenly.

"I don't want to get you in trouble," she said, "but think about it: the minute we're gone, the navy is off your tail. And this boat is perfect. It's small enough that we can hide. It's fast, and if we use the wing masts, no one's going to catch us. You've said so yourself." She could see a gleam of approval in Santher's eye.

"Well . . . ," he said slowly. "I do need to get back to the workshop. But before I go, I should explain one last thing to you guys. There's a trick to getting a ship out of the cargo doors. . . ."

They leaned closer to listen.

Herbie made his way down the hallway, looking desperately at every group of Arghs for some sign of Laika. He had already checked the aerie and the dining hall twice; he'd even waited for ten minutes outside the girls' bathroom door. Now he was wandering up and down the hallways. He didn't know where her bedroom was, or he would have gone there.

"Hey," he said to a young boy who looked familiar. "Have you seen Laika?"

The boy shook his head and kept walking.

Herbie sighed heavily as the last group of Arghs went by.

He was just about to go back to the dining hall when a door opened at the end of a long corridor and a girl stepped out. He recognized Laika from her tangle of mousy hair.

"Laika," he said breathlessly, running toward her. "I've been looking everywhere for you. I just wanted to say goodbye before—" He was brought up short when she turned to face him. She was wearing a large woolen coat, and she had a small backpack slung over her shoulder. She looked scared.

"I, uh . . . are you going somewhere?" he asked, afraid to hear the answer.

"Yes," she said a bit petulantly. "Santher told me that you and Emma are sneaking away tonight, and I've decided that I'm coming with you."

He was too shocked to speak. As she took off down the hallway, he scrambled after her. "Wait," he said. "You mean, you're . . ."

"I'm coming with you," she said, her voice quavering. As she hitched the backpack higher on her shoulder, he noticed her hands were shaking. "I've made up my mind. I know this is crazy. But I've packed my stuff. And I already said goodbye to the birds, and Flawn knows how to take care of them. He does."

"Flawn does not know how to take care of the birds," Herbie said.

"He can manage," she said. "I've told him everything. By the way, you have Chester, right?"

"Yeah, he's here. I was going to give him back—" He took the screech bat out of his pocket and handed it to her, but she refused it and continued down the hallway. "Laika, wait." He stopped her. "I know you want to come, and I would love it if you came, but . . . it's going to be dangerous."

Laika gave a sniff. "Look, I know you told me never to tell Emma that I know who her mom is, but sheesh, everybody knows already. And if it's true, and her mom really is Halifax Brightstoke, then I have to do this. The Queen killed my parents, and she almost killed all the Arghs!" She glared at Herbie. "Getting Halifax back is the only way that the pirates are going to come out of hiding, and that's more important than taking care of birds."

"What if the pirates are dead?" he said.

She gave him a cool look. "Don't be silly." Turning on her heel, she kept walking. Herbie watched her, half in amazement, half in dread before running to catch her.

When Emma saw Laika climbing onto the *Markab* with a backpack slung over her shoulder, she instantly realized two things. One, that Laika knew everything. And two, that there was no getting rid of her now.

When Herbie came closer, Emma gave him a glare, but Herbie shrugged and mouthed: *She wanted to come.*

"Hi," Laika said, trying to look brave.

"Hi." Emma glanced at Herbie again. "So I guess Herbie told you."

"No. I figured it out myself." She was blushing. "I can help," she said. "I know how to navigate in space, which you probably don't. And I'm really good with animals. I know how to fish, and I brought a net, in case you didn't have one." She patted her backpack. "I figured you would need any help you could get. And . . . I know it's important to find your mom."

"Okay," Emma said. "But Lovesey told us not to go."

"I know," Laika said. "But I have to do this. This is the only way the pirates will ever come out of hiding. Once they realize that your mom is back on the seas . . ."

Emma still wasn't sure what to think about the whole pirate army thing, but she liked the idea of finding someone who could help them. She glanced at Herbie. "Well," she said, "we've got to leave now. The monkeys are going to help us get the *Markab* on the water."

Laika dashed off with a *squee* and went below to stow her bag, while Herbie stayed with Emma.

"I'm sorry!" he whispered. "I didn't have a choice."

"It's okay," Emma said. She knew she ought to be worried, but she was quietly pleased that someone on the *Argh* was willing to come with them.

A loud groan drew their attention as the monkeys began to open the great cargo doors. All around them the hold was dark, but as the doors opened, the light from a nearby star peeked in. It shone blue and bright, and it lit the room like moonlight.

The monkeys had rigged the *Markab* to a complicated pulley system. Now one group of monkeys was pushing the ship forward along a pair of rollers toward the cargo doors. Another group stood by a dozen thick lines that were hanging from the wall. Letting out the lines would lower the boat into the water.

When they reached the edge of the hold, Emma felt a stiff, warm westerly wind begin to tousle her hair. She stood next to Herbie and Laika, the three of them staring at the sea some ten feet below. The water was smooth and dark.

THUMP! The boat swayed, and the monkeys squawked. Santher hauled himself over the railing, tossing his own backpack onto the deck. He smiled at them.

"Santher!"

"I thought you could use some extra help," he said. "And I thought Laika might be coming. I figured if she had the nerve to come on this crazy expedition, then I did too."

"But you can't go," Laika said. "You're the best shipwright on the *Argh*!"

"I know," he said happily. "But you're going to need me more than the *Argh* will."

Emma didn't protest. She was secretly delighted. Santher would know how to fix the ship if they encountered any problems, and besides that, she was glad to see him.

The monkeys managed to get the pulley system working smoothly. They lifted the boat off the deck and slid it out the door. Hanging from a pair of wooden arms, the *Markab* was lowered slowly into the water below, where it landed with a gentle *splish.*

They cut the lines from the *Markab*'s hull and waited as the monkeys pulled them back in. Once the boat was free, Herbie went to the mast and let out the mainsail. The wind filled it gently, and with silent motion, the *Markab* set off into the night.

CHAPTER 18
Memory Water

As much as Emma loved the new cabin, she was far more interested in the goings-on above deck. They had only been on the water for one morning, and already they'd seen two mermaids, a school of marletts, and a burping dog whale. After turning off the Strand to Cepheus, the *Markab* was now more than halfway down a much shorter Strand that would lead to the Lacerta system. They had also seen two ships, but those had kept their distance. Every sailor on the Strands knew better than to approach a dragon-of-war, no matter how small it was.

A stiff, warm wind spanked the *Markab*'s backside, and she was making good time. According to Santher's *Navy Manual,* it would take three more days to reach Lacerta's main star, Alpha Lacertae. Two planets were there, and they would be able to dock on either one—and, hopefully, get information about Emma's parents. Everyone was worried that the navy would have ships posted at the vostok zones on Alpha Lacertae, just like it had on the other systems. The Markabs had no choice but to wait and see.

Herbie and Laika had spent most of the morning at the wheel, reading the *Almagest* and untangling the fishing net that Laika had brought in her backpack. Santher puttered about below, fixing odd things, while Emma sat at the bow, enjoying the warm air and the sight of the great Strand spread out before her. Herbie and Laika were prattling on, but when they got to the subject of Emma's parents, her ears perked up.

". . . and their yacht was the *Markab,* of course," Herbie was saying. "It's funny, I always thought Emma's dad was suspicious. It doesn't surprise me that he was a pirate. I probably should have figured it out a long time ago. But I never thought Emma's *mom* was the dangerous type."

"She was supposedly more dangerous than Mad Jack!" Laika said.

"I know," Herbie exclaimed. "Crazy, huh? It's just, she always seemed so nice. She did yoga and she baked these really awesome granola cookies. I hate granola, but these were amazing. You have to spend time on them to get them that good. The craziest part, though? She hated sailing."

"What?"

"Seriously. She was totally afraid of the water. She never went sailing. She could barely manage to walk down the pier at the marina. Emma said she had all kinds of phobias—" They glanced at Emma in case she wanted to contribute, but she was pointedly ignoring them. "She was especially afraid of the water," Herbie went on. "Although of course she showered. . . ."

Emma realized that all this talk about her mom was making her worry even more, so she decided to join Santher below.

Climbing down the stairs, she found him standing in front of the faux porthole—a strange object that Dad had always kept hanging on the wall above the captain's desk. The foot-wide circular mirror was set in a golden frame. Yet the mirror reflected nothing of the room around it. Emma used to like touching it as a kid; it was soft and squishy, like there was some kind of goo inside. It was one of the objects that hadn't broken when the *Markab* had crashed onto the floor of the *Argh*'s cargo hold.

"What are you doing?" she asked.

Santher looked surprised. "Oh, I was just wondering why you had an empty mesmer."

"That's a mesmer?" She came closer.

"Yeah," he said. "I guess your parents didn't tell you about this either."

"No," she said. "It's one of those communication devices, right? Laika told us about them."

"It sure looks like it," Santher said. "I've been watching it for weeks now, ever since I first saw it. I kept meaning to ask you why there was no mesmer guard in it, but I figured he'd been scared away when the boat was damaged."

"What's a mesmer guard?" she asked.

"A guard occupies every mesmer. It's usually an animal, sometimes a person. They live on the other side." He touched the surface and the liquid in it rippled mysteriously. "You've really never seen anything in here?"

"No."

Santher looked disappointed. "I was hoping we'd find a guard. It's our only way to communicate with the outside world."

Laika popped her head through the window. "Could you guys help us? We're ready to catch some fish."

They went above to find that the net was fully untangled. Emma took the wheel, Santher reefed the sails, and the *Markab* gently slowed. Together, Laika and Herbie tossed out the net. Everyone watched it sink.

It only took a few minutes before the net line gave a tug. Laika leaned over and began hauling it in, while Herbie and Santher scrambled to assist. The net rose out of the water, flopping with long, skinny bright-blue fish and weighted by barnacles. They dumped the catch on the deck and began peeling the fish from the net.

"Look," Laika exclaimed, seizing a barnacle. "Vostok!"

"That's vostok?" Herbie asked. "It looks nothing like what we've been eating. On Earth we call those barnacles."

"Don't eat it," Santher said. "It's dangerous raw."

"So, not sushi," Herbie said.

They watched as Laika struck the barnacle against the deck, cracking it easily in half. A blue blob of jelly spilled out like an egg from its shell.

Herbie recoiled. "Okay, not eating it."

Laika was grinning. "Hand me that line," she said. Puzzled, Herbie handed her the rope and watched as she tied one end to her leg, the other to the railing.

Santher moved closer. "Laika, this is a bad idea. . . ."

She laughed and popped the vostok into her mouth. Judging from her face, it wasn't as tasty as regular vostok—in fact, it smelled like brine—but immediately the jelly skin began spreading over her body. This one had a faintly iridescent sheen.

"I don't see how it's diff—" Herbie's comment was cut off when Laika began floating. She lifted up off the deck, still seated with her legs crossed. She was grinning happily as she floated up and up until the line went taut. Herbie got to his feet and grabbed the line, apparently afraid that it might come loose, in which case Laika would float up into the sky. Santher was shaking his head.

"How is that happening?" Emma asked.

"It's just what happens when you eat raw vostok."

"So the stuff we ate was cooked?"

"Sort of," he said. "I'm not sure what they do to it."

Emma remembered eating vostok and feeling a strange lightness, as if she could float. It made a kind of sense that Laika was floating now, bobbing above them like a helium balloon. Herbie was staring up at her with a mixture of worry and amazement.

"Come on, Herbie. Try it!" she called.

"Not into the raw stuff," he said.

Laika spent another few minutes dangling above them before the effect wore off. The floating didn't last long, but the shimmering jelly coat remained for the rest of the afternoon.

That night, Laika and Herbie came topside, carrying plates and silverware and a giant bowl of stew. "We're going to eat out here," Laika announced. "I promised Herbie I'd show him the Lacerta conjunction. That's when you can see the stars of Lacerta with Cepheus in the background. It looks like a giant river. Anyway, I saw it when we came down here on the *Argh* last year. . . ."

She carried on happily while Herbie laid down a blanket and everyone sat on the deck. The others must have been hungry, judging by the way they tackled the stew, and Emma, who hadn't had much of an appetite for days, found that she was starving. She finished off one bowl and started on another.

"So," Herbie said excitedly to Emma, "I finally figured out why we can understand each other."

"Oh. How?"

"Laika explained it. It's because of the vostok. Apparently, it affects the parts of your brain that understand communication. I mean, I don't think anyone understands it entirely, but it kind of downloads a universal translator into your head or something. That's how I think of it, anyway. It works on everyone."

Emma slowed down her eating long enough to say, "Wow."

"But it only lasts for a couple of months," Herbie said. "After that, you have to eat more vostok."

"Do we have more vostok?" Emma asked.

"We have a whole box of it," Herbie said, looking pleased by this. "The cooked stuff," he added. Since they needed vostok to communicate with Laika and Santher, Emma figured it was a good thing they had such a big supply.

The conversation carried on, and Emma ate another whole bowl of stew before Santher spoke up.

"I'm curious how you got away from the navy," he said. "You told me they chased you all the way from Monkey. I noticed the bullet holes in your mast when I was repairing the ship."

Herbie leaned backward to grab his backpack and take out the scuppers in the old bait jar. He showed them to Santher, who whistled through his teeth.

"They look like bullets to me," Herbie says. "Only I got hit by one and—"

"You did?" Santher was amazed.

"Yeah." He shuddered, not wanting to explain. "Another one hit me, and I got changed back right away. But it's nothing like a real bullet or it would have gone through me. I mean, what is it?"

Santher shook his head. "Scuppers are bullets dipped in memory water. If they hit something inanimate, like a mast, then they just act like regular bullets. But the minute they hit a living thing, they transform it into something else."

"How?" Emma asked.

"Memory water can do that if it's really concentrated," he said. "The navy does something to the water before they put it on the bullets."

"It's horrible when someone gets hit by a scupper," Laika said. "The worst is when they turn into a fish. They flop around on the ground and you have to put them in water or they'll die. Usually the closest water is a Strand, but if they get in a Strand, then they swim away and they're gone forever."

"So when you're a fish," Emma said, "you're really a fish. You don't remember your human self?"

"That's right," Santher said.

Herbie shook his head. "I was only a dragon for a few seconds, but I had no idea what was going on. . . ."

Emma looked at the others. "He was an *iguana*."

Santher laughed. "We are on the lizard system. You should feel right at home."

"Very funny," Herbie replied. "So I take it not everyone turns into an iguana?"

"No," Laika said. "You never know what you'll turn into. One time, this boy on the *Argh* got turned into a hammer!"

"It does seem completely random," Santher added.

"So . . . ," Emma said, looking down at the remains of their meal, "one of these fish we just ate could have been human?"

Laika put a hand to her mouth.

"Probably not," Santher said, but he didn't seem convinced.

"I still don't understand how a memory can be trapped in water," Herbie said.

"No one understands it," Santher replied. "Touching it with your finger can mess up your mind. Imagine what would happen if your whole body fell in."

"What would happen?" Emma asked.

"When you touch it," Santher said, "the memories trapped inside the water become yours. They become like your own memories—you can't really get rid of them again. But in the memory seas, you would get millions of memories all at once. . . ." He trailed off, uncertain how to explain.

"So your brain would explode," Herbie said.

"Kind of," Laika said. "No one but your mom has ever survived being thrown in the memory seas."

Emma felt a horrified awe imagining her mom drowning in memory water. When she had touched the memory water on Delphinus, she had been drawn into a song that felt as real as if Herbie had been singing it beside her. And that was only one small memory. She couldn't fathom what it would feel like to submerge her whole body, and to have to absorb millions of memories at once. This might explain why her mother was so afraid of the ocean and of sailing. For a sharp, sad moment, Emma regretted not knowing this before. In all the years she'd grown up, she'd only seen her mother as a coward.

Suddenly, an idea popped into her head. It was so simple and obvious that she smacked her forehead.

"I've got it!" she said. "I know a way to find out where my mom is right now!"

"What?" Herbie said.

Emma snatched up the jar of memory water. "I can use this!"

"What—you're going to touch the *scupper* water?" Herbie yelped. "What if it turns you into an iguana?"

"He's right," Laika said. "That's an extremely bad idea. I mean, eating raw vostok is one thing, but *memory water* . . ."

"When I touched the water on Delphinus," Emma said, "I got a memory about my mom. And then afterward, I could hear all the animals at the tables around me, but I could only hear them when they were talking about my mom. It's almost like the memory water *knew* what I needed to hear. Maybe if I touch it again, it will know now too."

Herbie gave a sputter of protest, and Laika said, "You can't just touch it and get what you want. I don't think that's how it works."

"And didn't you say that scuppers were dipped in *concentrated* memory water?" Herbie asked Santher.

"Yes," Santher replied uncomfortably.

"So this would be stronger than normal memory water?" he asked.

"Maybe."

"Besides," Herbie said, turning back to Emma, "you're looking for information about what's happening right now. But memory water is, by definition, going to give you, uh . . . *memories?*"

"Okay," Emma said, "but a memory can be a few seconds old. It doesn't have to be ancient."

"But if it's a few seconds old," Herbie said, "then your mom would have had to touch some kind of memory water recently, right?"

"Actually, I don't think that's true," Santher said. "Once you travel down Eridanus, the water makes some kind of connection with you, so it's not just the few memories from your journey that get left in the water, it's everything about you. All your memories get put in the water, even ones from childhood. It seems possible that it would keep that connection to you, and it would keep storing your memories even after you've left the system."

Herbie shook his head. "All I'm going to say is: *What if she turns into an iguana?*"

"That's not going to happen," Emma said. "Berenice touched the water in the tavern on Delphinus, remember? A drop landed on her wrist, and nothing happened to her."

No one replied.

"Look, I have a feeling this could work," Emma said. "And I really need to know where my mom is. I mean, what if we're going in the completely wrong direction right now? She could be in the Queen's hands already. And what if the Queen executes her?" She stopped talking, feeling her throat grow tight again. She wanted to say: *I can't believe I didn't think of this before.*

"I think you're right," Santher said. "You should try it."

Everyone was staring at her. She took a deep breath and gently unscrewed the lid of the jar. Herbie's lips were set tight, and he was frowning.

"At least this water's cleaner than the stuff we touched on Delphinus," Emma said, setting the jar lid on the deck beside her. Her comment did not seem to soothe him. "And if I *do* turn into an iguana, just get a pair of tweezers and drop one of the scuppers on me right away so I can turn back."

"Sure thing," he said coolly. "Once I'm finished having a heart attack, I'll get right on that."

"Just touch it with the tip of your finger," Laika said, looking anxious. "It will be stronger than normal."

"And before you touch it," Santher said, "I think you'd better concentrate on what you want to know."

Emma followed their instructions, shutting her eyes and thinking about Mom. *I need to find out where she is right now.* She reached into the jar and carefully touched the water with the very tip of her finger. She retracted it immediately and set the jar on the ground, quickly screwing the lid back on.

At first, nothing happened. She looked at her friends. Each was staring at her with anticipation and fear.

"Anything?" Santher asked.

Emma shook her head. She was about to open the jar again, but when she looked down, she was struck by an awesome sight: at the edge of the dinner blanket was a five-hundred-foot drop to a chasm below. She gasped and startled, and the blanket tipped, dropping her over the side.

She fell as dead weight, too terrified to scream. With a sudden jolt, she stopped and opened her eyes. It was like waking from a nightmare. Her heart was still racing and she was covered in sweat, only now she was in an unfamiliar world. She looked around, trying to comprehend the scene.

She was on a ship—she could tell by the rocking, the way the wood squeaked and groaned, and a distant splash of water against the hull. She was walking down a narrow corridor behind three people: two guards in navy uniforms who were escorting a prisoner between them. The prisoner had a bag over his or her head, but when Emma caught a glimpse of the hands, which were tied behind the prisoner's back, she recognized Mom's wedding ring.

"Mom!" she cried. No one seemed able to hear her. She tried touching one of the guards, but he didn't respond.

The guards brought Mom to a fo'c'sle. It was a dark, narrow space with hardly enough room to stand up straight. The floor was covered in damp straw, and the whole place smelled of mildew and bilgewater. Emma watched as the guards untied her ropes and locked her in prison cuffs. The cuffs were heavier, and with the weight on her arms, Mom nearly fell over. She looked around with an air of utter confusion, shuffled to the wall, slid down weakly, and drew her knees to her chest.

Emma tried sneaking into the cell before the guards locked the door, but there wasn't enough room between the two burly men, and she was left outside staring through the bars at Mom's crumpled form.

"Mom," Emma croaked, tears burning in her eyes, "I'm so sorry. I'm going to get you out of here." She knew this was a memory, and she suddenly felt an urge to find out how long ago it had happened. She forced herself to think. Mom was wearing her wedding ring, and Emma had seen pictures of their wedding at San Francisco's city hall. Had she gone back to space since then? Probably not. The navy hadn't captured her until recently, or they would have known she wasn't dead. The memory Emma was seeing must be recent.

But what if it was already a week old? Or more? That still left plenty of time for the Queen to have executed her. Emma rushed back down the corridor, hoping to find some way to tell what day it was or what ship they were on, but at the end of the hallway the door was locked.

From above she heard voices. People were coming down the stairs. She waited for them to unlock the door, and she stepped back as they came through.

First came the doctor, Bezerbee Vermek. Although Emma had never seen him before, she knew his name in an instant, and she knew that he was a doctor. She figured this was because she was inside a memory, and that whoever it belonged to must know him too. A limp swag of hair hung over the doctor's ghastly white face. His suit had undoubtedly once been fine, but it looked to have been worn daily for the better part of a decade, and now it was decorated with loose-hanging threads. Behind him came a scrawny young man with greasy blond hair. He was carrying the doctor's black leather bag, so she figured he must be the loblolly boy, an assistant.

She followed them down the dank corridor to Mom's cell. They stopped there and peered through the bars at her.

"She's sleeping," the loblolly boy whispered.

Dr. Vermek snorted and fumbled in his pocket. He drew out a key and unlocked the cell door. "Have you brought the correct instruments?"

"Yes. But I don't understand why—"

"Wake her up," he said.

"Yes, sir, but—"

"Wake her up." Vermek slid a vial from his pocket and held it to the light for inspection.

The loblolly boy stared in stupefaction. "Is that a grisslin?"

"Yes," Vermek said, grinning fiendishly. "This is a particularly rare and deadly grisslin that is prized among seers for its ability to absorb memories from the human mind."

The two men squeezed into the fo'c'sle, and the loblolly boy knelt beside Mom. She might have been dead but for the gentle pulsing of a vein in her neck.

"Is this really necessary?" the loblolly boy asked, regarding the grisslin as if it were intended for him.

"All the information the captain needs is *right down there.*" Vermek pointed at Brightstoke's head. "We simply have to retrieve it."

"But isn't it going to kill her?"

Vermek simply smirked. "Wake her up."

The boy knelt beside Mom and shook her arm. She didn't respond, so he touched her cheek. She sprang to like a wildcat, leaping to her feet with enough fierce energy to throw him backward. Vermek whipped out his pistol, but Mom was still shackled. She looked at the boy, then at Vermek. She stepped back until she touched the wall.

"Welcome back," Vermek said. He moved closer, inspecting her tattered clothes and mangled hair.

Mom scrutinized him.

"Do you remember me?" He brought his face closer. "I was there when we captured you on Rigel. I was there when Captain Gent put you in the bag. Do you remember the lynx?"

Mom caught sight of the grisslin in the vial. She seemed to realize what was going on, and a look of fear crossed her face.

"We know all about the Pyxis transmission," Vermek said. "We're taking you to the Queen for execution. We're very close by—only a few more days to Fairfoot. Enough time, I think, to strike a deal. If you tell us how to start the Pyxis, then we won't have to do this." He wiggled the vial. "We might even consider releasing you before then."

Mom narrowed her eyes. "Who is the captain of this ship?"

"Why, funny you should ask," Vermek sneered. "None other than your old friend Tema Gent. Would you like to see her? I'm sure she'd be glad to extend the offer herself."

Mom's face grew stubborn. "You'll never let me go."

Vermek began to unscrew the vial. Inside, the grisslin scrabbled against the glass, its legs working furiously. Mom tried to pull back, but Vermek motioned to the loblolly boy to step closer, and he did, reluctantly. "Hold her head," Vermek commanded.

"You're going to regret this," Mom said.

"Oh, so you remember the grisslin? You collected them—or should I say you stole them? Are you wondering where I got this one?" He held up the vial. "I had to search far and wide to find it. Quite painful, these smaller ones. They can really do some damage." He held the vial to Mom's temple. She resisted, but the boy held her firm. "So what are you going to tell us?" Vermek asked, lifting the lid.

Mom pressed her lips together in an attempt at defiance, but Emma saw that her shoulders were trembling.

"Nothing," she spat.

Vermek pulled back the lid, and the grisslin sprung out, its greedy legs finding purchase on Mom's skin. It scurried into her hair and came straight back out, its blind body furiously seeking an entrance to the brain inside, for there was a brain inside, and a million memories calling to the creature. It was only a matter of getting in there. The grisslin ran a manic figure eight on her forehead, and raced down her nose. Mom thrashed, and it took

Vermek's help to hold her in place. The grisslin stopped at her nostril and sent one of its antennae delicately inside, savoring the moment as a drunkard would savor his first drop of crocky after a long drought. Then, with such speed as seemed impossible, the grisslin darted into her nose.

Emma clapped a hand to her mouth.

Mom screamed, but it was cut in half by a sudden jerk of her body. She fell to her knees, looking surprised, then slumped forward, unconscious.

The loblolly boy knelt beside her and opened the doctor's bag. He took out a stethoscope and pressed its diaphragm to her head, listening intently.

"I think it's penetrated the cortex," he said grimly.

Vermek handed him the empty vial. "Good. When it's done, collect the grisslin."

CHAPTER 19
Fairfoot

Emma came to, shouting, *"Mom-mom-mom-NO!"* She awoke with a jolt and found herself lying on the dinner blanket. The plates and silverware were gone, and her friends were kneeling over her, looking concerned.

She forced herself to sit up. Her head was pounding, but she managed to speak. "They gave her a grisslin!"

Santher and Laika were dismayed.

"What's that?" Herbie asked.

"It was some kind of beetle," Emma said, "and they said it could eat the memories from her brain!"

"Sounds gruesome," Herbie said.

"I saw it. They put it in her nose, and it went inside her head." Emma forced herself to stand up. The ship was moving gracefully, but she swayed anyway. "They wanted to get information about the Pyxis, but she wouldn't give it to them."

Santher gave her a blanket because she was shivering. "Did you find out where they were?" he asked.

"Fairfoot," she said. "They were heading to Fairfoot. Where is that?"

"That's on Pegasus!" Laika said. "It's not very far!"

"They said they were bringing her to the Queen," Emma said.

"What?" Santher said. "The Queen is on Fairfoot? Why?"

"I don't know."

"Then we have to be careful going there," Santher said. "The Queen usually travels with a huge retinue."

"Not to mention she'll probably have the navy posted at the vostok zone," Laika put in. "How will we get around it?"

"I don't know," Emma said. "But we're going to Pegasus. They've got my mom, so that's where we're going."

Silence fell.

She turned to Santher. "How long will it take us to get to Fairfoot?"

"Uh . . . four days in good wind."

"That's not fast enough."

"Well," he said, grinning, "we could get there a lot faster if we fly. . . ."

"Oh no." Herbie put his hands on his face.

Laika smiled and made a small "*wheee*" of excitement. "I love flying," she said.

"But you said we needed to test-run the wings first!" Herbie said.

"Nah," Santher replied bluffly. "They're the best wings we've ever made. I'm sure they'll be fine."

Emma looked at the three of them and made up her mind. "Okay," she said, "first thing tomorrow, we fly to Pegasus."

✦ ✦ ✦

Emma and Herbie were standing beside the captain's wheel, the wind in their faces. Laika grinned as the *Markab* soared majestically over the Pegasus Strand. Thanks to the yacht's streamlined body and massive wings, it was proving itself a light, fast ship, and the tailwinds along Scheat were giving them a phenomenal boost.

Everyone was strapped to a line that was tied to a railing or the mast. Herbie was clutching the rope around his stomach and turning various shades of green. He might have mastered climbing to the aerie, but flying was a new and turbulent experience. When the ship dropped in the strong winds, his knuckles went white, and when it soared higher, he squeezed his eyes and muttered, "Please no, please no . . ." Emma was still shaken from her experience the day before, and she couldn't stop thinking about what had happened to her mom.

"We're going to find her, no matter what," Laika said. But Emma knew that she was just saying that to make her feel better. Deep inside, she had a horrible feeling that it was too late.

Santher was standing at the propelling generator, a wooden box with a wheel on it. By spinning the wheel, he was able to generate the energy to raise the ship off the water and keep her wings flapping.

"How are we going to land?" Herbie called out.

"We'd better check our position!" Laika cried.

Emma hauled Santher's *Navy Manual* from beneath the bench and flipped it open to Pegasus.

"Look for landmarks!" Laika said.

Emma scanned the pages of text until she found Scheat.

"There should be a giant split in the Strand just before the vostok bridge to the star Markab!" she shouted over the wind. "One Strand turns left to Homam, and the other goes to Algenib."

"That's it?" Laika asked. "No islands or rocks or banks?"

"Nope."

"Okay, but how are we going to *land*?" Herbie said.

Laika pinched her lips. "I think we're going to reach it pretty quickly. Once we see the split in the Strand, we'll set her down."

"Right, but HOW?"

"Well," Laika said. "We just kind of spread the wings and float down." She stretched her arms to demonstrate. Emma had never been on a flying ship—she had never even been on an airplane—and if it hadn't been for the feeling of gloom about her mom, flying would have been exhilarating. With every flap of the wings, the *Markab* pulled slightly higher with a remarkable feeling of boundless space. It reminded her of swinging at the park as a kid.

Herbie shook his head, muttering to himself. "Float down. Just like that. I knew I should have stayed on the *Argh*."

Santher had a devilish gleam in his eye. "You should see what it's like flying on the *Argh*!"

For a brief, queasy moment, Herbie looked as if he might vomit.

✦ ✦ ✦

When they saw the split in the Strand, Santher shouted directions for shifting the wings. Laika and Emma leapt to action, adjusting the wooden knobs on the generator until Santher was satisfied. The wings stopped their flapping and now spread out widely as the *Markab* began a gliding descent. Herbie, who had gone below groaning, was nowhere in sight as the boat glided down to the water. It finally touched down with a great, satisfying splash, carving waves in the waters that shot up behind them. They heard Herbie give a terrified yelp below.

"It's okay!" Laika shouted. "We've landed!"

Herbie climbed topside, looking around warily. Santher scampered to the mainmast and let out the sails, while Laika and Emma went to make sure the wing masts folded in properly.

They were surprised to discover that the vostok zone was empty. There was no sign of the navy at all, and the vostok bridge was rapidly approaching. Fifty yards ahead of them, the massive bridge stood high and wide. It was easily big enough for six *Argh*-sized ships to pass through side by side.

"Why is there no navy?" Laika asked.

"They must be on the planet," Santher said. "Probably because the Queen is here." He steered the *Markab* toward the bridge and called for everyone to vostok up. Emma ate hers and braced herself for another plunge into darkness.

"Cannons on my count!" Santher cried.

Emma and Laika stood behind the cannons, which were aimed at the wide blue horizon ahead.

"Three . . . two . . . one!"

Emma pulled the trigger cord. The cannons gave a boom and a rearward lurch, shooting their vostok cargo into the clear blue sky. With a bright explosion, the shots seemed to hit an invisible barrier and explode into a million glittering particles. Emma held her rope as the ship lurched forward into the green light, falling helplessly for a terrifying minute through the strange, wild void. This transition was more of a surprising *whoomph* that hit her like a blast of fresh air. Then, with a hearty splash, they found themselves sailing on a dark-blue sea, their vostok skins gone, their hearts still aflutter. The great harbor of Fairfoot was gleaming before them.

And directly ahead stood a fleet of navy ships.

"Good grace!" Laika jerked. "That's why there were no guards at the vostok zone—they're all down here. There must be three hundred of them!"

Herbie had gone utterly pale.

Santher was studying the ships. "They're not going to attack," he said quickly. "They don't even notice us. Look." He was right. None of the ships seemed to be responding to their presence. In fact, they looked empty. "Just remember: nobody knows who we are. And conveniently"—he grinned at them—"we belong to the Draco system, one of the Queen's favorites."

Ahead, twenty Virgo men-of-war were anchored side by side, their colors gleaming in the bright morning sun. The *Markab* sailed forward with the delicacy of a man tiptoeing through a nest of sleeping scorpions. Cast in momentary shadow, Emma gazed up to see a Virgo bowsprit looming overhead, a sinister look on her peasant face.

Beyond the first row of ships, they saw another line.

"I can't believe we're doing this," Laika whispered, her face frozen in shock. She turned to Santher. "Don't you think we should go back?"

"I thought you wanted to help find Halifax," he said.

"Shhhhh!" Laika hissed. "Don't say her name so loudly."

"There are hardly any Pegasus ships," Herbie said.

"How can you tell?" Emma asked.

"None of them have wings. These are all navy ships. . . . But I think Laika's right. We should hide or something."

"Look!" Santher pointed at a cluster of ships ahead of them. Three Leo craft were plowing their slow way through the harbor. They were large galleons like the *Argh.*

"What, those Leo ships?" Laika asked. "They're not going to recognize *us.*"

"No, look between them!"

And there, sitting happily on the waves, was a very elegant, exquisitely white ship, looking all the more lovely and delicate surrounded by its powerful Leo guard. The first impression Emma had was of a woman gliding across a ballroom in the arms of the wind. The ship was sleek and narrow, delicately constructed with three slender masts holding tricornered sails and two side masts that hung above the water like wings. The sails were silky and iridescent, almost like a chiffon dress. The sound they made was not the heavy *flap-flap* of the *Markab*'s rigging, but a thin *whip-whip.*

"That's an Andromeda ship," Laika said nervously. "Oh, good grace . . . is that . . . ?"

"Yup." Santher was gaping at it. "With the Leo guard . . ."

"I can't make out the name," Laika put in. "But if it's the *Chained Lady* . . ."

Santher turned to Emma and Herbie. "That's Queen Virgo's ship."

They were aghast.

"Shouldn't we go—I don't know—in the *other* direction?" Herbie squeaked.

Santher steered them gently away.

"Why would the Queen be on an Andromeda ship?" Emma asked.

"She kept it as a war prize when she defeated Cassiopeia," Santher said. "That's Princess Andromeda's mother."

"Santher," Laika whispered, *"we ought to hide now."*

But Santher's eyes had taken on a quality of devilish determination, and he shook his head. "No," he said. "I think this means we'll find exactly what we need."

CHAPTER 20

The *Chained Lady*

Fairfoot's harbor was built in a natural inlet. Two outstretched arms of land embraced each new arrival, and ships from every system were lined up on its shoulders, elbows, and wrists.

Santher steered them straight into the center of the harbor. With ships packed on every pier, there was little room to dock, but the *Markab* was small. Santher found an unobtrusive place beside a longboat from Ursa, and the four of them quickly disembarked, tying the yacht to a post.

Emma followed the others down the pier, where they encountered a group of Ursa sailors. They were a mixed crowd of bears and men, the lot of them smelling like pipe smoke and the oily stench of fur. The bears stood upright and were remarkably tall. The men were tall as well, and dressed in fur coats that hung down to their boots. Emma felt tiny among them—she barely reached their waists. She moved delicately beside Herbie, afraid of getting trampled.

One of the men had great, hairy hands and a thicket of beard that sprang sideways from his ears.

"Ursell," he called to a friend of his, "think the Queen'll want some pelts?" He was holding an armful of wolf skins, and when he raised them in the air, Emma ducked. A swipe from a single one of the skins could have knocked her into the harbor.

"Only pelting she'll get will be a smack across the face," Ursell grumbled. The other men laughed. "Don't see what we're doing here anyway."

"We don't have a choice, do we?" the first man said. "You see what she did to Lynx—you want her doing that to Ursa?"

Laika stopped abruptly and looked up at the man. "Do you know any pirates?" she asked.

The man froze and looked down at her. "Don't know what you're talking about," he said. Stiffly, he moved past her and hurried his men forward, glancing back at her as if she were dangerous.

Laika turned to Emma and Herbie. "See how afraid everyone is to talk about pirates?"

Emma was surprised. "Maybe it's because there's so much navy here," she said.

"But they're always like that," Laika replied.

"It's just because they think you're crazy," Santher said. "Come on."

They had reached the center of the wharf. The *Chained Lady* docked on a long, lone pier that extended out into the middle of the harbor. Red carpets had been laid out for her, leading straight ahead to a grand building that dominated the shoreline. It was a veritable pantheon with a dome roof, a stone facade, and imposing marble columns. Ministers from all over the galaxy had lined up along the carpet to greet the Queen. Emma and her friends crept to the front edge of the crowd and watched as the Queen's ship laid down its gangplank.

Silence fell as a large shadow passed over the crowd. Everyone looked up to see a flock of flying Pegasus horses heading for the carpet, their great wings outstretched. Two by two, they landed on the carpet and ran forward, clearing the way for those behind. On their backs, smartly dressed soldiers sat upright, sternly ignoring the applause that broke out from the crowd.

When all the Pegasus horses had landed, sailors from the Queen's ship began marching down its gangplank.

"Draconi sailors," Laika whispered to Emma and Herbie. The Draconi guards moved in a tight formation, their short, stocky bodies draped in coarse fabrics, their arms and faces browned by the sun. "They look like Riders."

"They ride dragons?" Herbie asked.

"Normally, yes. But those ones were sent to protect the Queen. She has her own dragons. But I don't see them. Sometimes they fly alone."

A trumpet blared, and everyone fell silent. The Queen appeared at the top of the gangplank, flanked by her guards. Regally, she walked down the plank. The crowd fell in a sweeping wave as every creature knelt before her. Emma bowed halfheartedly. She wanted to get a better look.

Queen Virgo was a surprisingly small figure, but her clothing more than made up for her size. She wore a long royal-blue dress that seemed to spread out for miles behind her. Her great tier of blond hair was drawn up in waves, and a crown of objects was placed artfully around it. They looked like bright-blue ears of wheat. A gigantic diamond hung around her neck.

Once the Queen had passed and the crowd had risen again, Emma heard a clanking. Straining to see, she caught sight of a dirty young woman in white rags. Her legs and wrists were bound in heavy chains, and she was being dragged, stumbling, behind the Queen.

"That's the princess of Andromeda," Laika said, her big brown eyes wide with sympathy. "It's how she's being punished for rebelling against the Queen."

They got a look at Princess Andromeda's face as she passed. She might have been lovely once, but now her cheeks were sunburned, her lips were cracked and bleeding, and her eyes were swollen. She moaned.

"Just one drop of water, please!" she begged. One of the guards turned, raising a whip in his hand. She cowered. The guard yanked her chains and dragged her, stumbling, into the hall.

Santher gave a low whistle, and they turned to see him ten feet away, slipping into a crowd of young servants from one of the warrior systems. It so happened that the warrior's beige uniforms matched the ones that the four of them were wearing. As the ministers began moving into the great hall, Emma and her friends followed, blending in seamlessly with the servants.

CHAPTER 21

Every Last Little Yipping Fox

The Queen of Virgo, whose real name was Elemin Marchpane, was sitting on a high silver throne. She exuded an air of cold regality. Draconi guards stood to the side along with her personal dragons—a nervous one in front and a vicious one in back who liked to bite off hands but never swallowed them. The front one was her favorite dragon, Simmah. He paced to and fro like a vigilant guard, even if the Queen herself knew better—he was nervous with so many people in the room, anxious to get away from the crowd and fly off on his own. To the royal soldiers, Simmah looked like the fiercest guard in the room. They admired him, stepping back only when he belched a wisp of flame, hoping not to scorch their bright-red uniforms or shiny white tuskets, each festooned with an ear of wheat.

Around the Queen, spreading out like a river delta, were the many guests she had invited to the Royal Hall. Every system that paid fealty had turned out for the event. It brought her pleasure to notice that, despite the great mixing of every sort of creature, the representatives from various systems tended to congregate in sensible groups. She saw the warriors from Ras Algethi, tall, meaty men in fur capes and jagged-tooth crowns. She saw the ministers from Regulus on Leo, their lions circling them watchfully, and nearby the heavy-framed shipbuilders from Canopus on Argo mingled comfortably. The head of the Hercules delegation was wearing a dead brown bear on his back, and when the great bears from Ursa noticed the man's garb, there was a roar and a scuffle, and a group of Draconi guards intervened, dispatching the bears to the other side of the hall.

Beyond that group, she caught sight of the bright-purple cloaks of the judiciaries from Libra, and beside them, three magnificent sprays of feathers announced the triumvir from Pavo. There were scientists, undoubtedly from Gemini, as well as the doctors from Ophiuchus, with their colorful snakes coiling around their bare arms. And there too were the royal hares of Lepus, who, although short in this crowd, stood out because of their great jeweled ears, and their minister, a red rabbit whose name she always forgot. A few more merchants from Argo and an artisan or two from Sculptor stood at the edge of the crowd.

The central part of the room was given over to the water systems: people from Cetus, Pisces, Aquarius, and Delphinus. Their clothing was colored in bright indigos and jades, some shimmering with phosphorescence. The only things to tell them apart were the unique patterns of their constellation sewn onto their vests, sleeves, and hats. That, and the Cetans were taller than the others, thicker, and less inclined to mingle.

And finally, to her right the clan systems had gathered: the tall warriors from Corvus, their birds jessed and perched proudly on their shoulders; King Razliman's son, Lusit, and his Draconi ministers, who had brought their own contingent of dragons; and the queen of Antares and her carapaced Scorpio, who trolled through the crowd like a lost dog. There was a minister from Pegasus with a white stallion at his side. (He was not a handsome man, she noted, and she wondered again why the women from Pegasus were so beautiful when their men were so boorish.) In any event, from this side of the room came the greatest noise, a veritable swell. It was the rising cacophony of human voices and animals braying, snorting, and squawking, their energy doubling upon itself to create an even greater excitement. Birds from Cygnus were shrieking, birds from Tucana were yawking, and birds from Columba were cooing. The rams of Aries were bleating, the crabs of Cancer *tick-tick-tick*ing on the colored tiles. She noted with consternation that the bears from Ursa didn't mix with this crowd either; they kept their distance, as if expecting an ambush.

She contemplated the systems that had not arrived for the event. Eridanus. Monkey and Lynx. Aquila, Canis Major—and Andromeda, of course. And there was no one from Hydra. She hadn't expected their presence, but their absence was loud, for even if they were not on good terms with Virgo, the crowd that gathered had come to discuss an issue of importance to everyone, in every system. No system was isolated; none could pretend not to be affected. No, it was time to put all disputes aside.

The Queen, summoning her strongest presence of mind,

rose from her throne and waited until the last of the chatter had died down, until every last fox from Vulpecula had finally stopped its yipping and yapping and sat obediently at its master's feet. *Cats,* she thought, *we are only missing small cats.* Once she had the attention of every last soul, she sat back in her throne and exchanged greetings with the crowd before realizing quite suddenly that members of the Chamaeleon delegation were missing. She believed they too had failed to arrive until after a general search, a bear from Ursa spotted them at the back of the room, blending nicely with the tapestries.

When she had finally dispensed with the formal nonsense, she turned to the most pressing topic, her voice rising darkly over the room.

"As you all know," she intoned, "we are gathered here for one purpose today, and that is to discuss the depletion of our galaxy's most valuable resource—our memory water."

There was a cold, stifled applause and murmur of consent. She went on: "As you also know, we are down to our last strategic reserves. Without this water, our galaxy will have no medical cures, no energy systems, no hubbles or scuppers, and, crucially, no mesmers, and thus a failing communication system all across the galaxy. Our systems are becoming desperate, paying ever more dearly for a diminishing supply. Very soon, we will have no more memory water left."

The Queen paused to take in her crowd. They were listening attentively. Some looked desperate, others skeptical. The only movement was Simmah's tail, swishing nervously at her feet.

"Many of you have already begged my generosity in sharing more than I am able to. I have heard a great number of pleas, and I have had to reject them all. Nothing so far has been able to abate the great disaster we all fear is looming ahead of us."

Another murmur from the crowd, and some nervous squawking of wildlife.

"As you all remember, the dread pirate and traitor Cascabel was responsible for ruining the memory seas of Eridanus—" At this there was a great hissing of contempt from the back of the room. "He stole the water from an honest system and smuggled it into the great portals of the Shroud, leaving behind a single way to open those doorways. And that is the Pyxis."

She let this word hang in the air while she studied each of her guests with a stern gaze.

"We have been unable to open those doorways and access the resources we so desperately need, for the Pyxis has been lost to us." A quiet thrill was stirring the crowd. "But just two weeks ago, a Pyxis transmission signaled throughout the galaxy for the first time in over twelve years. And we have determined that the signal was authentic."

A triumphant roar rose up from the crowd, followed by waves of raucous cheering.

"For many years," she said in a darker voice, "we have strained to preserve our resources. For many years, we have worried desperately about our futures. But it is only memory water that will save the galaxy. And now, finally, a solution is within reach. Therefore, I would call on each of you here to commit a part of your fleets to the hunt for the Pyxis, and to guarantee its safe return to my palace on Spica."

More applause broke out, followed by cheering.

The Queen raised her hand, and the room fell silent again. "The Pyxis is a dangerous, mysterious object. Very few understand how to operate it successfully. However, we are fortunate to have the guidance of the finest philosophers, the counsel of the finest judges"—she motioned to Libra—"and the strength of the greatest armies in the galaxy." Here, with a royal sweep of the arm, she included the warriors from every system, to general applause. "We feel, with all these strengths on our side, that Virgo's actions are the best possible decisions to be made for the betterment and safety of all your systems, as well as ours."

This was greeted by more thunderous clapping.

The Queen stepped aside and the ministers from Pegasus began making announcements. She remained by her throne, listening. Whispers became clear, directed by the memory water in her blood. And what she heard translated from mouth to ear, from one species to another all across the great hall, was that the notorious pirate and former Virgo princess Halifax Brightstoke had been captured and taken into the Queen's custody. (Think of it! After all this time! How *did* she survive? Where was she hiding?) Like the expansion of the galaxy itself, rumors began to drift outward, pulling every idea farther and farther apart. Rumors that Halifax had escaped her execution with Cascabel's help. Rumors that she had died, and that someone else was posing as Halifax. Rumors that the Pyxis had given her the power to stay alive. There were rumors that the old rumor was true—that good pirates never die—which sparked a minor series of debates: What *was* a good pirate? Weren't pirates by definition very bad? The scoundrels of the Strands? Thieves and whatnot? The rumors continued: rumors that Halifax had a baby boy. A baby girl. A baby monkey. Rumors that she'd been living on Draco. On Eridanus, imprisoned in the dark, occult waters.

There was no one to dispel the many myths and lies, and so they expanded outward, unfettered by the gravity of truth.

Suddenly, the Queen caught sight of a woman at the back of the crowd—shabbily dressed, bright-red hair, someone she hadn't seen in years. Captain Artemisia Gent. It disturbed her very much.

Queen Virgo stood up then. Her work in the Royal Hall was complete, and Gent's presence was annoying and unexpected. The entire room bowed as she strode off the dais, dragons in tow.

CHAPTER 22
A Squilch

Tucked amid a troop of Hercules servants, Emma and the others strained to see what was going on. During the Queen's talk, they stood and listened, unable to see the Queen herself. They were too short, and the crowd was pressed too tightly together.

Once the Queen had finished her speech, the crowd in the great hall broke into chatter. It only took a few minutes for Emma to become attuned to the important sounds. They reached her ears with the familiar whisper of memory water voices.

"The *Newton Eel* arrived last night," a voice said. "It's hidden up the coast."

Emma broke away from her friends and ran into the crowd, pushing past one minister after another.

"Emma!" Herbie called, running after her.

She ran, straining to follow the voice before it disappeared.

"Halifax is really here?" another voice asked. It was coming from a different direction. She quickly changed course to follow.

The others came up behind her.

"What's she doing?" Santher asked.

"I don't know," Herbie replied.

"Shhhhh!" Emma said. "I'm listening. . . ."

"How can you hear anything above all this babble?" Laika asked.

"I think this might have something to do with the memory water . . . ," Herbie suggested.

"Yes," a stranger said. "Although grace only knows where they're holding her."

Emma was just about to reach the man she believed was speaking when the conversation died. It must have carried on, but the sounds of it evaporated into the crowd. She stopped, looking around, dizzied by the great array of people, while all around her rose the memory water whispers of the great Halifax Brightstoke.

"That old pirate ought to be executed. . . ."

"I always suspected she was a fraud. . . ."

"Word is, she's still sailing free on the Strands. . . ."

But Emma knew this wasn't true. Mom was in the hands of the navy now.

Frustrated, she took off in a new direction. She heard a faint voice, a whisper almost. It drew her attention precisely because it was so quiet, and yet it reached her ear as if it had been spoken there.

"Go back to the ship and keep an eye on the doctor." It was

a woman who spoke. Emma froze in place, straining to hear more. Behind her, Herbie and the others waited in suspense.

"Captain, she's well watched," came the reply.

"I don't care," the woman said. "I want you to make sure that the prisoner is safe and that the doctor hasn't done anything foolish. The Queen will be furious if anything happens to her."

"Did you hear that?" Emma asked.

The others shook their heads.

Emma bolted toward the sound. There was only one person the Queen would care about that much. Mom.

"Take three of your best," the woman went on. "And be discreet."

"Yes, Captain."

Emma ran, knocking over two servants and pushing a minister aside. She reached the very back of the room and went tearing around a corner—but she stopped short. The hallway in front of her was empty. The woman was done talking, but Emma could just make out the clack of her boot steps. They seemed to be coming from a hole in the wall near her feet. It looked like an air vent.

Emma climbed into the hole and began crawling.

"Emma, where are you going?" Herbie called behind her.

The passageway was long and made of stone. The deeper she went, the colder it became. She heard the others climb into the passage too, and only hoped they had the sense to stay quiet.

Up ahead she saw a bright light in the passageway. She approached it with caution. The tunnel continued, but along the right-hand wall was a long grille that revealed a meeting room below. Emma crawled up to it and peeked through the metal slats. The Queen was there, attended by two handmaidens, who were adjusting her headpiece and straightening the back of her dress.

Herbie came up behind her, followed by Santher and Laika. The three of them lined up along the grille beside Emma and watched the scene below.

"It's the Queen's chamber," Laika whispered.

"Shhhhh." Emma could see the Queen's face now. It was surrounded by a high collar, but there was something very familiar in her eyes and her small, pointed nose. Emma realized that she looked a lot like Mom.

A pair of boot clacks grew louder, stopping outside the door. A moment later, the door opened and a guard came in.

"Your Grace," he said, falling to his knee. "Captain Gent is here to see you."

The Queen didn't reply, but her handmaidens shrank away. "Leave us," she commanded. They scurried out. "Send in the disobedient Captain Gent."

The guard left.

A moment later, Captain Gent entered the room. From so high up and behind, Emma couldn't see her face. All she could see were the long blue coat of a navy commander and a pile of flaming red hair.

Gent fell to her knees. "My apologies, Your Highness. We encountered some weather."

The Queen waited for Gent to rise before speaking. "I understand you have Halifax Brightstoke in your possession," she said.

Emma felt a desperate panic lumping in her throat. She grabbed Herbie's arm.

"Yes, Your Grace," Gent replied.

"And have you confirmed her identity yourself?"

"Yes, Your Grace."

The Queen scowled at her. "That's remarkable, Captain. I was under the impression that Brightstoke was dead."

"So was I, Your Grace." Gent swallowed hard. "We did sew her into a Party Bag. There were thirty men watching when we threw her overboard. The only thing I can figure is that she must have found a way to get out."

"Obviously," the Queen said drily. "And I believe I commanded you to take her to my prisons on Hydra."

"Yes, Your Grace . . ."

"And you have failed in that duty as well."

"Your Grace, may I explain—"

"You will leave Pegasus immediately. I am sending a fleet of Draconi ships to escort you. They will rendezvous with you outside Markab and guide you to Hydra, since clearly you are unable to get there by yourself."

Gent seemed to feel the sting, and she stammered. "You understand—Your Grace—that my delay—I mean, by switching course—was because of the possibility of finding the Pyxis."

The Queen glared at her. "And how exactly did you plan to do that?"

"We have the vagrants who captured Halifax on Monkey," Gent said.

"Do *they* have the Pyxis?"

"No, Your Highness, but I was hoping that their knowledge might assist me in—"

"Captain Gent, I believe I gave you direct orders," the Queen said. "Half the fleets in the galaxy will be searching for the Pyxis now. They may be able to find it, but the only person who truly knows where it is, is Halifax herself. So from now on, you shall leave the hunt for the Pyxis to other captains. It is of foremost importance that Halifax makes it to the prison on Hydra safely. That is the only place where we can extract the truth from her. Do you understand me?"

"Yes," Gent said grudgingly. From the sound of her voice and the way she squirmed in discomfort, Emma thought she was hiding something. "I will bring her there, Your High—"

Gent was cut short by a pounding behind her. The door flew open and the guard burst in, apologizing while two men pushed past him. The guard made a feeble attempt to introduce Dr. Vermek and the loblolly boy, who were coming in on his heels.

Vermek fell to his knees, prostrating himself. The poor loblolly boy stared in stupefaction before Vermek grabbed his coat and yanked him down.

"Please forgive us, Your Highness," Vermek muttered, his nose nearly touching the floor. "Please forgive us for this intrusion. We have important news. . . ."

"Get up," the Queen commanded.

Vermek climbed to his feet, once again dragging his loblolly boy along.

"How dare you barge in here?" asked the Queen.

Vermek fidgeted. "I'm so sorry, Your Highness, I was only looking for my captain. It is a matter of some urgency." He spun nervously on Gent. "She's dying," he said. "We haven't much time."

"Who is dying?" the Queen demanded.

"Uh . . . Halifax Brightstoke, Your Highness." He cast a worried glance at Gent.

"What's wrong with her?"

Vermek gaped at Gent, hoping she would explain, but she was clearly in the mood to watch him writhe. "Er . . . she's been infected by a squilch, Your Grace. She is *extremely* ill—"

"A squilch!" The Queen looked surprised. "How did that happen?"

"Uh . . ." Vermek looked helplessly at Gent, but she didn't reply. "Er . . . she was kidnapped by Draconi mercenaries," he said. "They traffic in all kinds of medicines, you know. And we believe that they were the ones who gave her the squilch."

"What's a squilch?" Emma whispered.

"It's a virus," Laika said. "It eats your memories."

Emma was thrown back to the kidnapping. She remembered Mom fighting like a ninja, and Caz and Laine getting the better of her. It made Emma angry to learn that they had poisoned her too.

"But unfortunately," Vermek went on, "the squilch they gave her was tainted somehow. It's done much more damage than the average squilch."

The Queen looked skeptical. "This is very strange, Doctor," she said. "Would you care to explain why two Draco mercenaries would give Halifax a squilch? They ought to have been trying to collect her memories, not destroy them."

The doctor fumbled for an answer. "Well, Your Highness, they weren't the brightest criminals. . . ."

"They would have to have been incredibly *stupid* criminals. And how did you discover the presence of this squilch, Doctor?" the Queen asked.

"Your Highness, we were looking for the memories of the Pyxis for you. The grisslin that we gave her came out infected with the squilch, and then it died."

"So you've learned nothing."

"No, Your Highness," Gent replied.

"And you've potentially crippled Halifax's mind."

"I'm sorry, Your Highness—" Gent began.

The Queen spun on Vermek. "Do you have a cure, Doctor?"

"Uh . . . no, Your Highness. We only have memory water, but that can't last much longer."

The Queen regarded him with a pair of icy-blue eyes. "If she truly is dying, then we're going to have to take more drastic measures than *memory water*—and fast. I'm afraid we need that information, and you must do whatever it takes to get it from her. Do you understand me?"

Vermek nodded vigorously.

Gent managed to squeak, "I'm sorry, Your Highness. I did mention to Lord Whelp that Halifax was ill. I didn't realize she was dying. . . ."

The Queen eyed her gravely. "Captain Gent, I am sick of your misunderstandings. You will change your course at once. Instead of sailing to Hydra, you will gather the Draconi armada and head to Draco immediately."

Gent hesitated, but she forced herself to say, "Yes, Your Highness. May I ask—"

"There are sorcerers at the royal palace on Rastaban who will be able to get the information from Halifax before she dies. For them, grisslins are child's play. And if Halifax is as sick as you say, then she won't make it to Hydra."

"Yes, Your Highness."

The Queen leaned menacingly over the kneeling captain. "I don't trust you, Gent. You're hiding something from me. But I am going to make one thing perfectly clear: finding out everything about the Pyxis is the most important thing in the galaxy right now. You will probe Halifax's memories again, and you WILL get that information for me—I don't care what you have to do. Can you do that, Captain Gent, or should I find someone else?"

"I can do it, Your Grace."

"Good. Now get out of my sight."

"Yes, Your Grace," Gent said with a bow that was designed to conceal the panic on her face. "I am your servant."

"And hopefully an adequate one," the Queen spat. "Now get out."

Gent rose and went scurrying from the room.

CHAPTER 23

A Doubleheader

With astonishing speed, Emma and her friends crawled back through the passageway. Emma's heart was thumping so loudly that she felt it in her neck. All she could think of was Mom. She was dying. Right now, probably on a ship at the docks. But she was here!

Those stupid kidnappers had given her a squilch! How long before it killed her? Emma couldn't stop thinking of the screechy panic in Dr. Vermek's voice when he'd said, *"She's dying."*

Reaching the end of the air vent, she scrambled out of it and saw her friends looking panicked.

"We have to find her—now!" Emma said.

She could still hear Captain Gent's boot steps making their way across a marble floor, so she went running after the sound. "This way!" she cried. The four of them dashed back into the great hall, catching sight of Captain Gent's red hair just as she strode out the door. They ran after her.

Emma reached the main door and burst out, determined not to lose Gent in the crowd. The plaza in front of the Royal Hall was packed. Emma darted down the stairs and plunged into the fray. She was too short to see anything, but she knew the direction Gent had gone, so she pushed through the crowd ruthlessly, elbowing ministers and crushing the odd foot. She managed to cross the plaza before spotting Gent.

Gent was standing by the water's edge. She had been waylaid by a dignitary, who was fawning over her. Emma slowed and crept closer.

Just then Gent happened to look around, and for the first time, they saw her face.

"Nisba?" Santher blurted rather too loudly.

Gent froze. She looked exactly like the *Argh*'s cook, Nisba, only more gaunt. Her red hair was longer, and most telling of all, she wore a calculating sneer.

"It's not Nisba," Emma whispered.

"I know, but who is it?" Herbie asked in amazement. "She looks just like—"

They stared unabashedly. The woman's resemblance to Nisba was extraordinary, and for a brief, horrifying moment, they imagined that it *was* Nisba and that somehow during the course of the past few days Nisba had changed.

"They must be twins," Laika whispered. "I guess Nisba's from Gemini."

"Okay, let's go." Emma tried to draw her friends back into the crowd, but Gent's guards came up behind them, and Gent herself swooped in.

"Pardon me," she said sweetly. "You called, but I didn't hear what you said."

Herbie was unable to take his eyes from Gent's face. "Sorry," he said. "We thought you were someone else."

"Yes." Gent put her finger on her chin. "But who *exactly* did you think I was?"

"Oh, just this old friend. *Really* not important—"

Something black and hairy poked out of Gent's sleeve. It looked like an insect leg. They watched in horror as another leg slid out, then another. Finally a fat-bellied tarantula popped onto her hand. Emma stood back. The tarantula's large, beady eyes gazed challengingly at her.

"I am Captain Artemisia Gent." She stuck out her tarantula hand for a shake, but no one took it. She tucked her other hand deep into her coat pocket and wrapped her fist around something. "And may I have the pleasure of *your* names?"

"Uh . . . I'm Ragnar," Herbie said.

"And does this young lady have a name too?" Gent asked, motioning to Emma with a sickly smile.

"Um, yes." Herbie made to move away, but Gent removed her hand from her pocket and opened it, revealing a jar of beetles. They came scurrying out and leapt onto Herbie's shirt. Laika shrieked. Herbie jumped back and tried to swat them off, but the bugs held on fast, burrowing furiously into his shirt. One of the beetles ran up his collar and onto his neck, where it bit deep enough to send up blood. Herbie grabbed his neck, but another beetle latched onto his fingers.

Emma tried to help him, but quick as a cat, Gent grabbed her arm. A dozen beetles leapt onto Emma's neck and raced into her collar. They bit her viciously, and she let out a cry.

It seemed as if the plaza had emptied. There was no noise but the terrible clicking of the bugs' pincers and a ringing in her ears. She looked up and saw Gent's cruelly familiar face looking down at her with gleeful, wicked eyes.

"I know who you are," Gent said. "You look just like your mother."

"I don't"—Emma gasped—"I don't know what you're talk—"

"Don't deny it," Gent said, drawing her closer.

"Don't . . . *touch* . . . me!" Emma sputtered. There was a ringing in her ears, and she couldn't understand why it was so hard to speak. Her arm was hot with pain. She looked around for her friends. They were thrashing clumsily as beetles crawled over their clothing and skin. "Let me go!" she tried to shout, but her voice came out in a squeak.

"Slurch beetles," Gent explained. "They carry a numbing poison. It won't last long, but if you try to resist, I'll open another vial." She motioned to her other pocket.

Gent's guards seized her and, leaving the others behind, hurried Emma down the dock. She wanted to resist, but every movement was difficult. She finally wrenched herself free and tried to run, but only fell to her knees. The guards hauled her to her feet and dragged her on.

"Tema!" a voice cried from the end of a pier. With great effort of will, Emma turned toward the sound and saw Dr. Vermek climbing out of a longboat. Small green sparks began to pop behind her eyes.

"Look at this," Gent hissed. She grabbed Emma's chin. "Just look at that *face*."

The man locked eyes with Emma. "This is remarkable. I—"

"Get her on the longboat."

Emma blinked madly to clear the sparks from her vision. The beetles' poison wasn't wearing off.

The next few moments went by very fast. Vermek took Emma's arm. Emma lunged forward, blubbering, "No!" Then one of the guards noticed a surprising thing—Gent, who was standing in front of him, was also coming out of the crowd behind him. Confused, he looked back and forth. Gent noticed the commotion and spun to face the woman behind her.

Nisba.

In that moment everything came to a halt. The two women froze. Their mutual stares were so thick with disgust that even the tarantula scurried for cover in the folds of Gent's coat. Emma stared. Nisba had found them, and it couldn't be a coincidence. Maybe the other Arghs were nearby. . . .

"What do you think you're doing?" Nisba said.

"Don't you know?" Gent taunted.

Nisba's face turned an angry red as she glared at her twin. The women seemed locked in an emotional force field, unable to break gazes.

Emma, who had been struggling to stay out of the longboat, suddenly found herself pulled away as Gent snatched her arm. The captain dragged her along and began circling her sister like a lion. The tarantula drew the courage to peek out of her coat, but stayed well within it.

"I always hated being inside your head," Nisba said. "But now it's a particularly disgusting place."

Gent grinned. "Well, I have news for you: it's not *my* head—it's *our* head. You can't just leave because you don't like it."

"Yes, I can," Nisba said. A bead of sweat slid down her nose. "I broke that link long ago."

"Then how did you find me?" Gent gave a cold laugh. "I suppose you intend to stop me?"

"Yes."

Gent drew the pistol from her weapons belt and pointed it at Emma's head. "Try it and I will shoot the girl."

A look of panic crossed Nisba's face.

Emma froze. As she was suspended in a strangely quiet world where things seemed to have slowed to an insect-like crawl, one realization came to her clearly: Nisba had been sneaky indeed. She must have recognized Emma as Halifax's daughter and realized that she might be carrying the Pyxis. And she must have pretended that none of it was true. Because Captain Gent was her twin. Because if Nisba knew it, then Gent would know too. Nisba had been trying to protect Emma.

Gent seemed to have read something in her sister's thoughts, for she turned decisively to Vermek. "Search the girl," she commanded.

"Captain?" he asked.

"Just do it! She's got something on her. Something important enough that my sister would come all this way to make sure I don't find it."

"Don't be foolish!" Nisba snapped. "She doesn't have anything!"

Vermek knelt before Emma and felt her sleeves and shoulders.

"Wait," Emma said, pulling away. "Wait, I'll get it for you."

They looked at her in surprise.

Emma slid a bloodstained hand into her trouser pocket and closed her fist around the jar. It was the one with the bullets and the scupper water inside. Pretending to fumble with all the things in her pocket, Emma secretly unscrewed the jar's lid.

As she removed the jar from her pocket, she looked at Gent. "My mom made me promise never to show this to anybody," she said. "But I guess I don't have a choice. . . ." As quickly as she could without spilling it, she took out the jar and tossed the whole thing at Gent. The memory water hit the captain's face with a splash, and the ruined bullets clattered into her collar.

Instantly, Gent's face went deathly pale. Her eyes jerked open wide and she gasped, stumbling backward. She went as rigid as a board and let out a horrifying scream. It was so loud and startling that it drew the attention of everyone nearby. Even Emma, who dearly wanted to run, couldn't help gawking.

Gent's guards rushed to their captain's side, acting quickly to catch Gent as she tumbled backward and collapsed.

Emma knew this was her chance. Still woozy, she stumbled toward her friends. They were standing in a group, looking disoriented. They seemed to have gotten the last of the beetles out of their clothing, but they were covered in bite marks and bloodstains. Herbie was looking around for Emma.

Emma nearly tripped over Nisba, who was lying in a heap on the ground, just as pale as her sister.

"Herbie, over here!" Emma called. He saw her and motioned to the others.

Nisba was unconscious, but Santher and Herbie managed to hoist her up and carry her between them like a sack of grain. They moved into the crowd, still dizzy from the beetles' poison. Fortunately, there were so many people in the plaza that it was going to be difficult for the navy to find them.

"What happened?" Santher asked.

"I threw the rest of the scupper water on Gent," Emma explained. "And Nisba fell over too."

"You threw the whole *jar*?" Laika gaped.

Emma nodded. "I had to do *something*. She was about to find the . . . uh . . . necklace in my shirt."

"Oh." Laika nodded. "Good thinking."

"We've got to get to the *Markab*," Emma said, checking nervously over her shoulder to make sure that no one was following them. They were hauling Nisba along as best they could, but they were getting some curious stares.

A shot rang out, and everyone ducked.

"They're over here!" someone shouted.

They began to run, but it was difficult with Nisba's limp body. Emma prayed furiously that the navy hadn't found the boat, that they weren't waiting at the dock. More scupper fire whizzed past as they ran alongside a giant catamaran and headed down the pier.

It was quiet there, and to their relief, the *Markab* was just where they'd left it. Emma raced ahead. She leapt onto the deck and went straight for the engine, digging in her pocket for the key, shoving it into the ignition, and firing the boat to life. Laika untied the rope and leapt onto the deck just as the others hauled Nisba on board. They set her down by the wheel.

"Hydra fire!" Laika shouted. "Get down!"

Everyone ducked as a shower of scuppers came tearing at the boat. Raising her head long enough to check that the coast was clear, Emma gunned the engine, and the *Markab* went shooting out of its slip. She spun the wheel to turn toward the harbor just as another round of scuppers hit the boat. Emma looked back and saw a navy sailor on the pier aiming a giant, nine-headed Hydra rifle at the *Markab*. It could shoot plenty of bullets into the air, but they didn't go very far. The next spray fell short of the boat.

"I think we'd better head to the vostok bridge!" Santher said.

"Wait, no! We have to get my mom!" Emma cried.

"We don't know what ship she's on!"

Desperately Emma scanned the harbor around them. There were hundreds of ships, and she had no idea where to start.

The *Markab*'s engine sputtered and gave out. They'd been low on gas since arriving on Delphinus, and now it seemed it was finally gone.

"I'm letting out the sails!" Herbie said. Laika scrambled to help.

Santher, who was standing at the stern and watching the navy activity behind them, cried out, "We're going to need more than sails to get out of this!" Both Emma and Herbie spun around. "They're sending a bunch of Muscan junks our way. Those are flying ships. They'll be on us any moment." He raced forward. "We've got to get her in the air."

"No!" Emma said. "If we fly, we'll never find Gent's ship!"

"We certainly won't find it from a navy prison!" Santher cried, starting up the generator.

Behind them, the Muscan junks were taking flight.

While Santher pumped the generator, Herbie and Laika unleashed the wing masts, extending them wide. The wings began flapping, and with a few great strokes, the *Markab* lifted into the sky.

The *Markab* was a remarkable flyer. It zipped over the harbor and reached the vostok bridge before the Muscan junks could catch it.

Emma looked at her friends and felt an overwhelming urge

to shout: "*WE HAVE TO GO BACK! I'm not going to let her die!*" But the junks were still close behind. There were three of them, each with black sails puffed out like an insect's carapace. Light in the air, their wing masts drove them swiftly ahead. Their bulging fore windows stared directly at the *Markab* like the horrid, immobile eyes of flies. Emma's heart filled with bitter despair. They were going to chase the *Markab* straight out of Pegasus. Soon the whole navy could be coming after them—she could already see more junks alighting—and if they didn't get away now and find a safe place to hide, every ship in the galaxy would be right on their tail.

But down there, somewhere in the harbor full of ships, was Mom.

She turned back to her friends and said in a desperate, quavering voice, "I need to go back. I'll go by myself."

"We can't let you off now," Santher said.

"They've noticed us," Laika said, looking grim. "I know this is horrible, but you've got the Pyxis. If you go back there and they catch you, the Queen will have everything."

Even as her heart roared in furious resentment, Emma knew they were right. There was no way to go back, and she had to protect the Pyxis.

The winds were stronger up here. Santher was pumping the generator so hard he was sweating. Laika was straining to keep hold of the wheel, and even Herbie was adjusting sails, despite his obvious queasiness with flying. Emma watched it all in disbelief, the thoughts in her head surrounded by a great, impenetrable wall of agony.

A cannon shot shook the *Markab.*

"They're firing!" Santher shouted.

"Guys," Laika said, "we have to get to the *Argh.* It has to be nearby. Nisba is injured—and the *Markab* is too small to fight this many ships!"

Emma turned from Fairfoot just in time to catch a vostok stone that Herbie tossed at her. Behind him was the vostok bridge, so large that it startled her. They were barely fifty yards away. Through the bridge's thin screen, they could see the bright-blue waters of the Strand. There was a ship dead ahead.

"Eat the vostok!" Herbie called. Reluctantly, she slid it into her mouth. As the jelly coated her skin, she could hear the muffled sounds of shouting above the wind.

"I think that's the *Argh*!" Laika said. "But it's moving away from us!"

"What do we do now?" Herbie cried.

"Get to the ship as fast as possible—they'll be waiting for Nisba, but they've probably seen us and they think we're the navy!"

"Yeah, but I mean how are we going to *land*?"

"They'd better have the cargo door open!" Santher exclaimed.

With a *whoomph,* the *Markab* plunged through the bridge.

CHAPTER 24

Dragon-of-War

The *Argh* was straight ahead, and they flew madly toward it, the Muscan junks getting closer every second. One of them had nearly come in range of the *Markab*'s stern.

"Can't this thing fly any faster?" Herbie cried.

Emma had taken over the wheel, and Herbie was helping Santher with the generator. Scupper shots rang out and everyone ducked.

"The cargo door's not open!" Laika cried, pointing ahead at the *Argh*.

"Can we hail them?" Emma shouted.

"They see us!" she shouted back. "If the cargo door isn't open in sixty seconds, we'll have to land on the top deck!"

"The *top deck*?" Herbie screeched. "We'll kill everyone!"

Arghs spun about in confusion as the *Markab* approached. People shouted and quickly ran for cover.

"Clear the deck!" Laika screamed below.

The boat crested the *Argh*'s railing and slammed into the deck. The reverberations knocked Emma off her feet as the *Markab* crashed and crunched and slid inexorably forward, tearing a massive gouge in the wood. It tilted, creaking, and a wing snapped off before it finally ground to a halt just a few feet short of the forward mast. It gave a last groan and fell to the side, its mast smashing into the railing with a terrible splintering of wood.

Just behind them, a powerful boom sent up a cloud of choking black smoke. The Muscans were firing their cannons at the *Argh.*

Emma and Laika had managed to hold on to the wheel, and Nisba had been buffered between the benches, but Herbie and Santher had gone skidding down the stairs and into the cabin. Emma and Laika scrambled to their feet just as Herbie and Santher climbed up through a broken window.

"Hurry, those junks are coming back!" Laika shouted.

"What about Nisba?" Emma asked.

"We'll need some help to get her down!"

The four of them stumbled and slid off the *Markab* and onto the *Argh,* taking cover behind some barrels just as the Muscans swooped in for another pass. The small ships pounded the *Argh*'s port side with cannons. Explosions hit the railings and the hull, rocking the ship and sending up thick, lethal clouds of smoke. Screams came from below.

They ran down the deck, heading for the command room. Just as they reached the gallery deck, Lovesey burst through the command room door, shouting, "Arghs, prepare to fly!"

"We can't, sir!" someone shouted. "The port wing sails were damaged in the last pass!"

"Well, get them fixed! *Now!*"

Three Arghs raced off to do his bidding.

"Where's Nisba?" Lovesey barked.

"She's still on the *Markab,*" Laika said. "She's unconscious, and we couldn't get her down. . . ."

Lovesey shouted at more Arghs to get Nisba off the *Markab* and take her below. Laika and Santher ran back to assist. "What happened to Nisba?" Lovesey asked.

"I threw memory water in her sister's face," Emma said.

Stricken by this, Lovesey went running toward the *Markab,* but Mouncey stopped him.

"Sir," he screeched from the command room window, "the Muscans are back! And six more ships have just come through the vostok bridge!"

Lovesey rushed to the railing and leaned over. "How long until the wing is fixed?" he shouted.

The squawking of a dozen monkeys came up from the side.

"That's too long!" he shouted back.

Another gaggle of squawks conveyed a mutual panic.

All was chaos as another troop of worker monkeys raced up the stairs. They carried canvas and ropes, and scurried over the railing and down to the port wing. Above, there was a screech, and Emma and Herbie looked up just in time to see half a dozen eagles leaving the aerie, each clutching a canvas sack in their talons. They dove ferociously, their bodies as sharp and rigid as metal projectiles. As soon as they got within range of the Muscan junks, they released their sacks, and the cannonballs fell, hitting the black ships violently. One cannonball landed in the center of a mast, cracking it clean in half. The junk tipped and began falling out of the sky. The Arghs let up a cheer.

"Garton, Yee," Lovesey barked, "take cover somewhere!"

Emma and Herbie ran to the gallery deck and flew into the stairwell. Going down would take them to the dining hall and their old rooms; going up would lead them to the command room.

The minute they were inside, Emma turned to Herbie. "Are you okay?" she asked breathlessly.

"Yeah," he said. He was still covered in wounds from where Gent's bugs had bit him, and bloodstains were beginning to dry on his sleeves and collar, but he didn't seem too banged up from the crash. "I'm all right. I'm sorry we didn't get your mom."

Suddenly they heard a shrieking. *"Navy!"* It sounded like Nelson, the spyglass. *"Navy ahead!"*

Emma and Herbie rushed up the stairs. They found the command room door open, so they went inside. It was a large space with windows all around and cubbies above, each filled with scrolled maps. In the center of the room was an enormous table, also covered in maps. Mouncey was at the wheel, and Nelson was bobbing frantically by the front window.

"Navy dead ahead!" he shouted.

"I know!" Mouncey cried in annoyance. "I can see too, you know!"

Emma and Herbie went to the window. Just ahead, a fleet of enemy ships was heading straight for the *Argh.* Emma's stomach dropped, and she and Herbie shared a terrified look.

"They're in front of us too?" Emma asked. "I thought all the Queen's navy was back on Pegasus."

"Maybe they were late to the meeting," Herbie said, dry-mouthed.

Lovesey came bursting into the room with Arghs on his heels. He grabbed Nelson and studied the oncoming fleet.

They could make out a Leo vessel, the *Zosma,* a cousin to the *Argh.* Beside it were two Virgo men-of-war, their bowsprits carved with staunch Virgo women, peasant gowns and all. Without wings, they weren't as speedy as the Muscans, but their masts were twice as high, and even from a distance it was possible to see the battery of cannons protruding from their sides.

Poking out of the water was a Cetan vessel, the *Tunsley.* Stout and dark green, it was shaped like a whale with a great square maw and a flat, water-smacking tail. Its rounded hull had a slick, scaly coat, as if barnacles had fastened to parts of its frame. Seaweed seemed to be dripping from its bow.

There was much to fear among the four ships. The Leo and Virgo crafts could blow a few holes in the *Argh.* And the Cetan vessel was solid enough to plow clean through the *Argh,* split her in half, and sink her in a moment.

The captain studied the ships through Nelson while everyone held their breath. "The Virgos have forty-eight guns apiece, the Muscans fourteen," he muttered. "The big one in the center—she's a Leo craft, as big as the *Argh.*" He lowered the spyglass, appearing to be calculating the odds.

"I guess the *Argh* is only safe when it's up against one ship," Herbie whispered in Emma's ear with a squeak. "That's a whole fleet!"

"It's the Cetan ship that's really dangerous, sir," Mouncey said nervously.

Lovesey, who returned to staring through Nelson, said, "Actually . . . she's not the one we need to be worried about. Look behind her."

It took a moment for them to see it, but sliding around the

back of the *Tunsley* was the smallest but deadliest of the ships, the *Darknall.* She was a real dragon-of-war. Like the *Markab,* her spiked beams were red and black. The ship itself was as skinny as a dragon if you took off the wings and the scales and the long, deadly tail. But the sheer size of its rigging made it imposing. There must have been two dozen great sails and twenty smaller ones, all sharp, triangular, and somehow clawlike. At the top, her sails were tilted rearward to resemble the spikes on a dragon's back. With her massive wings, she could lift herself into the sky with lethal speed. Yet the most dangerous part of her was the protruding, snoutlike bow. All her cannons were concentrated there, stacked up in layers like fearsome black teeth. When fired together, they spat out a veritable meteor of fire and steel.

The Queen's colors flew from every ship, announcing their loyalty to Virgo as well as their intentions to capture the *Argh.* Not a soul aboard the *Argh* thought otherwise, but all eyes turned to Lovesey anyway.

"If it weren't for that Draconi craft, I'd say we could take them," Lovesey said. "But that Draconi cannon, she'll be our end."

"What about going to submarines, sir?" Wardle asked.

"We've still got that Cetan craft to contend with. She'll be much stronger than us underwater." Lovesey gritted his teeth. "Damn! Araby, go tell Shucks anyway, make sure he's prepared. And summon more monkeys." Araby went racing out of the room.

"Mouncey, keep a straight course," he said. "Just as soon as that wing is repaired, we're taking to the sky. We don't have a choice." He strode out of the room and left a stunned silence behind. The Arghs' faces were a study of confusion and fear. The captain was taking the fleet head-on? There was a time for bravado, but this wasn't it, not when the odds were so plainly against them.

"What is he *thinking*?" Mouncey asked. "That dragon-of-war can fly twice as fast as we can!"

Emma felt her stomach sink. Everyone was looking at her. She knew what was on their minds—it wasn't every day that the captain would put the whole ship in danger. This was all her fault.

Summoning her nerve, she turned and put her question to Mouncey: "What can I do?"

The wing masts unfolded, stretching outward with terrible slowness and a creaking of wood. Dozens of Arghs scurried onto their frames, unfurling the canvas. The sails gave a round of angry *crack*s as they caught in the wind. Once the Arghs had returned to the deck, six of the biggest Arghs—three of them girls—climbed into the propelling generator, a contraption of gears with a giant wheel at its center. The Arghs pushed the wheel like oxen in a mill. The wings began to flap in slow, heaving motions, up and down, as the deck started to shake.

At first it seemed that nothing more would happen. Looking across the water, Emma saw the Muscan junks joining the rest of the fleet. The Draconi craft alighted to meet them. They were small ships, easy enough to lift into the air. But the *Argh*? It was impossible! The wings beat faster. The whole ship began to shudder. Windows rattled and maps fell from their shelves. The vessel groaned.

"Here we go *again,*" Herbie said, grabbing on to a desk. Emma had to admit she was frightened this time too.

"Batten down!" the captain shouted on deck. "Everyone to the lines!" There were ropes coiled at every corner and curve, beneath every pile of wood, and Emma knew now that they were meant for strapping yourself down. Each line was fixed firmly to a railing or mast, and all the Arghs took a line and strapped themselves to it.

Mouncey held out two lines. "Take them!" he shouted. Emma and Herbie quickly tied the ropes around their waists and pulled themselves to the front windows.

The ship jerked out of the water. Emma sucked in her breath as it began a slow climb, its body turning upward, its wings flapping with more power. Beside her, Herbie muttered a prayer. For a dizzying moment, it seemed that the ship would plunge back into the water, but with an ease that surprised her, the bow nosed upward yet again, and Emma felt the horrible shuddering give way to a sudden lightness. She seized Herbie's arm, but as the ship tipped higher, they both lurched backward.

Desperately, they pulled themselves back to the window. A cannon shot broke the silence, and the *Argh* shook with the force of a blow. Emma could smell the first tang of gunpowder.

The scene below was a messy network of lines and people. Arghs were running about, getting tangled with one another. She saw Laika scrambling to load a cannon.

A Muscan blew past the *Argh*'s bow and shot its guns at her masts in an attempt to push her into the Draconi ship's range. The *Argh* banked to the right to avoid the Muscan. More cannon fire ripped the air. It was coming from below. Judging by the sound, they were Leo cannons.

"Take her higher!" Lovesey called to the bridge. He was roped to the mainmast, red-faced and shouting. "Get her out of the *Zosma*'s range!"

Mouncey tilted the wheel back and they went higher. Emma watched the Muscans follow. The *Argh* was at a terrible disadvantage. She was a gigantic ship. She couldn't swing around half as quickly as the dragon-of-war, and with the Muscans closing in, she was a sitting duck. A cannon shot hit the stern. A terrible crunching of wood was met by shouting and a horrified scream. Smoke began to fill the command room. In the alarm, the *Argh* faltered and fell right into the Draconi ship's sights.

The *Darknall* was athwartships, heading straight for their port side. Mouncey tried to maneuver, but cannon fire sprang from the Draconi ship's muzzle like a belch. Twenty square feet of fire and metal hit the *Argh*'s mainmast dead on and blew it in half. The monolithic mast splintered with a sound like thunder and came crashing down, all thousand pounds of wood and iron. It fell to the port side, cutting through the top deck as if it were cake and barely missing the wing before sliding over the side. Emma thought of all the birds. Had they been in the aerie when it fell?

She had no time to consider, for a second later the command room windows exploded inward, showering everyone with glass. One whole corner of the room was torn away. Emma would never know if the explosion was from the *Darknall* or if it had come from a Muscan cannon shot. She felt a shock wave and fell over, tumbling through splintered wood and broken glass.

The ship was off balance, falling forward and to starboard. The *Argh*'s wings were still flapping in long, sure strokes as it struggled to right itself. The ship was roaring, faster than she'd ever gone on the water. Emma groaned and forced herself to stand up. She couldn't seem to focus on anything, so she kept her eyes on Herbie, who was getting up beside her.

The command room's wooden wall had been blown away, and the wind was pouring in freely now, whipping the charts out of their cubbies. Paper was flying wildly about.

Mouncey was the only other person on the bridge. His face and clothing were blackened, and his shoulder was bloody where shattered glass had torn his neck and arm. The look in his eyes was one of pure determination. The Draconi ship was a good distance behind them. Emma could see its black wings whipping furiously.

"Where's Lovesey?" Herbie cried.

"I don't know!" Mouncey said over the wind. "Everyone got blown to the deck. Look there. The captain's down!"

"What's happening?" Emma asked.

"We're outrunning them!" Mouncey replied. "The Muscans don't have the wing power to keep up with us, but that dragon-of-war is still behind."

Emma spun around. The *Darknall* was indeed coming closer.

"Check the atlas!" Mouncey shouted. "We're supposed to be heading toward Pisces, but it doesn't look right! I'm afraid we took the wrong Strand!"

Herbie and Emma scrabbled through the books on the floor, looking for the atlas. Most Strands were marked with their name and destination painted on a large wooden buoy. They had probably missed the buoy sometime during the battle, and now they had no way of knowing what Strand they were on without consulting the book.

Herbie seized the atlas and set it on the table. Emma helped him find Pegasus, and they held down the pages to read.

"Look for any Strand that has black and gray islands to the port side!" Mouncey shouted. "And dark-blue waters. And fat pelicans!"

"Black and gray islands to the port side. Dark-blue waters. Fat pelicans," Herbie said. They flipped the pages until they found it. Herbie looked up. "It says this is the Strand to Orion. We're heading toward Rigel."

"What?" Mouncey spun around, his knuckles white on the wheel. "That means we're heading straight for the navy blockade!"

There was a roar behind them, and they saw that the dragon-of-war was in firing range. Mouncey jerked the wheel again. The *Argh* lurched, dropping altitude and rising again as it tried desperately to get the *Darknall* off its tail.

"There's more navy ahead?" Herbie exclaimed.

"Yes!" Mouncey screeched. "The biggest fleet in the galaxy! We'll never make it through there!"

"What kind of ships are they?" Emma asked, coming closer.

"Virgo men-of-war and Leos!"

"Any flying ships?"

Mouncey's expression was one of frozen fear. "I don't know!" he said. "No one in their right mind would ever go there!"

He brought the ship higher, and the *Darknall* quickly followed.

"It looks like there are no exits on this Strand," Herbie said. "Shouldn't we turn around?"

"We can't—not with that dragon-of-war behind us!"

"Well, we have some time before we get to the blockade," Herbie said. "This is a very long Strand!"

"It goes ten times faster when you're flying!" Mouncey said, his voice cracking.

In fact, they could see the navy blockade up ahead. It was a terrifying sight. Large buildings had been set on floating docks, and ships were stationed around them all. There were dozens of vessels at the first row of buildings alone. As Mouncey had anticipated, they were mostly Virgo men-of-war and Leo craft. The blockade extended as far as the eye could see. There were hundreds of vessels laid out for miles.

"Can they reach us with their cannons?" Emma asked.

Mouncey shook his head. "We're too high! But keep an eye out for Draconi ships. . . ."

Herbie, who had been looking back anxiously at the *Darknall,* said, "Guys, I think they're about to fire!"

Behind them, the dragon-of-war gave a screech as its cannons shifted into place.

"Mouncey!" Emma cried. "If we make it through the navy blockade, then won't we be in . . ."

"Yes, Eridanus!" He banked so sharply to port that Emma fell against the wall. She quickly scrambled back up. Mouncey was turning back and forth, trying to see the *Darknall* and steer the ship at the same time. The *Argh*'s wings flapped harder. Emma felt it surge forward, desperate to outrun the small dragon-of-war.

When she looked forward again, she got a shock. About one mile ahead, two enormous metal poles stuck up out of the Strand. Between the poles hung a gigantic piece of netting that was clearly designed to stop flying ships from entering Eridanean waters.

"Mouncey!" she shrieked. "Look out!"

He saw it and jerked the wheel back, desperately nosing the

Argh upward. The ship was flying so fast that they reached the netting much more quickly than anticipated. Emma couldn't see how they'd be able to avoid it. Up close, she got another shock. It wasn't netting—it was metal. Enormous chain mail. Hitting any part of it would destroy the ship.

The *Darknall* hissed and screeched again.

Mouncey pushed the *Argh* upward. From beneath, they heard a terrible crunching of wood as the *Argh*'s lower hull hit the metal.

"They're firing!" Herbie shrieked.

Emma spun and stared straight into the *Darknall*'s maw.

The Draconi ship fired. The explosion—so close this time—seemed to blow straight through her head. She heard nothing after that—not the screaming of the wind, not the groaning of the *Argh,* not the distant cries of the crew below. She could only feel the strange sensation of falling. . . .

CHAPTER 25

Fluvius Eridanus

The wind was still blowing, but everything else on the *Argh* was eerily quiet as Emma lifted herself off the floor. She coughed, choking on the pungent smell of burning wood and smoke. Herbie was climbing to his feet near the table. She went over to him.

"Are you okay?" she said over the wind.

He gave a dry laugh, wiping blood from his arm. "Once again, I am okay. . . ."

Mouncey was still clinging to the wheel. His shirt had been torn off and his back was speckled with blood, but he had managed to keep the *Argh* up. Emma looked out at the deck and caught sight of the starboard wing. Its tip was torn off, and the rest was cracked and smoking.

"The wing!" she cried.

"It got hit by the Draconi cannons," Mouncey croaked. "She can't fly anymore. We have to set her down."

"Where's the dragon-of-war?" Herbie asked.

"She hit the netting," Mouncey said. "Crashed into pieces!"

The wind was softening as they descended. The wing workers had realized that the starboard wing was disabled, and they had stopped the wings from flapping. Now the great ship was gliding. From what they could see below, the Strand was empty of buildings and ships. They'd left the blockade behind, and around them was a great sea of green, brackish water dotted with islands in the distance, and beyond that—darkness.

"Shouldn't we land before we get to all those islands?" Emma asked.

"We have to get as far as we can," Mouncey said. "The navy will be coming after us."

"But it's getting dark!"

Santher came barreling onto the bridge, looking panicked. His face was scratched and smoke-blackened. "You can't put her down!" he cried. "We've got a hole in the hull large enough to sink us!"

"We're landing," Mouncey snapped. "We have no choice."

"But we'll start taking in water," he said. "*Eridanean* water! *Memory water!* Do you know what that means?"

"We'll probably get past those islands," Mouncey said. "But we can't land in darkness. There are too many islands, and I won't be able to see."

"He's right," Nisba said, appearing in the doorway behind them. "We have no choice but to land." They all turned to her. She was still deathly pale, and she moved terribly slowly, as if every gesture was painful. "Set us down in the light. And don't hit the rocks. She's already got enough holes in her."

Only the wind made a noise as everyone looked nervously out the broken windows, watching the waters of the Strand get closer.

"Santher, come with me," Nisba said. "We've got to help land this thing."

They went down to the deck. Emma watched them tie themselves to lines on either side of the bow. The ship was very close to the water now. All Arghs who could stand were holding tightly to their lines and hunkering down away from the railings. Santher waved an all-clear sign and shouted, "She's about to touch down! *Three ... two ... one!*"

The *Argh* hit the water with a terrific shudder that rattled Emma's skull and shattered the remaining glass in the windows. Water sprayed out behind them in an enormous jet as they skimmed along the Strand, slowing one painful second at a time.

As soon as the ship came to a halt, the crew burst into action. Santher ran toward the stairs, shouting for all able-bodied Arghs to follow him. He took them downstairs to seal up the ship's lower decks. Nisba gathered a group of monkeys to fold up the wing masts and set out the sails on the remaining masts. There wasn't much wind, but if they sat still for too long, they would surely get captured by the navy.

The *Argh* sailed ahead, its crew crouched behind railing poles, nervously scanning the waters around them for any sign of the navy. Aside from the wind, the Strand was strangely quiet. The Eridanean air was warm and close, and it stank of the repulsive elements of the sea: black kelp, rotten fish, and stagnant brine. A thin fog lingered all around them. There were so many islands that they formed an unbroken chain on either side of the ship.

Their shores were dark and craggy, like prehistoric figures rising from the mist. If there were ships here, they were well hidden in the islands' many coves and inlets.

After having their wounds bandaged in the infirmary, Emma and Herbie had gone straight up to the *Markab.* It was still on the top deck, lying on its side like a beached whale. It was a heartbreaking mess. All the sails were torn, the captain's wheel had come off, and there was a split in the hull. During the *Argh*'s flight from Pegasus, the *Markab* had slid even farther down the deck, tearing off one whole wing mast and snapping the main.

Emma tried not to cry as she surveyed the damage. She and Herbie climbed into the cabin and looked around. The captain's desk had come out of the wall, there was glass everywhere from the broken windows, and bilgewater had spilled into the room, creating a horrible stench. Every new injury she discovered filled her with an even stronger despair—one more thing they would have to fix before they could even think of setting off again to find Mom. Restoring the *Markab* would take a week at best, and that was only if Santher and the monkeys could work on it full-time like they had before. Right now, they were busy repairing the hole in the *Argh*'s hull.

When she saw Dad's binoculars broken in half, Emma snapped.

"This is all because of the stupid Pyxis!" she said. "What's the stupid Queen going to do with it, anyway?"

"Oh, I don't know," Herbie said. "Maybe just have ultimate power over the galaxy. I really don't think we should be worried too much."

"It's not funny!"

Herbie looked at her as if she'd lost her mind, then said very carefully, "Your mom thought the Queen was greedy and cruel. She gave up a lot to keep the Pyxis away from her."

"I know," Emma squeaked, her anger abruptly turning back to despair. She could vividly remember how defiant Mom was when Dr. Vermek forced the grisslin up her nose. Mom had proved herself willing to give up anything—her own safety, maybe even her own life—to keep the Pyxis out of the wrong hands. Emma could never betray that. The very thought of it brought tears to her eyes, and her lip began to tremble. "But I have to get her back, and the only way I can is to fix the *Markab*."

Herbie looked grim. "We're going to get it fixed, just like we did last time."

"But it's going to take too long," she said. "And you heard that guy in the infirmary—they're using all the extra wood to repair the *Argh*."

"Yeah," Herbie said quietly.

A few minutes later, the dinner bell rang. Herbie coaxed Emma out of the boat. She followed him to the dining hall, wiping angry tears from her cheeks. They ate in glum silence. The room was only half-full, and all that was on their plates was a strip of dried fish and a slice of stale tack. Herbie offered his to Emma, but she declined.

After dinner, Emma wanted to go back to her room, but Herbie said it would be better to stay on the *Argh*'s upper levels, preferably near one of the life rafts.

"Things could get all *Titanic*," he said. "We'd better wait until they repair the hull."

Emma was beginning to feel resigned and helpless, so she

followed him topside. Most of the Arghs were huddled in their own corners on the deck. The Strand around them was unusually quiet. Without her mainmast, the *Argh* was slower than ever, and the wind that had pushed them away from Rigel had now dwindled to a teasing whisper.

A few lights were on in the command room and they could hear the murmurs of conversation. Curious, Herbie went closer. Emma followed him onto the gallery deck and up the stairs.

The command room door was shut, so they stood for a moment, staring nervously at the carved lion on the giant oak door.

"Maybe we shouldn't bother them," Emma said.

That moment, the captain emerged, nearly running them down. "Oh!" he exclaimed. "Garton. Yee. Glad you're on your feet. I was just coming to get you. We need to discuss what to do about your boat. We might need some of your wood."

This made Emma's throat tight. Numbly, they followed Lovesey into the command room.

The bridge was dark except for a pair of lanterns flickering over the large wooden table in the center of the room. Mouncey was seated there, studying a chaos of maps. Someone had tidied up, and most of the maps were back in their cubbies.

No sooner had Herbie and Emma walked in than Nisba arrived with Laika and Santher on her heels, and Nelson bobbing anxiously beside them. Lovesey looked a bit discomposed as he shut the door and asked for an update.

In short order they learned that the infirmary was out of medicine and bandages, and that the kitchen was down to its last sack of dried fish and a single barrel of water. The hole in the hull had not been fully repaired, since part of it was below the waterline. The ship's Pisces scales were not enough to protect it from the dangerous Eridanean water that was sloshing in. And although the birds had not been in the aerie when the mast had tumbled over the side, Laika was still upset.

"Two of them came back," she said, eyes glistening with tears. "Kipple and Corsar. Corsar's the eagle. I sent him behind to keep an eye out for navy ships. The navy hasn't come after us yet."

Mouncey looked perplexed. "That's odd," he said.

"Not really," Lovesey remarked. "They're just as afraid of these waters as we are."

"Then we should pull up behind one of these islands," Laika said. "We can hide the *Argh* and wait for the rest of the birds to come back."

"Just because we haven't spotted the navy yet doesn't mean they're not coming," Mouncey replied. "If we stop, we'll be sitting ducks."

Laika frowned. "Why haven't we found any pirates yet?"

"Not with the pirates again!" Mouncey moaned.

An awkward silence filled the room.

"Our first concern right now is what's going to happen to the ship," Lovesey said.

"Because of the waters, sir?" Santher said.

"Yes. The hole in the hull is not our biggest problem." Seeing Emma's and Herbie's confusion, Lovesey explained, "The memory seas give things strange properties. Like scuppers. They're soaked in memory water: it's what makes them work. Memory water is great for nets and smaller things, but when something big like the *Argh* gets sopped . . ."

As if she had heard his remark, the ship beneath them gave a monstrous groan. Then she rumbled like thunder before giving an earthquake-like jolt. It was as if the ship had just stretched out her neck.

"You mean," Herbie said, "the ship is coming *alive*?"

No one could sleep that night. The Arghs were terrified that the ship would sink and they'd drown in the deadly waters of Eridanus. They were just as scared that the ship would come alive, now that it had taken on so much memory water. They'd heard stories about what happened when ships came to life, in particular how they always seemed to turn on their crew and start killing people. A dropped ceiling, a quick toss out a window . . . who knew what the *Argh* would do?

When the crab watch began, news spread that the largest hole had been mostly sealed. There was some question whether the repairs would hold, but for now, the ship wasn't taking in any new water. Lovesey made all the Arghs go to their rooms to sleep.

Lying in bed, Emma couldn't sleep. She kept reliving the horror of the Arghs being hit by shrapnel and scuppers and cannon fire. She imagined the ship sinking with more than a hundred souls on board, all of them screaming for rescue. Visions flashed through her mind of Mom being thrown into the memory seas and drowning, of Mom being shoved into a dank, dark cell. When Emma remembered the way Mom thrashed when the nasty little grisslin had climbed into her nose, her heart wrenched open with the most exquisite pain. As the visions grew stronger, she even began to hear voices. They might have been from a dream.

"She died here, she did."

"Evil people enjoy lying. It's what they do."

"Halifax was a liar, and a very good one."

She tried ignoring them, but they wouldn't go away, so she pressed her hands to her ears, buried her face beneath the pillow, and began humming to herself. It worked for a while, and she fell into a restless sleep. . . .

✦ ✦ ✦

She woke a few hours later to a terrific roar. She scrambled out of bed and met Herbie in the hallway. The noise sounded again—the angry roar of a lion. They rushed topside and saw Arghs gathered at the bow.

Pushing through the crowd, Emma and Herbie stuck their heads through the railing and saw that the lion on the bowsprit was moving. The great wooden creature had come alive in the night. He was still attached to the bow but squirming uncomfortably to get free, growling and lashing out with his paws. One swipe over his head sent the Arghs scrambling backward in a panic.

Behind them, the captain's voice called for attention.

"Arghs!" he boomed. "It's time I called a general announcement. And give me my hat." Mouncey hurried to assist.

Even though it was the dark of night, the water around them gave off a greenish glow. There was very little wind, and the *Argh* inched along, stirring nothing but the occasional cry of a gull or the splash of an eel. Once the crew had assembled, Lovesey spoke.

"As most of you know," he said, "the memory seas are deadly. While we are here, you must treat the water like poison and keep on board at all costs. If something falls overboard, it will be left behind. *No exceptions.*"

The Arghs stood listening with grim faces.

"If it rains," Lovesey went on, "I expect everyone to go below and stay there until it stops. The rain won't hurt you unless you stay in it for longer than a few hours, but we're not taking any chances. Because of water contamination, no one is allowed on the lowest two decks."

"What about food?" someone asked.

"I'm sorry to say that we'll be on dried-fish rations until we can find a food source," Lovesey said. "As you might have guessed, we can't eat the fish from these waters either. You've handled yourselves very bravely these past few days, and I need you to keep doing so.

"Also, you may have noticed that our bow figure has awakened," Lovesey went on. "For that reason, I'd like everyone to stay away from the bow."

Laika was wringing her hands. "Yes, Leashingwell?" Lovesey asked.

"I'm sorry, sir. I sent Kipple forward to scout for pirates, and now I'm afraid he won't come back, what with the lion roaring and all. Do you think we could do something to make him a bit . . . quieter?"

Lovesey reflected. "I'm afraid that lions are rather loud when they're hungry. Perhaps we should feed him."

"But we don't have enough food for ourselves," someone said miserably.

"Yes," Lovesey said. "Well, bow lions don't eat human food, do they?" He walked toward the bow and peered over curiously. "I suspect he only eats monkeys and children."

A few of the younger Arghs looked startled.

"But since we're not going to give him any of those yet," Lovesey said, "why don't we give him some sawdust instead? That should fill his stomach."

Herbie made a disgusted face.

"Yee, do you have something to say to that?"

"No, sir," Herbie replied.

"Mouncey, gather a group to get some food for our lion. And, Leashingwell, since you're so good with animals, would you please come up with a name for our newest Argh?" He motioned to the bow with a wave. And with that, he left.

Silence fell. The lion had stopped roaring. They walked to the railing and peered over at him. Like an unhappy baby, he hung there, frowning.

"I think we should call him Crowler," Laika whispered. "Because all he does is crowl."

"Crowl?" Herbie asked.

She made a long *HA-WOOOOOO* sound, and the lion crowled again.

Suddenly they heard a faint splash and looked up. A black silhouette was emerging from the blanket of fog ahead. It was a small rowboat.

"Quiet," Laika whispered. They all crouched behind the railing.

There was no one in the boat, but the oars were rowing rhythmically, rising and falling like the legs of some grotesque insect.

Emma's heart was pounding. She heard more splashing and turned to see three more rowboats approaching from the side, all of them empty.

"Oh no," Herbie squeaked. "They're alive!"

The lion crowled again, and the rowboats came closer.

Emma leaned carefully over the bow railing. "I think they're trying to communicate with Crowler."

"You mean, they're swarming?" Herbie shuddered.

They did seem to be drawn to the noise, and when Crowler stopped moaning, the rowboats lost interest and sailed back into the fog.

✦ ✦ ✦

Emma and Herbie weren't tired anymore, so they went to the *Markab*'s side and sat down. Herbie was strangely quiet.

Emma regarded the bandages on his arms. He had twice as many as she did, although perhaps that was because he had insisted that the nurses cover every single scratch.

"I'm sorry you got bit by all those bugs too," she said.

"Yeah." He shrugged. "Captain Gent can suck it. But listen, when I was lying in bed, I was thinking about everything that happened since we left Earth. Mostly my parents, like they have no idea what happened to me. They probably think I was kidnapped."

"You kind of were."

"Totally. But I started wondering what happened to Caz and Laine, and I came up with a weird theory." He sat up now. "Remember when Gent was talking to the Queen and she looked all guilty?"

"Yeah," Emma said. "But don't you think that's because she's, like, a total loser?"

"Yeah. But I was thinking: Gent captured Caz and Laine, so she must have captured the fake Pyxis too."

Emma sat up. "You're right. I forgot about that!"

"If it's true," Herbie said, "then Gent has had the fake Pyxis this whole time, and she probably thinks she has the real one. I mean—think about it—the Queen called a whole meeting for every system just to ask them to help her find the Pyxis, and Gent strolls right in and doesn't give it up."

"She's going to use it herself!" Emma said.

"But she can't," Herbie said. "Because it's a fake."

Emma's eyes opened wide. "Herbie, this gives me an idea."

"What?"

"We have to contact Gent."

He snorted. "And say what—we have the real Pyxis?"

"No. We're going to tell her that we know she has the Pyxis, and we're going to tell the Queen about it unless she gives me my mom back."

"So—the snitch strategy?"

"Yeah."

"But you know she's going to laugh at you. Why would she believe you?"

"We tell Gent that I was the one who activated the Pyxis. And if she doesn't give my mom back, I'll activate it while she still has it, and the Queen will find out exactly where it is."

Herbie looked surprised. "Okay, I take that back. That's a smoking gun, cowgirl. But you have to be holding the Pyxis to activate it."

"Gent probably doesn't know that. Only my mom knew that."

Herbie narrowed his eyes appreciatively. "Maybe you're right," he said. "This is not a bad plan."

She smiled. "There's just one problem. How do we talk to Gent?"

"That's obvious." Herbie blinked at her. "Nisba!"

She let out a yelp and punched his arm gleefully. "You rock it, cowboy!"

CHAPTER 26

A Prick on the Skin

They found Nisba in the kitchen. She was standing at a counter, chopping the last of the dried-out bread. There were no monkeys and none of the typical activity they'd seen before, just Nisba angrily bludgeoning sea biscuits.

When she saw them, she stopped her knife in midair. "I know why you're here," she said, "and I don't have any information about your mother."

Emma strode up to her. "That's okay," she said. "We need to know where your sister is."

Slowly, Nisba lowered her knife and said, "She's on her ship. Why?"

"Where's her ship?"

"Why are you—?"

"Just tell me. Please? I want to know where her ship is headed."

"She's coming here," Nisba said.

"Eridanus? Why?" Herbie asked.

"To chase us, I presume. I didn't look too deeply into the subject! Now, what is this about?"

Emma glanced at Herbie for support. "I know this might be too much to ask, but . . . I really, really need to talk to your sister."

"What do you want?"

"I want to give myself up in exchange for my mother."

Nisba snorted and turned to face them, crossing her arms. "Why do you think I would let you do that?"

"Because your sister needs me. She has the Pyxis. But she can't activate it. And I can. My mom taught me how."

Nisba fell silent.

"You don't believe me?" Emma asked.

"I do believe you, and that's the problem. You shouldn't have told me that. Now my sister can access that information." Nisba took a deep breath and leaned against the counter. "I've known for a while now that my sister is frustrated because she can't start the Pyxis. But she shouldn't have it. And if she does figure out how to activate it, she'll be just as dangerous as the Queen. Maybe more so." Nisba looked at her kindly. "I'm sorry, Emma. I know your mother is dying. But this was something she was willing to die for. She would do anything—including dying—to keep the Pyxis away from the Queen and from people like my sister."

"But Gent's never going to start the Pyxis," Emma said quickly.

"How do you know that?"

"I can't tell you," Emma said, biting her lip, "because then your sister will know. You just have to trust me—she'll never be able to start it without me."

Nisba reflected on this. "You're right," she said with a sigh. "I shouldn't know anything. My sister will find out. I don't know how, but she does every time."

"Then will you help us?" Emma asked. "We just need to find some way to talk to her."

"No," she said. "I'm sorry, Emma. I'm with your mom on this one. I can't let you get close to my sister if you know how to activate it. She can never find out."

"I won't tell her," Emma said. "I promise that. I'm going to tell your sister that I know how to activate the Pyxis, and if she doesn't give my mom back, I'll activate it while she has it."

Nisba considered this. "That's not a bad idea."

"If I activate it, the whole navy will go after your sister," Emma said.

"But how are you going to get your mom back?" Nisba asked. "You're going to have to meet with my sister."

"I know," Emma said. "But I can do that. I have to do it. This may be the last chance I'll ever have to save my mom's life. She's *dying.*"

Nisba studied her, and slowly a look of resignation came over her face. "I guess it doesn't matter," she muttered. "My sister is coming for us. She's going to find you soon enough anyway." Taking a deep breath, she pushed herself off the counter. "All right, I'll help you. But we'd better act fast," she said.

Emma gave a muted *squee* of excitement while Herbie looked surprised.

"Here's what's going to happen," Nisba said. She pulled

open one of the kitchen cabinets, and a dozen parchments came spilling onto the floor. She sorted through them until she found the one she wanted, then kicked the others aside and brought the parchment to the worktable. "To communicate with my sister, I'm going to need a drop of my blood. It's not much, but sometimes this kind of connection is very intense and it knocks me out. Open the parchment."

Herbie unscrolled it while Nisba went back to the counter, yanked open a drawer of kitchen tools, and began clattering through it.

When the parchment was opened, they saw it was a chart of the constellation Eridanus.

"If this does knock me out," Nisba went on, "then I'll probably be out for a while, in which case you're going to have to talk to her on your own."

"We can do that," Emma said.

"But you will not—until you promise to obey these rules."

"Okay," Emma said uncertainly.

"Do not tell her where we are. Do not tell her what happened during the battle or anything about the Strand we're on. Do not arrange to meet with her anywhere near the *Argh.* We're going to find a meeting place on the map."

"Won't she know those things already, since she can read your mind?" Herbie asked.

"I only know we're on Eridanus," Nisba said. "I don't know specifics. Why do you think I spend all my time down here in the kitchen?"

She found what she was looking for—a hunting knife, black and shiny like a beetle's shell. Its handle was shaped like a scorpion's tail. She brought it to the table along with a small hand mirror, which she propped against a dish. Drawing up a chair, she sat down and rolled up her sleeve.

"Now we're going to find a meeting place, and you'll tell her to go there alone," Nisba said. "Tell her I will be coming with you, so I will know if she is truly alone. And don't you dare leave this ship until I regain consciousness—is that clear?"

They both nodded vigorously.

Nisba surveyed the tools before her and said, "There's just one more thing we need. Memory water."

"Oh no." Emma slumped. "I splashed the last of it on your sister. I'm sorry about that, by the way."

Nisba eyed them both with a bit of irritation. "We only need about a cup of water," she said with deliberate slowness.

They both realized their mistake at the same time.

Herbie smacked his forehead. "Right. Okay."

Emma was blushing. "We'll be right back."

They raced topside, grabbed a bucket from the deck, tied a rope to the handle, and lowered the bucket hastily down the side of the ship and into the waters of the Strand below. Although the water sloshed out of the bucket on its journey up the hull, they managed to get a sufficient supply of memory water.

"Careful not to touch it," Herbie said.

"Well, you know, I am kind of thirsty."

Herbie opened his mouth to protest but saw that she was teasing and rolled his eyes. With exquisite care, they made their way back to the kitchen, not spilling a single drop. Nisba was still sitting at the table where they'd left her.

"Good," she said when they set the bucket on the floor. "Come here. Stand beside me. I've found a meeting place." Looking over her shoulder, they saw that she'd unrolled another parchment beneath the chart of Eridanus. The second parchment was blank. "My sister is one day behind us. Her ship doesn't have wings, so she had to transfer to a Draconi vessel. She told the ship's captain that she was on Queen's business, so no one's asking questions. The ship is called the *Hargrim.* It entered Eridanean waters a few hours ago and set down just behind the blockade. They're sailing toward us, but they've just sent out scouts. Birds, from what I can tell, but they're not very good in the dark. They'll be lucky to find us, but there's always the chance they do, so we'd better act quickly."

"Wait," Herbie said. "Where are we supposed to meet your sister?"

"Oh, right." Nisba drew the Eridanus chart closer and pointed to a small inlet on the Strand behind them called Skullax Cove. "I think it's close enough that we can get there in an hour of rowing."

"What about your sister?" Emma asked.

"She's on a Draconi ship. She can get there in minutes."

"But if they're flying, won't they be able to see the *Argh?*" Herbie asked.

"No, not in this darkness. Now, if I faint, I'll be out for an hour or more. Tell Tema you'll meet her in two hours' time. That gives me an hour to come around, and then we have an hour to get there. No matter what you do, don't tell Lovesey about this. He'll try to stop it."

Herbie nodded, but Emma was rather surprised by this. "Why?" she asked.

"Because he'd rather die than put me in danger," Nisba said, a bit grumpily. She picked up the knife and slid the case off, revealing a sharp, glistening blade.

"Uh . . . what are you doing?" Herbie asked, looking a bit sick.

"I just need a few drops of blood," Nisba said. "This knife used to belong to my sister. Anything I can use that can strengthen my connection to her will make this conversation stronger." With a swift, certain slice, Nisba cut her palm. A few drops of blood pooled on her hand and she held it over the table, squeezing the blood onto the parchment. Five drops landed there before she pressed a cloth to the wound.

Nisba looked into the hand mirror and said, "I need to see my sister." She stared at her face, whispering sideways to Emma and Herbie, "The mirror helps me visualize her since she looks just like me."

"Hand me a ladle," she said. Herbie rushed to obey and came back with a serving spoon. With this, Nisba scooped a small quantity of the memory water from the bucket and dribbled it over the blood on the parchment. When the greenish water hit the blood, it turned a deep and cavernous black, spreading across the paper like a gentle wind stirring the sails. It began to cause movement, and soon they could make out shapes. Gaping at the parchment, they saw the first flicker of light.

Emma only noticed how this was affecting Nisba when she started sliding out of her chair. Emma yelped and grabbed her shoulders just in time. With Herbie helping, they managed to lower her gently to the floor. They propped her head on a chopping block and made sure she was breathing before going back to the parchment.

Like paper in a photo-developing solution, the parchment before them slowly resolved into a picture of Captain Gent. They seemed to have a view of her office. It was a small space filled with dark wooden furniture and cluttered with books and cabinets. Gent was sitting at a desk and looking into a jelly jar filled with beetles. On the wall behind her, an apothecary cabinet displayed hundreds of bottles of insects, most of which seemed to be moving so that the wall itself appeared to be alive. Herbie gave a shudder.

Gent picked up the jar. "Time for a bite to eat?" she asked sweetly. Opening the lid just a crack, she stuck her finger inside. Immediately two beetles leapt onto it, scanning her skin with their antennae, trying to decide whether or not to bite. The bigger one made up his mind and dug his pincers into the soft spot on her fingertip. She sucked in her breath, shook him loose, and quickly sealed up the jar. Sitting forward, she shut her eyes and took a deep, languid breath. Her rich red hair tumbled into her face.

Emma and Herbie exchanged a horrified look.

"Do you think she can hear us?" Emma whispered.

At the sound, Gent shot up. She leapt from the desk and came striding toward them. They both took a step back.

When she recognized them, she let out a short cackle. "Well, well," she exclaimed gleefully. "The little Miss Brightstoke and her boyfriend. I was wondering what my sister was up to. I knew she was plotting something."

Herbie gave Emma a sideways look. "Are we, like, on her wall or something?"

"Yes," Gent said. "You are on my wall. You are, in fact, inside my mesmer. And if my mesmer guard notices, she's going to hunt you down and report your location to the Queen, so I suggest you get to the point. I take it you've come to beg for your mother's life."

"No," Emma said crudely. "I came to tell you that I know you have the Pyxis."

Gent kept a steely gaze, but they could tell that the news unsettled her.

"And I know how to activate it," Emma went on. "I was the one who did it two weeks ago, when we were still on Monkey. If you don't believe me, you can ask the sailors of the *Arcturus Venture*."

This name seemed to tighten Gent's face even more.

"I could activate it right now if I wanted to," Emma went on.

Gent's eyes narrowed. "I don't believe you."

"Fine," Emma said. "I'll show you, then." She shut her eyes and pretended to concentrate on starting the Pyxis.

"Wait!" Gent looked furious. "I don't believe you, but I can't take that chance." She drew in her breath and said in a cold voice, "What do you want?"

"My mother," Emma said. "I want her back. Now. And if you don't give her back, then I will activate the Pyxis, and I will make sure that the Queen knows exactly how you lied to her. I will keep activating it until every ship in the galaxy has pinned you in a corner and you won't be able to get away."

Gent now looked suitably enraged. "You can have your mother back," she spat. "And you can try to keep her alive yourself." She said these last words bitterly.

The picture began to dissolve.

Emma looked at Herbie in panic. "It's fading!"

"Maybe we need more memory water." He grabbed the spoon and set another few drops on the parchment, but it didn't help. "We might need more blood," he said.

They both looked at Nisba.

"We can't cut her," Emma said.

"I know you're on Eridanus." Gent's voice came through. "Tell me where you are."

"No way," Herbie said. "We're going to meet you. And you'd better come alone, because Nisba's coming with us, and she'll know if you're lying."

"Where is my sister?"

"None of your business," Emma said. "Meet us in Skullax Cove in two hours. If you don't bring my mother, I'll activate the Pyxis."

"Two hours is too long," Gent said. "We have a Draconi fleet coming, and if they see you, it's all over. Meet me in one hour . . . otherwise, nothing."

Gent faded again. They could still see a vague outline of her form, but the voice was gone.

Emma spun on Herbie. "She said more navy is coming. We have to leave now."

"But we can't," he said. "Nisba won't wake up for another hour."

"Then we have to go without her."

"She said not to do that!" he protested, but Emma was already dashing out of the room. "Emma, wait!" She heard him calling, but she was through the dining hall. In the hallway, he came running up behind her. "We can't DO this," he panted. "Nisba's the only one who will know if Gent is going to meet us alone or not!"

Emma kept up her brisk pace. "You heard what she said—she can't take the chance that I might activate the Pyxis."

"But wait, we—" He stopped abruptly, and she turned around.

"What?" she said.

"We didn't ask for proof that your mom is even alive."

Emma waved her hand. "Of course she's alive."

"You're being very cavalier—"

She cut him off. "She's *alive*."

He could see from her expression that it was pointless to argue.

"Wait—wait—wait!" he said, forcing Emma to stop. "I've got to get something. We're going to need it. Will you promise me you won't leave this ship without me?"

There was such an earnest demand in his eyes that she couldn't help nodding. "Okay," she said.

"You promise?"

"*Yes,* but hurry!"

"Wait!" he said. "One more thing. You have to give me the Pyxis."

She looked dumbfounded. "Why?"

"We can't bring it when we meet Gent. She might get her hands on it. I'll hide it here while you go get a rowboat. I know a good hiding place."

"I don't think that's such—"

"You *have to,*" Herbie said.

She knew he was right. Reluctantly, she slid the Pyxis off her neck and handed it to him. He tucked it into his pocket, and giving her a final look, turned and ran off.

The cargo hold was empty when Emma arrived. She went to the cargo doors and hauled them open, looking down at the waterline. It was not too far to lower a rowboat. With clever use of ropes, they could swing down into the rowboat and they'd be off.

A noise above startled her and she looked up to see Crowler still hanging limply at the bow and muttering to himself. She hadn't realized before how close he was to the cargo doors. Whatever she did, she would have to be quiet about it.

After carefully shutting the doors, she raced around, looking for a suitable rowboat, but there was none. Not so much as a canoe remained in the hold. The Arghs had used every scrap of spare wood to seal up the hole in the ship's hull. Emma grew increasingly frantic as she tossed aside canvases, desperately searching every corner, hoping fervently that something had been left behind.

A renewed bout of despair was just sweeping over her when Herbie arrived with Santher and Laika on his heels.

"We can't go alone," he said, forestalling Emma's protest. "We can't row for an hour all by ourselves. We'll need help."

"Herbie told us everything," Laika said. "We want to come."

Santher noticed Emma's desperate, speechless state and said to everyone, "But there are no more rowboats. We used them all!"

Herbie was horrified.

"What do you mean?" Laika said. "There are plenty of rowboats."

They stared at her in amazement. Laika raced to the cargo doors and pulled them open. "Get me something to throw," she said. Santher came up with a broken hammer. "No, not that! It's too heavy. Something else, like a small stone."

Herbie fished in his backpack and drew out some vostok.

"Perfect!" Laika said. Emma was beginning to understand what Laika had in mind. She went over to the doors just as

Laika tossed the vostok at Crowler. He jolted and opened his eyes, looking around.

"Another one!" Laika said. "I have to keep hitting him." Herbie handed her the whole sack of vostok.

Laika threw another one at Crowler, and he snorted. The third one caused a mewl—and a silent cringe from Laika, who didn't like throwing stones at animals—and by the fourth one he was howling properly again.

It took a few minutes, but soon the rowboats began appearing out of the mist. They came like dolphins, a little shy and mostly curious. Slowly they gathered around the ship's bow, falling alongside the *Argh.* When Crowler made a particularly loud roar, they startled and scattered briefly, but they came back.

"That's brilliant!" Herbie said. Grinning, Santher was already tying up a line they could use to lower themselves into one of the rowboats. Emma went first. She grabbed the rope with both hands and slid carefully into the boat.

"Gentle," Laika warned. "It's alive, you know."

When Emma set her foot on the boat, it gave a small start, but it didn't seem to mind her presence. She motioned the others down. First Herbie came, then Santher, and finally Laika. Once Laika had stopped pelting Crowler with vostok, he settled into an unhappy mewl, and by the time she was in the rowboat, Crowler had fallen into glum silence. The rowboats, seemingly at a loss, began to disperse into the mist around them. Their own rowboat sat nervously by the side of the *Argh.*

"How do we make it move?" Herbie whispered.

Laika was studying the boat, touching its interior walls and wiggling its oars. It didn't seem to be responding. "I think it's kind of like a Pegasus horse," she said. "It's waiting for a command."

"Take us to Skullax Cove," Santher ordered.

The rowboat didn't move. Laika clucked her tongue. "That was too harsh," she said.

"Take us to Skullax Cove, please," Santher said.

Nothing happened.

"I think it needs a gentler touch." Laika ran her hand along the edge of the hull, but the rowboat seemed to find this annoying and it gave a stiff jerk, nearly throwing them overboard. Everyone gasped.

"Take us to Skullax Cove *now,* you sack of maggots!" Santher snapped.

With a gentle whip, the rowboat took off. Everyone stared in surprise as it turned away from the *Argh* and sailed in the direction of Rigel.

CHAPTER 27

The *Maggot*

That was incredible," Herbie said.

He and Emma were sitting at the bow. Emma was finally feeling a little hope—but it was offset by a lot of anxiety. This could be the craziest thing she'd ever done.

"You were so tough with Gent," he went on. "I mean, it was like you were an adult, the way you talked to her."

"Thanks."

"You kind of reminded me of your dad," he said. "A little scary."

Emma managed a half smile. On any other day, the idea would have thrilled her.

"And what the hell with those bugs in Gent's office?" he asked. "Did you see the way she let them bite her, and then she was *enjoying it*? She's like a bug addict."

"She's probably a bug dealer too."

Herbie laughed. "I want a bumper sticker: 'Just say no to bugs.'"

Emma was glad he was talking. They had been sailing for almost an hour, and she kept feeling frantic. Were they going to miss Gent? Would she be there with Mom? Was Mom still alive? Was the rowboat even going in the right direction? It was hard to tell where they were in all the mist, but the occasional island appeared on one side or another, glowing green in the water's eerie luminescence. For every one of these concerns, her friends had given her reassurance. She took comfort from their confidence.

"I think we should give the rowboat a name," Laika said.

"How about *Maggot*?" Santher suggested.

"I like it," Herbie said. Laika rolled her eyes.

The cove came upon them suddenly. There was no sign marking it; the *Maggot* merely slowed and turned into an inlet. Emma figured it resembled the sketch on Nisba's chart of Eridanus, but she was more interested in scanning the coastline for some sign of Captain Gent.

"Is this Skullax?" Herbie whispered. His voice echoed strangely in the still air.

"I don't know." Emma thought she heard a faint *splish* but saw nothing moving.

Their rowboat stopped just as a longboat emerged from the low, thin fog ahead of them. Even from a distance, they could make out Gent's form and detect the sheen of her bright-red hair. A cloaked figure was sitting beside her. Emma watched intently as they drew closer and could just see a narrow bit of blond hair at the front edges of the cloak. She couldn't tell if it was Mom.

"Put your hands in the air," Santher called out. "Or we'll activate the Pyxis."

Gent did as she was told.

"Guys," Herbie said, "I have a bad feeling. That doesn't look like Emma's mo—"

He was about to finish when something whizzed past his head. A small object splintered the hull in front of him.

"Scupper!" Laika cried. The word hit them like a shock. Everyone spun to see a pair of ships coming through the darkness on the port side. They could just make out the Draconi bowsprits, glowing viciously red and fiery. All around them were more rowboats, each filled with navy sailors, each carrying tuskets and pointing them straight at Emma and her friends.

Gent gave a laugh. "It's too bad you didn't bring my sister," she called. "Although I doubt she could have helped you. She's so easily fooled." The cloak of the person beside her dropped away, revealing one of her crew members—a stout man with blond hair. He wore a malicious grin.

In no time at all, the rowboats were upon them, hauling everyone into the Draconi longboats and kicking the *Maggot* to send it back on its way.

Emma felt the boat sway and saw Gent step on board. She came straight to Emma, hauled her to her feet, and pulled her to the stern. The sailors ignored them.

Gent forced her into the seat there and sat across from her, her eyes narrowing wickedly. From her pocket, she removed the fake Pyxis and dangled it in front of Emma's face.

"Start it," she said.

Emma was shocked. "You don't want to do that," she replied. "The whole galaxy will come after you."

"It doesn't matter. We're on Eridanus. The navy won't follow us here, and neither will any mercenary vessels. They're too afraid of these waters."

"Then the pirates are going to find you," Emma said.

Gent gave a snort. "There are no pirates. We killed them all. *Now start it.*"

Emma was panicking now. "You don't want to do this—" Before she could finish, Gent grabbed her arm and pushed her backward so that she fell over the side of the boat. Emma yelped. The only thing preventing her from falling into the water was the firmness of Gent's grip.

"Start it," Gent said.

"I can't," Emma gasped. "I can't start it. I don't know how."

Gent hauled her back into the longboat and dumped her roughly on the floor. "That's what I thought," she said. "But don't worry, you'll come in handy in another way."

Shaking in fright, Emma curled into a ball and let the Draconi sailors begin tying her up.

CHAPTER 28

The Revenge of Artemisia Gent

Emma sat on the top deck of the *Hargrim,* a large Draconi craft. She was shivering violently in her thin tunic. It had begun to rain, great sheets of water slicing like guillotines from the sky. Her hands were tied together with cord, and they were aching. Herbie was beside her, his black hair plastered to the bruises that marred his bleak face. Laika was next to him, looking cold and miserable. They were all in shackles and lashed to the railing poles.

No one knew what had become of Santher. They'd each been thrown into a longboat and brought on board separately. But Santher had never arrived. When Laika tried asking what had happened to him, she got a kick in the leg.

Emma's hair had been cut short by the surgeon's knife. She hadn't cried when the filthy loblolly boy dragged her head over the side of a table and sliced it all off, but it hurt her soul just as if she were a cat whose tail had been chopped off. No one else had lost their locks this evening, and it was obvious why: the captain was going to make an example of her.

Now Emma was wet, cold, and shaking. She kept thinking of Mom. Was she here, on the ship? Was she lying in some dank, cold brig, infected by a squilch and dying?

"Maybe Santher will rescue us," Laika said.

"Laika," Herbie said, "we have to rely on ourselves. Even if he managed to get free, how is he going to rescue us by himself?"

"He may have a plan." But even Laika didn't look hopeful about this.

Emma glanced at Herbie. He was staring at the sailors with a terrible look of disappointment.

"I don't like Draconi ships anymore," he said numbly.

Emma felt tears welling in her eyes and she couldn't seem to stop them. *I've failed everyone,* she thought.

Captain Gent strode onto the deck. She was wearing the overcoat of the Virgo navy. Her head was cloaked against the rain, but they caught a glimpse of her thicket of red hair. She planted herself in front of the mainmast, while behind her a dozen sailors assembled in a half circle, their tuskets pointed at the Arghs.

There was a scuffle at the stairs. She looked over to see two sailors dragging Mom onto the deck. Emma's heart gave a terrific leap—she was alive!

"Mom!" she cried, forcing herself to her feet, shackles clanging. A blow from a tusket butt cut her short, and she fell to the deck. Emma grabbed her head and struggled to sit up again.

They had cut Mom's hair too. Emma had never seen her

look so bad. She was wearing a prison robe, which hung on her withered frame like a sack. She seemed tiny and frail beside the burly men, and her face wore a look of grinding pain. Captain Gent motioned the men to release Mom. They let her go, and she stumbled, dragged down by the heavy chains on her wrists.

Captain Gent came forward, looking smugly at Emma and her friends. "You all know why you're here," she called out. They stared back at her grimly. "You are being charged with aiding and abetting piracy on the high seas. The Queen has given me permission to expedite proceedings, so instead of the requisite three days of waiting, I am now obliged to perform the trial this evening. Believe me," she said with a false attempt at a smile, "I don't want to do this, but my hands are tied." To emphasize her point, she held out her hands.

No one moved.

"Ringrose," she said. "Read the judgment." One of her men nodded solemnly and opened a scroll of parchment. Emma's heart knotted in her throat.

"'Emma Brightstoke Garton of Monkey,'" Ringrose began. "'After judicious decision by the maritime configuration of a war seas council, you are hereby charged with treason and piracy. . . .'"

"What judicious decision?" Herbie shouted.

"Wait! Wait!" Mom cried. "What do you want? Tell me. I'll give you anything."

Gent turned to her in mock surprise. "My, this is familiar," she said. "Only last time you were not so eager to cooperate."

"I'll tell you anything," Mom said, her voice cracking. "Whatever you want."

"Very well," Gent replied. "I have tried to activate the Pyxis, and nothing has happened." She reached into her collar and pulled the Pyxis from her shirt. "This infamous object is said to lead its bearer to the Shroud's very doorway. These dials and gears"—she flicked them angrily—"are supposed to align to the Shroud's coordinates. And these blue stones are said to open the gate itself. And yet this powerful, incredible object has done absolutely NOTHING. So you see, Halifax," Gent said, coming closer, "it seems to be entirely useless."

Mom blinked rapidly.

"I believed that," Gent said. "And then I remembered how good you were at lying."

Mom was fighting to stop shaking.

"So what I want you to do," Gent went on, "is tell me how to start the Pyxis, or your daughter dies."

Mom turned to Emma, a look of horrible anguish on her face. Tears were streaming down her cheeks. Emma knew that she had spent most of her life protecting the secret that Gent wanted so badly, and to reveal it now would be the most brutal defeat.

"I don't know the answer," Mom said.

"Oh well," Gent said lightly, motioning to her men.

Ringrose picked up the scroll and continued reading. "'By law, your punishment is immediate execution. . . .'"

Mom looked panicked, her eyes flashing to Emma.

Suddenly there was a scuffle from the stairs and two men appeared, hauling a large cage. There was a lynx inside, snapping and clawing at the iron bars. Emma and her friends stared at the lynx in wonder.

"Is that . . . ?" Laika whispered.

The sailors jammed their tuskets at the beast, and one

speared its shoulder. The lynx yowled in rage and lashed out with its claws as blood spurted down its leg. Another sailor delivered a savage blow to the animal's head, and it fell down with a thump.

"Better hurry up," Gent said to Mom.

"You've got to use the Pyxis with a map," Mom blurted.

The deck fell silent.

"What map?" Gent demanded.

"It's a special map. An old one," Mom said, looking around in confusion. "I don't know where it is. Someone else hid it. . . ."

"I don't believe you."

"I don't know what they did with it!" Mom's voice quavered. "You have to believe me!"

" 'In a manner,' " Ringrose continued, " 'to be determined by Captain Artemisia Gent of the sloop *Newton Eel,* now on board the Draconi vessel *Hargrim,* in Her Majesty's service. Graces to the Queen.' "

"Noooo!" Mom cried. "You can't do this! You just have to find the map! The Pyxis won't start without it!"

Emma felt as if the world were shrinking. The deck, the crew, the faces of the Arghs all seemed to be growing smaller and darker. She had to force herself to breathe. Two men undid her shackles and dragged her to a sheet of canvas that was lying on the deck.

"Stop!" Herbie cried out. *"No!"*

A sailor knocked him with the butt of his tusket, and Herbie too fell aside.

Mom was sobbing at Gent's feet.

"Mom!" Emma cried. "Don't cry! It's going to be okay!"

The sailors threw her into the center of the canvas. She felt a burst of adrenaline and began struggling against their grip, but their fists were like iron bracelets. Two more men laid six large rocks against her legs. She tried kicking them away, but the men held her fast.

"Please!" Mom cried. "I swear I'll help you find the map. I swear it!"

"I think you know exactly where it is," Gent said coolly. "And you'd better tell me fast, or your daughter is going overboard."

"I *don't* know where it is!" Mom shouted.

Tears sprang to Emma's eyes.

The sailors went for the lynx. They dragged it from its cage and tossed it down beside Emma. In two quick moves, the men folded the canvas over her and rolled her together with the bloody, rain-sopped beast, squashing them so tightly that she felt nothing but wet fur in her face.

Outside she heard the clatter of rain on the canvas. It jerked as the sailors hastily sewed it shut. "Hurry up, hurry up," one of them grunted. "Before the cat wakes!"

Emma squirmed and kicked against the canvas. She was going to die. She would never see her parents again, or Herbie or Laika or Santher. And she would certainly never get the Pyxis back. There was a sudden flash of light and the deafening boom of tuskets. Emma gasped. They were going to throw her over the railing.

Struggling, she managed to get her hand into her pocket. She touched something cold and it startled her. She still had a few vostok. They were icy. She took them out and tried to get them into her mouth, but she couldn't. The bag thumped as the men dragged her across the deck. The big rocks banged against her legs. There were protests in the distance, the sound of Mom crying. The jolting was so harsh that she felt certain it was designed for one purpose: to wake the angry lynx before they reached the railing.

It worked. The lynx awoke with a roar and a vicious explosion of hissing. Emma was pressed tightly to its back, but she screamed nonetheless—which only upset the animal more. Its claws slashed wildly at the canvas, but it was so thick that it would take another few minutes to break free even if the animal knew what it was doing. And they didn't have the time.

Emma felt the lynx twisting and thrashing. She had never been so terrified in her life as when its claw nicked her arm. She cried out in pain and struggled desperately to put the vostok into her mouth, but in the bumping and jouncing the stone flew out of her grip.

And then a startling thing happened. She felt the lynx's wet fur transform into soft, wet fabric. She gripped it in disbelief.

"Emma," a voice gasped.

"Oh!"

"It's me—Santher."

"Santher?" She fumbled to touch his face. "How did you—?"

"No time. Do you have anything sharp?"

"No!" she gasped. "They took every—" They felt themselves being lifted over the railing. "Santher, what do we do?" With a great shove, they were loosed over the side.

They hit the sea with a heavy splash. Emma could just feel the water seeping through the canvas when suddenly a different kind of pain overtook her. Her whole body began shaking as the coldness swept through her. She cried out.

They were sinking rapidly. Emma saw herself drowning, a corpse being dragged into a poisoned sea. Worse still was the thought that she had dragged Santher into this, and that he was suffering the same agony as her. His body clunked against hers like a slab of ice. The choking, the horror of the darkness, and the weight of the water as it pressed her to the bottom. There were only minutes, perhaps seconds, left.

CHAPTER 29

Whispers of the Living and the Dead

Emma looked around. She was standing on the deck of a ship. It was the *Markab,* she realized with a sudden burst of relief, the *Markab* before it had been turned into a baby dragon-of-war. She was sailing with Dad and Herbie, and they were heading through the Golden Gate strait out into the open ocean. It was just like the other times they'd done it, only this time she was filled with the most extraordinary feeling—that everything she had ever wanted to know was *just right there,* and all she had to do was reach out and grab it. Every question she ever had. Every desire. Every hope. It could all be grasped at the slightest thought.

She tested it. She thought of Dad. What did he look like when he was her age? All at once he appeared before her, a tall boy with jet-black hair and a piercing gaze. He was riding a chestnut-colored Pegasus horse, and there was a mallet in his hand, almost like a polo stick. He met her eyes and she stared at him in wonder, trying to imagine him going to school and doing homework and sailing on the weekends just like she did.

Anything, she thought with giddiness. *I can ask for anything!*

Her mind wheeled through the possibilities. She could ask about Mom. About how she grew up. About what it was like being a princess, and why she ran away to Eridanus. About being with pirates. About how she met Dad. Quickly, she thought of more pressing concerns: How had they stolen the Pyxis? How had Mom survived the execution? And where was Dad now? It occurred to her that she ought to find out what was *going* to happen. Was Mom going to die on Gent's ship? What would happen to Dad? And Emma and Herbie and their friends—what would become of them?

Suddenly, Queen Virgo loomed before her, grandest of all figures. She said sternly, "These waters are dangerous." But she herself was drinking from them—clear blue memory water. It was making her skin glow. "These waters can kill you," she warned, water dripping from her mouth. "They spread lies."

Emma felt a violent swirling clap, as if someone had just yanked her from behind. The picture changed. Now she saw a man leaning over her mother. They were both very young, and her mother looked glamorous in a silky blue gown and a tiara of diamonds, her white-blond hair flowing down to her waist. The man's eyes were filled with such a look of sweet surrender and weakness and desire. Mom shifted nervously when he leaned over to kiss her.

CLAP!

Another picture. This time a horse was running joyfully toward her. It was Dad's horse. It had wings, and they were going to fly. . . .

CLAP!

Sitting at the kitchen table, Herbie was laughing so hard that flakes of carrot came flying out of his nose.

CLAP!

A violent maelstrom in a stormy sea. Ships were getting caught in the swirl of water. Voices screaming. Emma gasped. Of course she couldn't see the future—these were memories! She realized that she was still underwater, without air.

This is how it kills you, she thought wildly. *You believe it's real. And you stay here, fascinated by all the pictures, and you drown.*

She forced her eyes open and saw nothing but darkness. She felt Santher beside her. He was struggling with something. With a sudden rip, the canvas split and fell away, dragged down by the rocks. They were in a green and rocky underwater world, near the bottom of the sea. The floor was covered in sand, and great streamers of kelp were swirling about.

She was captivated by the water. It was full of light and motion. Images were flickering everywhere she looked, and sounds came to her ears as if they were spoken there—soft voices, loud shouts, whispers of the living and the dead. She could see these visions, hundreds of them moving through the waters all around her, and she was filled again with the feeling that everything she had ever wondered about or wanted to know was right there at her fingertips—all she had to do was reach.

No, she thought viciously. *I have to get out!* She gave a swift kick, desperately pushing herself back toward the surface, but her head hit something hard. It was Santher's foot. He was falling on top of her. He must have tried to swim to the surface and gotten swept away by the memories.

She grabbed him, feeling a desperate burning in her throat and lungs. She needed air. The memories were coming back for her too. She could see them swirling closer, a great dance of ghostly forms. She saw her parents clearly. They were standing on a platform above her, beckoning her, waving. She wanted desperately to go to them, but she knew they weren't real.

She might have been able to make it to the surface on her own, but with Santher in her arms it was hopeless. She looked back at her parents. Perhaps they were real. . . .

Just in front of them, her eyes fell on a small black stone. She dropped Santher and reached for it. It was vostok! Knowing she only had seconds left, she cracked it open and squished half of the jelly into Santher's mouth. She tried to squish the other half into her own, but when she pressed it between her lips, water came pouring into her mouth and she panicked, choking, inhaling a great lungful of liquid. . . .

CHAPTER 30

The Dragon and the Roach

Emma's mom was lying on the deck. As soon as she'd seen them throw Emma overboard, she had collapsed. The doctor had come up with the loblolly boy, and now they were lifting her up.

Herbie was sitting rigidly against the railing, tears spilling from his eyes and blurring the world around him. A small black cockroach crawled out of his pocket, but he barely noticed. All he could think of was Emma's face as they had sewn the canvas closed. Her desperate kicking and clawing. The bag disappearing over the railing with a terrible finality. A moment of expectant silence followed by a cruel splash.

Down the deck, the navy sailors were talking, but all he heard was the sound of Laika sobbing and the sloshing of waves against the ship. The cockroach burrowed its way into a hole in the knee of his trousers. He felt it scratching and looked down. It disgusted him to see a roach on his leg, but he couldn't swat it off—his hands were tied firmly behind his back. And anyway, the poor thing was probably looking for shelter from the rain.

Then he remembered the screech bat. It was still in its vial in the pocket of his coat. If his hands were free, he would be able to release it. He would unscrew the cap and set the bat free. In one great swoop it would knock everyone out. It gave him a faint glimmer of hope to think of the entire crew falling over, but there was only one problem: he and Laika would fall unconscious too. And then they'd all wake up just where they were now, and what good would that do?

It was hopeless.

A noise across the deck made him look up. He blinked. He thought he must be dreaming. He saw a pair of slanted red eyes. A great smoking muzzle and the scaly, iridescent skin of a reptile. Herbie blinked away his tears so he could get a better look. It was a dragon. He was colored a deep, rich green, and his face held an expression of dignity and coldness that sent a shiver down Herbie's arms. The dragon was perched on the railing as his rider spoke to one of the crew. The dragon seemed to be looking right at Herbie. All at once he felt a jolt of amazement.

A *dragon*!

With a flap, the beast turned and flew into the darkness. Herbie stared at the railing. He looked around at Laika. Suddenly, her tragic face seemed out of place. *Stop crying,* he wanted to say. *Didn't you SEE that?*

Two sailors were walking by, talking casually.

"What are we going to do with the little ones?" one sailor asked.

"Captain says she's going to trade them to a Corvan vessel on Rigel," the other replied. "They're healthy. They'll fetch a fine price."

Laika overheard this and burst into renewed sobs.

Herbie knew what had to be done. His feet were shackled to the railing, but his hands were only tied with rope. He twisted his fingers to try to reach the rope. He tried wiggling his hands free. Nothing was working—the rope was tied securely. He looked around for something sharp. The closest object was about three feet away: a metal ring around a barrel that was next to the railing. The ring was broken, and a jagged strip of it protruded from the barrel. It was low enough that he could probably reach it.

Carefully, he moved away from Laika while keeping an eye on the guards. They were busy talking and didn't notice as he slid like an inchworm, using his legs to push himself sideways and back.

He was just about to reach the barrel when his shackles gave a *clink*. He'd pulled as far as he could go. Looking behind, he could see that there was only about a foot of distance between him and the strip of metal. Straining, he raised his wrists and managed to set them on top of the metal strip. With a gentle motion, he began to saw away at his binds.

As they rose, water came pouring out of Emma's mouth, and she felt her ears popping as if some kind of pressure were lifting from her body. She clung desperately to Santher's leg, but halfway to the surface his body gave a jolt and he kicked her free. The pressure change must have been affecting him too, because now he was thrashing as the vostok lifted them up. She could see his skin rippling strangely. Fur was sprouting from his arms, and his hands were shrinking, turning into paws.

Emma needed so badly to take a breath that she had to clap a hand to her mouth to keep it shut. Her chest was jerking in spasms, begging for air. Her vision was getting dark at the edges and she knew she was blacking out. She looked up one last time to see the surface, but it seemed much too far away. . . .

Herbie had sawed through the rope. The guards were not paying attention. They were huddled against a new onslaught of rain, wiping it nervously from their hands and faces and muttering about what it might do to them. Captain Gent was standing beneath an awning, talking to the Draconi ship's captain. She was looking at Laika but too busy talking to notice what was going on.

Herbie slid back toward Laika and untied her ropes. She looked back in surprise.

"Just pretend to keep crying," he whispered.

She hung her head. "What are you doing?" she whispered between sobs. "We can't go anywhere!"

"I'm going to try. I just need to get these shackles off. . . ." Hiding his feet behind Laika, he felt around the shackles. There didn't seem to be a lock, but his fingers touched a pin. He pulled it out and the shackles fell open. He slipped them off his ankles.

"Stay here," he said to Laika. "I'm going to take care of Gent." He climbed to his feet.

Captain Gent noticed at once. She motioned her men to make him sit back down, but before they could reach him,

Herbie took off running. He went heading for Gent, every fiber of his body surging forward. One of the sailors tried to stop him, but he dodged. The sailor nicked him. Both of them slipped on the wet deck. It sent Herbie into a slide, and he went careening into Gent.

He knocked her over with a crash.

She grunted as she fell. Herbie was up in an instant, scrambling onto her, seizing her throat. But he was yanked away and hauled to his feet by a pair of angry sailors.

THUMP! Something hit the *Hargrim,* and everyone turned to the starboard railing. A figure had landed on the deck. The men gave a startled gasp. Gent leapt to her feet, her face a mask of disbelief. A lynx was standing by the starboard railing, dripping wet and poised to attack. He bared his teeth in a growl.

"It's the lynx!" someone hissed. The sailors backed away. The animal was drenched, but his fur stood on end, every part of him coiled to spring. There was a look of madness in his eyes as he gave a vicious snarl.

Now everyone was backing away in terror.

Then they saw a hand reach up to grab the railing. It was small, a girl's hand slick with rain. She pulled herself up—a tangle of clothing and limbs—and slid through the railing, struggling to her feet. She stood to the astonished face of every person on board. She was panting and rain-soaked, looking furious and wild. It was Emma!

The sailors were dumbstruck. They lowered their weapons, frightened, wondering by what miracle this young girl had survived being sewn in a bag with a beast and thrown into the deadliest waters in the galaxy.

"She *is* a pirate!" one of the crew hissed.

"Just like her mother!"

"They'll come for her, then—ye watch!"

"Nonsense," Gent said, although she didn't seem so certain herself.

Herbie stood unsteadily, staring at Emma. She touched her arm where a spot of blood was forming. She looked at the blood and wiped it on her shirt. When her eyes met Herbie's, they were furious and triumphant.

"She's bleeding," someone murmured. "Look at 'er leg!"

"Pirates ain't supposed to bleed," someone else said.

"That's because she's not a pirate." The voice was Captain Gent's. It was a bit unsteady, but it contained enough authority to snap the men to attention. They stopped whispering and raised their weapons again.

"Look!" one of the men said, pointing at the lynx.

The lynx was stumbling backward dizzily. His rear slumped down; then his head fell to the deck with a *thunk.* His body seemed to be flickering between two shapes. One moment he was a lynx; the next he was Santher. Finally the form settled on the boy, lying half-naked on his side, moaning.

There was a moment of stunned silence. No one could believe it. Even Laika was amazed.

Gent came forward smugly. "And this magical beast is only a man," she said, stopping above him and nudging him with her foot. "So don't be surprised when he dies as one too."

Herbie knew what he had to do.

"Don't anyone move," he said. They all turned to see him holding the jar with the screech bat inside. "We're leaving this ship peacefully," he said, "or I release the bat."

Slowly, Gent's mouth formed an irritated smirk. She motioned to her men. "Shoot him."

The sailors turned their weapons on him, so he threw the jar against the deck. The moment it cracked, an impossible, piercing scream filled the air.

SCREEEEEEEEEEEEEEEEEEEEE!

Herbie saw people collapsing around him, but he didn't remember much after that.

CHAPTER 31

Drool and Fire

Herbie was standing in an open desert. Rolling sand dunes spread out before him, and the sun was beating down with relentless intensity. He was parched, sweating profusely, and pulling at his clothes to get away from the choking heat. Suddenly something wet hit his face. He reached up to touch it and his fingers came away covered in goo. . . .

He opened his eyes. Something wet was indeed dripping onto his face. As he wiped it away, he saw a great mouth hanging open above him. He sat up with a jolt and skittered backward. He had been lying beneath a dragon's jaw.

This beast looked a little older than the one he'd seen earlier. It had tired eyes and its breath was something foul. But it was drooling happily and gazing at Herbie with a look of expectant adoration.

Herbie's hair was singed and his face felt sunburned. His tunic was smoking, and there was a hole in the chest. He climbed to his feet in amazement, and the dragon shuffled closer, sniffing his shirt. Herbie stepped aside—away from the fiery maw—and with a shaking hand, touched the dragon's head. The dragon purred, which sent a hot burst of air sailing out of its mouth. Herbie spat out a terrified, awestruck laugh.

His head was throbbing, but he looked around. The Strand was deathly quiet. The only sounds were the creaking of wood and the splashing of water as the ships bobbed on the waves. Every person on deck was unconscious. The Hargrims all formed a big jumble. Emma and Santher were lying on the ground nearby, and Laika just beyond them.

Herbie was just wondering why he had woken up and no one else had when a few of the sailors began stirring nearby. He didn't want them to wake up yet, so he scanned the deck for the bat and found it. It was crawling up the front of Santher's shirt. He picked it up carefully and laid it in his palm. It was tiny and black and completely disgusting, but he touched it anyway. He discovered at once that when he pressed its backside, it gave another screech. Not as loud as the first one, but enough to make his head feel like exploding. The sailors groaned and passed out again. The dragon shuffled closer and licked his hair. Herbie gave a nervous laugh.

He stared down at the bat, not sure what to do with it. The glass jar was broken, and he didn't want to lose the little creature. He felt inside his pocket and his hand struck the cockroach. He tried to knock it away, but it only fell down into his waistband.

There are too many animals, he thought. He didn't want the bat to eat the cockroach while it was inside his shirt, but he couldn't think of anywhere else to put it, so he stuffed it in there. Then he turned to the dragon.

The dragon's rider had fallen off and was lying on the deck. The saddle was empty. . . .

A moment later, Herbie was kneeling beside Emma. "Hey," he was whispering. "Wake up!" He tapped her cheek. "Emma! Wake up!"

She simply wouldn't wake. The dragon came over to investigate. It leaned its giant mouth closer, sniffing interestedly. As soon as the drool touched Emma's face, her eyes opened.

"Hey, wow. Magic drool!" he said.

"Herbie?" She looked around in confusion. "What happened?"

"Get up before everyone else does, and check this out!" He helped her to her feet and motioned to the dragon.

When she saw it, she stumbled backward. "What the . . . ?"

"I know!" he exclaimed. "That screech bat knocked everyone out—and I think it tamed the dragon."

Emma looked around at all the bodies on the deck and then at the big dragon breathing heavily on Herbie's shoulder. She couldn't seem to make sense of it.

"Are you okay?" Herbie asked. "You were in the memory water. . . ."

"I think I'm good."

"Let's wake up Santher and Laika and go find your mom," he said.

"Okay." She started to lunge away, but Herbie grabbed her.

"Wait," he said. "Let's chain up the navy first, in case they wake up."

"Yeah," she said. "Good idea."

They dragged the shackles away from the railing and began clamping them around the sailors' ankles and wrists. Fortunately, the chains between each of the cuffs were long enough. It only took a few minutes.

"We should also get the fake Pyxis from Gent," Herbie said.

"Right." Emma went to retrieve it.

Fishing in his shirt, Herbie found the screech bat. By pressing on it gently, he was able to lure the dragon to where Laika and Santher were lying. When its drool touched Laika's face, she came around.

"Hey," Laika said, looking sleepily at the dragon. "That's a really big bird."

"It's not a bird, Laika. It's a dragon."

She sat up and clutched her head. "Ow. Was that a *screech bat*?" Herbie nodded. "We'll have headaches for weeks!"

"Santher isn't waking up," Emma said, tucking the fake Pyxis into her shirt.

They tried dropping more dragon drool on his face, but he didn't respond.

"Come on," Herbie said. "Let's leave him for now. We've got to find Emma's mom before the navy wakes up."

They followed him to the stairwell. It was well lit, but they went slowly anyway in case there were any Hargrims below. They couldn't be sure if everyone had been knocked out by the screech bat's cry.

At the bottom of the stairs, they encountered an empty hallway that ran the length of the ship. Moving carefully around each doorway, they passed a series of crew's quarters and a bathroom before coming to the surgery. It was a small, dark room filled with books and bottles. Dr. Vermek was lying just inside the door, his loblolly boy beneath him. Emma's mom was on a cot in the corner.

Emma fell on her and squeezed her hand. Herbie felt for a pulse while the others waited in terrible suspense. He slumped in relief.

"She's still alive," he said. "But we'd better get her back to the *Argh*."

"Yeah, but how?" Emma asked.

"I have an idea."

They lifted Mom carefully—it took all three of them to carry her—and navigated their way out of the small room, back down the hallway, and up the stairs. On the top deck, the sailors were still unconscious. Herbie led the others toward the dragon.

"Wait," Emma said. "You can't put her on the dragon!"

"Let's find a rowboat," Laika agreed. "It's much safer, and we've got to take Santher too."

"There are no rowboats," Herbie said. "I've been looking this whole time. I guess since this is a Draconi ship, dragons *are* their rowboats, if you know what I mean."

They all turned to stare at the dragon, who sat watching them happily.

Before anyone could protest, Herbie scrambled onto the dragon's saddle, climbing up the one stair, swinging his leg over the harness, and locking his feet into the stirrups, which were almost like ski boots.

"I'm on," he said, a bit breathlessly. "Now just get her up here, and we'll tie her to my back."

"Herbie . . ." Emma wanted to disagree, but they didn't have any other choice. Nearby, a few of the Hargrims were rousing.

"Hurry!" Herbie whispered.

The others scrambled to haul Mom up the stair and onto the saddle behind Herbie. They placed her there like a giant rag doll, wrapped her arms around his waist, and tied her securely with rope.

"Are you sure about this?" Emma asked. "I thought you were afraid of heights."

He nodded like a jackhammer. "I can do this. I have to." The dragon turned in a nervous circle, so Herbie took hold of the reins. "You guys better get Santher."

Emma and Laika rushed back to their friend and hauled him onto the dragon's back. It was difficult getting him strapped in behind Mom, and by the end, they were both sweating. Emma climbed up behind Santher and wrapped her arms around his waist. There was still plenty of room on the dragon's back for Laika to climb up behind her. Once everyone was situated, Herbie turned back to the reins.

Nothing had prepared him for this. He had no idea what to do. He tried kicking the dragon, but it only let out a sizzling burp and whipped its tail in irritation, causing Laika to duck. Herbie couldn't use the screech bat again. They'd all fall off the dragon's back.

He wrapped his fists around the reins and yanked once. The dragon breathed a bolt of fire so powerful it blew the railing off the *Hargrim.* Emma yelped and curled into a ball. Setting his chin, he took the reins again and pulled twice this time. The dragon's wings went out sharply, with military precision.

That worked, he thought. He yanked three times, and with a terrifying kick, the dragon took off.

Herbie gasped, swallowing air. The dragon swooped over the side and flew low to the water. Herbie gave a kick and it dove lower, its toes skimming the surface. He quickly pulled the reins back and the dragon lifted. Herbie's heart was beating so hard it felt as if it had come up into his throat.

They flew over three other Draconi ships. On each deck men were lying unconscious, piled in heaps. The screech bat had conquered the entire fleet.

He had no idea where the *Argh* was, but he steered them back in the direction they'd come, remembering gratefully that the *Argh*'s top deck was large enough to land a dragon. . . .

The journey that had taken them an hour in a rowboat only took five minutes on a dragon's back. They spotted the *Argh* sailing right alongside the islands. Someone had left the candles burning in the command room, and in this darkness, they lit up the top deck like a cruise ship. Herbie pulled gently on the reins while kicking the dragon's sides, and with a graceful flutter the beast set down right next to the foremast and curled up its wings, giving a happy, fire-tinged burp.

CHAPTER 32

Reunion and Ragnar

When the nurses finally allowed Emma into the infirmary, she saw at once how tiny Mom's form looked on the outsized bed. There was a teacup on her lap, but her eyes were closed, her breathing slow and silent.

Emma approached the bed, and Mom opened her eyes. Seeing Emma, she leapt up, throwing the bedcover aside, which sent the teacup flying, along with the medicine jars on the bedside table. She grabbed Emma in a fierce embrace. Emma was too startled to do anything but stand there.

It took her a moment to realize that Mom was crying. Her shoulders were shaking. Emma hugged her back and waited, embarrassed, until Mom released her. Mom's face was red and puffy.

"Emma," she said in a hoarse whisper, "I thought you were

dead. When they threw you over the edge, I thought it would kill me too." Choking on tears, she buried her face in Emma's hair and kissed the crown of her head. "You don't know what this means to me to see you alive. My whole life has changed in an instant." She wiped the tears from her face and sat down on the bed, pulling Emma closer. "Come here. Sit down next to me. Tell me what happened. How did you survive?"

Emma sat. She knew she ought to be crying too, but her emotions were stirring, kraken-like, deep inside. A bit nervously, she explained what had happened beneath the seas. All the while Mom studied her with deepening concern.

"That's remarkable," Mom said with some puzzlement. "You seem all right, but are you seeing things?"

"No."

"Have you been throwing up? Feeling dizzy?"

"*No.* But Santher is sick. He was in the water with me." Emma motioned to a bed across the room, where Santher was lying unconscious. "He got knocked out by the screech bat, and he hasn't woken up since then. Do you know what's wrong with him?"

Mom was chagrined. "Being exposed to so much memory water can damage your brain."

"Is he going to wake up?"

"I can't say," Mom said.

"Why am I okay?" Emma asked.

Mom shook her head. "I don't understand. It must be because . . ."

"What?" Emma asked.

"Never mind. It's just that falling in the memory seas is deadly. If you manage to get out alive, which, believe me, is extremely rare, it can have a dramatic effect on your mind."

"What?" Emma said. "Like now I'll be scared of everything?"

Mom gave a wan smile. "You think I'm scared of everything, is that it? You probably do. I'm so sorry, Emma. I never—"

"So you're not really scared?"

Mom pursed her lips. "There's only one thing I've ever truly been afraid of, and that's losing you. You are my greatest weakness, and I love you more than anything, Emma." Mom wrapped her in a hug, and Emma felt tears welling in her eyes. She wiped them away.

"You survived the memory seas," Emma said. "So what do you think is going to happen to Santher?"

"I'm not sure," Mom said gravely. "When they threw me in the seas, I had already grown accustomed to the waters of Eridanus. I had lived with the pirates and gone through their rituals so that I could tolerate the water. You and Santher had *none* of that, as far as I know. I'm afraid of what this might do to you. But let's not worry about that now. You look all right, and I'm just so glad you're alive."

Emma was thinking of all the things she had intended to say: "*Why did you lie to me?*" "*Why didn't you tell me you were from outer space?*" She wasn't sure how to say them. She reminded herself that Mom had been a hero, and now she actually understood why.

"I have the Pyxis," Emma said. "Herbie has it, actually. It's safe."

Mom shut her eyes, letting out a sigh of relief, but it was tinged with regret. "How did you get it?"

"It was behind Dad's bookshelf. He shoved us in there, you know."

"Yes, I figured. I'm so sorry for what happened on the ship with Captain Gent. I didn't know how to get them to stop. I don't think they would have, even if I had been able to give them the answer right then. They would have tried to kill you anyway."

"So is it true what you said?" Emma asked. "The Pyxis has to work with a map?"

"Yes," Mom said. "Your father had the map. He attached it to the inside of an old book."

"We have that too," Emma said. "At least I think so. But Captain Gent was surprised when you told her. It's like she didn't believe you."

"Nobody knows about the map. I've never told anyone, and Cascabel and I intentionally spread the rumor that the Pyxis was the only way to open the Shroud. We never mentioned the map."

"That was smart," Emma said. "But where did you get the map?"

"I stole it," Mom said. "It wasn't very nice of me, and in general you shouldn't steal things. . . ."

Emma rolled her eyes theatrically while Mom studied her with a seriousness that was new and intimidating.

"You're a pirate," Emma said. "You can't really tell me not to steal anything."

"But *sometimes,*" Mom finished, "you can have a good reason for stealing something."

"Did you have a good reason?"

"Of course," Mom went on. "Cascabel was becoming dangerous. We were losing the war, and he believed that the Eridanean fleet was losing its power because they had drained the water. He wanted to open the Shroud and seize the water back. He believed it was the only thing that would make him powerful enough to conquer the Queen."

"And you didn't think so?"

"No. I knew that if he opened the Shroud, the Queen would simply seize the water and all our work would be ruined. So there was only one thing left to do."

"Steal the Pyxis and the map, and run away."

"Yes," Mom said.

"And Dad stole it too."

"He was the only one I trusted with my plan."

"I saw a notice that said you were executed by the Queen," Emma said.

"I was. Cascabel realized immediately that I had stolen the Pyxis, and he was furious. Before I even managed to leave Eridanus, he struck a deal with Captain Gent. He told her what my ship looked like and where I was. He let her fleet come into Eridanus to find me. And they did. They captured me near Rigel." Mom shrugged. "I betrayed him, so he decided to turn me over to the Queen's navy. But I didn't have the Pyxis. Your dad had the Pyxis and the map, and he was on a different ship. I refused to tell Gent where they were, so she executed me."

"How did you survive?"

"Oh, that's a story for another day." Mom reached over and took her arm. "You're all right," she said. "And I'm so, so sorry for all this mess. I wanted to tell you."

"You mean, tell me about space and about being a pirate?"

"Yes." Mom lowered her gaze. "Sometimes lying is safer," she said plainly. "We wanted to protect you. We were wrong to lie."

Emma gazed at her. "You're a pirate," she said. "You can't really tell me it's bad to lie."

"But it is bad," Mom said.

"Unless you have a good reason."

"Right," Mom said regretfully.

Emma bit her tongue. Mom looked terribly vulnerable and pale. She took hold of Emma's hand again. "Do you remember when you were young and you had just come back from your first sailing trip with Dad?" Emma nodded. "We sat you down and told you that there was more to the universe than just Earth. That people lived in space too. That there were whole galaxies out there with millions of people and animals and all kinds of magical things. And do you know what you said?"

Emma only had a vague memory of this. "No," she said.

"You laughed at us and said we were making it up. The next day at school, you told your friends what we'd said, and that afternoon your teacher called us at home. She was concerned that we were filling your head with nonsense." Mom paused, clearly upset at the memory. "It wasn't your fault. That's just what happens when you grow up on Earth. We made the decision then not to tell you anything until we could be sure that you were old enough to understand. But as the years went by, it became harder and harder."

"You should have trusted me," Emma said.

"I'm sorry we didn't," Mom replied.

Emma felt another choke of tears rising in her throat. She knew she had to ask her next question, even though she was terrified of the answer.

"Where's Dad?" she asked. "What happened to him?"

Mom's face darkened. "Caz and Laine brought us on their ship. It was a Scorpio craft disguised as an Earth yacht. They sailed out to sea, blew open a vostok portal, and took us back to space. The whole time they kept us in separate rooms. I was so worried about him—they had shot him, you know—but then I could hear them interrogating him, and I could hear him talking, so I knew he was still alive." A triumphant smile stole over her lips. "It didn't take him very long to escape."

"He escaped?"

"Yes. After a few hours on the Strand, I heard Caz and Laine shouting at each other. They were fighting because your father had somehow gotten out of his cell and jumped ship." Mom looked at her differently now, Emma thought, almost with a strange relief that she could tell her everything. "He was always very good at escaping. It's because of him that we were able to disappear to Earth."

Mom seemed to find this quality admirable, but it reminded Emma too uncomfortably of how Dad had lied to her about his trip to Phoenix.

"I was hoping this whole time that he would find me," Mom said. "Now I don't know what's become of him. But we'll find him."

Emma nodded, uncertain what to say. Mom put her arm around Emma and gave her a squeeze. Quietly, Emma thrilled to her touch. Mom might have been a pirate, but she also needed protecting, and Dad wasn't around to do it. The only person who could do it now was Emma.

She put her arms around Mom's neck and hugged her.

Mom fell asleep, but Emma stayed by her side, watching the nurses putter about. The rest of the day passed in a blur. Arghs came and went from the infirmary, and Emma heard the rumors about the activity above, but it wasn't until Herbie came in that Emma got up to talk.

Herbie looked rumpled but excited. "Hi!" he said. "How's your mom?"

"She's okay, I think. The doctors have been giving her medicine."

"Cool." Herbie looked ready to burst. "Guess what! Lovesey said I can keep the dragon!"

"What?"

"He said he didn't have any problem taking goods from the navy, but he did expect me to learn about the dangers of dragons before I'd be allowed to fly him again. And of course I already know all the dangers. . . ."

"I can't believe Lovesey's letting you keep the dragon."

"He's on the top deck now. He likes to sit on the railing. I think that's where he used to sit on his own ship. But he kind of scared the birds off, and Laika got upset, so we're making a nest for them in the cargo hold. Oh, and Laika's going to come up with a name for the dragon, unless you have any ideas?"

"How about Drool?"

Herbie laughed. "But seriously, he's a dragon. He needs an awesome name. I was thinking . . ."

"Ragnar," they both said at once.

Emma smiled. "That's perfect."

Herbie finally seemed to be catching his breath. "But are you okay?" he asked. "You fell in the memory seas. I thought it was supposed to kill you! I mean, look what happened to—" They both turned to the bed where Santher was lying.

"He hasn't woken up yet," Emma said. "Nobody knows what's going to happen to him, not even my mom."

"But you're awake," Herbie said. "And you seem okay. . . ."

Emma shrugged. She did feel a little strange, but she figured this was because she'd finally gotten Mom back and she was trying to digest how everything was going to be different now.

"That was *so* amazing," Herbie said. "When you jumped on deck—just wow."

"You were the one who saved us with the screech bat." She smiled, remembering Herbie threatening Gent with that tiny jar. "You were totally Ragnar."

"Yeah." He was grinning. "Oh, by the way, I got the Pyxis out of its hiding place." He reached into his collar and drew the amulet out of his shirt, giving it to Emma. "I thought you should have it."

"Thanks."

"We should probably find another hiding place for it. I think a lot of Arghs have guessed that you have it."

"Yeah," Emma said. "You know, what my mom said is true—it works with a map."

Herbie raised an eyebrow. "Are you thinking *the map*?"

"Yeah. She said my dad hid it in a book."

"Then we should hide that too," Herbie said.

"Yeah." Emma tucked the Pyxis into her shirt.

"I have to get back to Ragnar," Herbie said. "Want to come?"

"Okay, but I have to talk to Lovesey first," she said. "I want to know how we're going to get out of Eridanus. I still need to find my dad."

Herbie sobered instantly at this. "We should ask the monkeys to get the *Markab* back to the cargo hold. They might be able to fix it up again."

Emma nodded. Fixing the *Markab* was about all she could

manage right now. She had no idea where to begin in the search for Dad.

She and Herbie said goodbye. Before leaving the infirmary, Emma gave Mom one last kiss on the cheek and whispered in her sleeping ear, "I'm going to go see about fixing the *Markab.* The doctors are going to get rid of that squilch in your brain or whatever it is. And then we're going to find Dad. And I'm going to keep the Pyxis safe. So don't worry. Everything's going to be okay."

She had no idea how wrong she was.

Glossary of Terms

Almagest: mysterious book about the constellations; contains a map

Argh: stolen ship from the Leo system, one of the largest in the galaxy

Artemesia (Tema) Gent: navy captain of the *Newton Eel,* famous for capturing and executing the notorious pirate Halifax Brightstoke

Berenice: barmaid at Job's Coffin tavern on Delphinus

bridge (jelly, vostok): wall of vostok that separates the waters of a Strand from the waters of a planet; in order to pass safely, you must be wearing a vostok coat

Cascabel: leader of the pirates, thought to be in exile on Eridanus; no one has heard from him in twelve years

Chained Lady: Queen Virgo's ship, a cutter from the Andromeda system

Delphinus: constellation in a region of the sky known as the Sea; the only system connected to Solacious in the Monkey system

Draco: dragon system that remains loyal to Queen Virgo

dragon-of-war: galleon-class ship from the Draco system; the deadliest of all ships

Emma Brightstoke Garton: daughter of Halifax Brightstoke and Jack Garton

Eridanus: river constellation; former home to pirates; its Strands are called the memory seas

Gemini: twins constellation

grisslin: small, beetle-like creature that eats memories from the human mind

Halifax Brightstoke: Emma's mother; the second-greatest pirate of the seas

Herbert Yee: Emma's best friend

Jack Garton: Emma's father; former pirate known as Mad Jack

Laika Leashingwell: crew member on the *Argh*; from Canis Minor

Leo: lion constellation

Lynx: lynx constellation

Markab: yacht belonging to Emma's father, Jack Garton

marlett: a fish with a long, sharp snout that likes to leap out of the sea and flick its sassy tail; also a name for a woman who has a high degree of cunning and impudence

memory seas: Strands of Eridanus; legend says they contain the memories of everyone who has ever passed through there

memory water: any water taken from the Strands of Eridanus; can turn inanimate objects into powerful tools (see *scupper, mesmer*)

mesmer: communication device used on ships; usually a framed mirror containing memory water and a mesmer guard

Monkey: galactic constellation shaped like a monkey; Earth is located here

Newton Eel: current ship of Captain Gent, from the Scorpio system

Nisba: cook on the *Argh*

Party Bag: type of execution in which a criminal is sewn into a canvas sack with a lynx and numerous bricks or stones

Pegasus: constellation of the mythical flying horse, Pegasus

Pyxis: magical object that can lead its bearer to the Shroud

Queen Virgo (Marchpane): ruler of the galaxy; hunting for the Pyxis so she can locate the hidden memory water and regain her power

Rudiman Lovesey: captain of the *Argh*
Santher Medleycatt: crew member on the *Argh;* from Lynx
screech bat: a small black bat; it produces a horrific screech that can knock people out; dragons love them
scupper: bullet dipped in memory water; able to transform people and living things into something else
Shroud: hidden realm where the pirates hid the memory water of Eridanus
Solacious: star in the Monkey system; sometimes called Sol
squilch: mind virus capable of erasing your memories
Strand: any of the great waterways that crisscross the galaxy and connect the stars
Trunchien: former ship of Captain Gent
tusket: long rifle with an ivory dagger at the end
Vermek: navy doctor on Captain Gent's ship
Virgo: constellation of the mythical maiden, Virgo
vostok: small edible object that looks like a rock or a meteorite; swallowing one will coat your skin with a protective jelly
vostok cannon: cannon designed to shoot vostok cannonballs, which are necessary for opening a vostok bridge

People, Places, and Ships

On the *Trunchien*

Halifax Brightstoke [from Virgo]
Artemisia (Tema) Gent [from Gemini]
Besnett, Tema's tarantula
Dr. Vermek [from Scorpio]

On Earth

Emma Brightstoke Garton
Herbert Yee (Herbie, aka Ragnar)
Halifax Brightstoke [from Virgo]
Jack Garton [from Pegasus]

On Delphinus

Berenice, server at Job's Coffin [from Coma Berenice]

The *Argh*

Captain Rudiman Lovesey [from Leo]
Nelson, the spyglass
Sofonisba (Nisba) Gent, ship's cook [from Gemini]
Santher Medleycatt, quartermaster [from Lynx]
Shim Mouncey, first mate [from Lynx]
Laika Leashingwell, aerie spotter [from Canis Minor]
Wardle Porkiss, crew [from Cetus]
Crowler, ship's bowsprit

On Pegasus

Queen Virgo

DECEMBER
NOVEMBER
JANUARY
JULY
MAY
JUNE

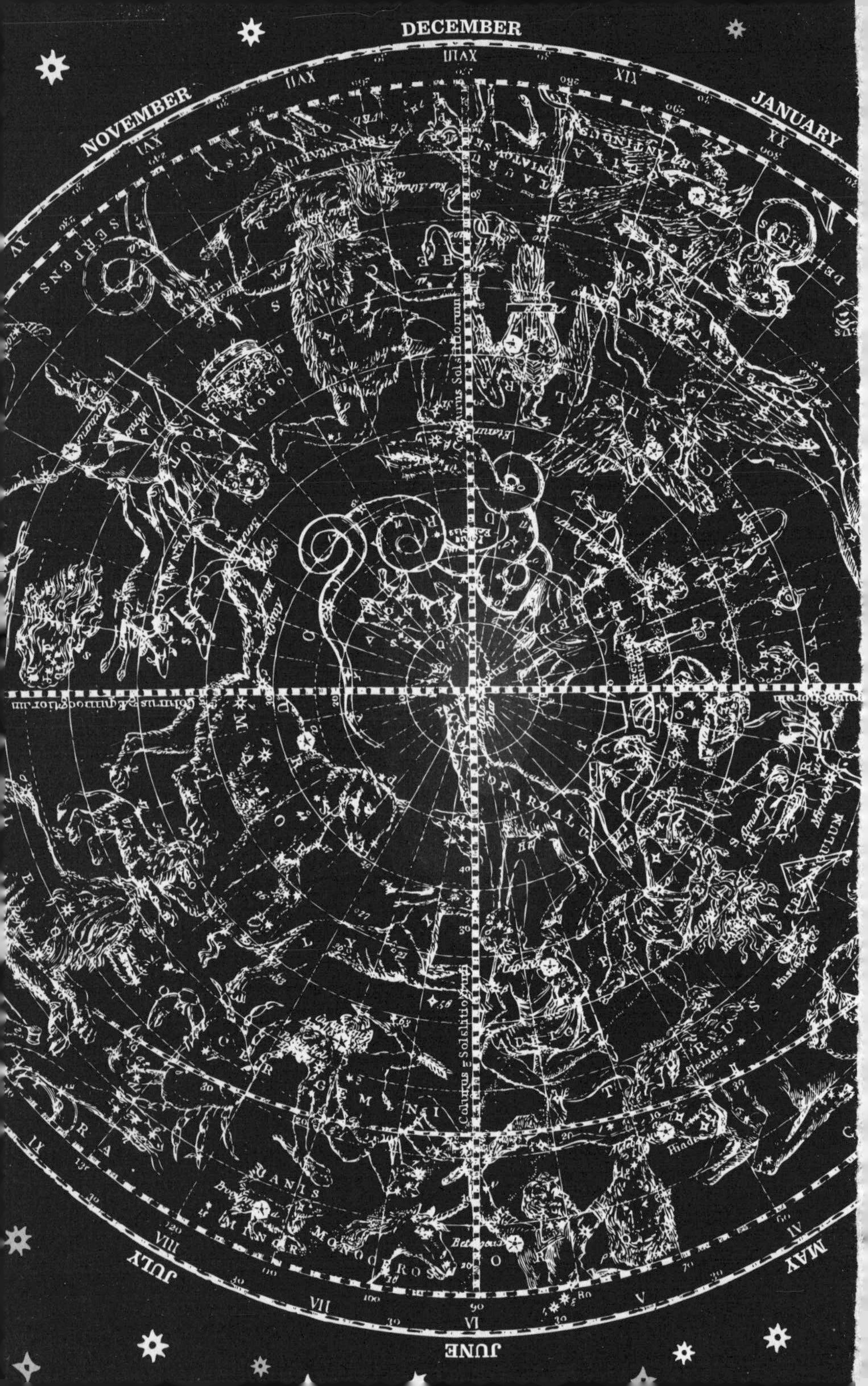

DECEMBER
NOVEMBER
JANUARY
JULY
MAY
JUNE
SERPENS
CORONA
HERCULES
DRACO
URSA MINOR
CAMELOPARDALUS
LYNX
GEMINI
CANIS MINOR
MONOCEROS
TAURUS
Colurus Solstitiorum
Colurus Æquinoctiorum